THINGS
I WANT
TO SAY
BUT
CAN'T

Carla Christian

The Things I Want To Say But Can't

Copyright © 2020 to Carla Christian

This book is a work of fiction. Any resemblance to any other persons, living or dead, is purely coincidental.

Editing, cover design and formatting by www.letsgetbooked.com

ISBN: 978-1-5272-6088-7

For the hearts I've broken, and for those who broke

my heart in return.

Prologue

A machine flatlines. Chaos. I'm counting coins into Mother's hand. Two, four, five, six-seven, eight-nine. Pause. A shiny five-pence piece suspended between thumb and forefinger over her upturned palm. 'Come on, Isobel.' Impatient Mother. 'Nine add five makes?' Somewhere in the background, my little brother sings a nursery rhyme. Wind the bobbin up, wind the bobbin up, pull, pull, clap, clap, clap.

The machine drones.

Nine and five makes, nine and five makes. I don't know. I can do the grubby brown ones, it's the silver ones that always get me stuck. I turn the coin over and over. I hate the way they make my hands smell. Metallic and dirty, like when Daddy starts the car and I'm standing at the wrong end, where all the blue smoke comes out.

1

'Nine and five makes?' Mother again. Think. Think. I don't know. The numbers don't make sense. Why did a silver one have to come along and spoil it? I was doing fine with twos and ones; those coins are easy. Nine and five. Nine add five. Nine plus five. Whichever way I say it, the answer doesn't come. Squeezing my eyes shut and saying a little prayer like we do in morning assembly at school doesn't help either. I even put two Amens and a pretty please at the end of it too.

Mother sighs, losing patience. 'Oh, come on, Isobel. You're seven now, surely you can do this. Nine and five, nine and five. Come on! You need to practise. Nobody ever got anywhere by just drawing silly little pictures. Now, for goodness sake, think properly!'

I throw down the coin into the pile on the floor in front of my crossed legs. Tears. 'I don't know! I don't know, all right? And I don't want to play your stupid game.'

Standing up. Turning away. Heat across the back of bare legs, just below where the hem of my skirt rests against my skinny thighs, and above where the elastic on my knee socks grips my calf. Red handprint. The go-to-your-room stab of a finger in the air and the crack of harsh words close behind. Running up the stairs, the slamming of a door. The world going back to normal downstairs while upstairs, all alone in my bedroom, I wonder how nine and five and pretty pictures could make Mother so mad.

A mask over a mouth, a blast of fire in the chest. Pressure. Counting. One, two, three, four, five, six, seven, eight, nine, ten. Nothing. An involuntary jolt. A violent reflex. Shock. I see a girl in a bed. Seventeen. Her dark hair a severe contrast against her pale face. A black-and-white movie all of her own. My best friend, the star of her own show. I knew this girl once, but now I can't place the stranger in the bed. Cheeks hollowed-out; eyes sunken. Skin hanging from bone. A horror story. Barely existing and fading into the bedsheets. I couldn't save her, and now she's leaving me behind. Going, going, gone.

Hurried trainers squeak on linoleum floor tiles. Machines that once beeped incessantly now whine in a constant state of high-pitched frenzy. A hand around my throat, squeezing. A final curse, a hateful word. A lifetime of endings, a million goodbyes. None of them right.

It's funny what you remember when you've got nothing else to think about. All those things you should've said while you had the chance. You never learned, did you? You never, ever learned.

Part One: Endings

Chapter One

It's my last day. If I'd known it was my last day, I might've thought less about the breakfast cereal and more about what I should do with myself.

But I don't.

Instead, I pour cereal into the two white bowls laid out on the kitchen worktop. And I frown. There's too much. They'll never eat all that. I scoop some flakes back out of the bowls roughly, using only my right-hand, and put them back into the box. My left-hand still hurts from yesterday. I concentrate hard. I have to make sure it's equal. Fair.

But now there's not enough in the bowls. They'll be hungry before lunchtime if they don't eat more than that. I tip the box again and pour cereal back in. Slowly this time, to get it just right. I transfer the bowls carefully to the dining table, staring for too long at the flakes of corn piled high inside until they blur into a bright-orange stain in front of my eyes.

There's a crack in one of the bowls. A fine hairline fracture running the length of the curved porcelain. It's fragile. That will break soon. And I think that there's too much cereal again. But too much is better than not enough, right? That's usually the way it goes. So I leave it at that and place the bowls gently onto the placemats laid out side by side on the table. One pink. One blue.

As I reach out my left-hand, the skin beneath the dressing around my wrist prickles with tight, itchy heat. I turn my palm upwards, clenching and unclenching my fist slowly, feeling the ache in the wound and the tautness of the skin. Raising my hand closer to my face, I pick curiously at the sticking plaster that holds the dressing in place. Fingernail scratching at the flesh-coloured fabric, raising a tacky corner bit by bit. I don't really want to see underneath, not if I don't have to. I saw enough yesterday. My stomach lurches, recoiling at the memory. I smooth the plaster down, but it's lost its stickiness, and the corner remains turned upwards defiantly. Are you mocking me? I think that it is. Maybe.

'Ruby. James. Breakfast's ready.' I sit at the table and call gently for the children. Once, twice. I wait, picking at the plaster again, more deliberately this time, thinking I will just remove it, then it can't silently taunt me anymore. I pull more and more away from my skin, leaving behind a sticky black residue, a gluey deposit across the protruding bone of my wrist. Now most of it has come away and the edge of the dressing is exposed, which means it will probably come loose too. I wish I'd left it alone now. I remind myself that I don't want to be reminded. I remind myself that I don't want to see. I remind myself not to listen to the mocking.

I sigh. I'll have to fix this now. The chair scrapes loudly against the ceramic floor tiles as I push it back and raise myself slowly, leaning my good hand on the table to help me. My heart pounds as though I've been running an imaginary race and my breathing comes in the quickened pants of an athlete waiting patiently to get his breath back. Momentary stars before my eyes. Slight feeling of light-headedness; the dizzy sensation of a drunken night out. Faint stirring of nausea deep in my stomach. I squeeze my eyes shut, wait for the moment to pass and I manage to walk to the cupboard beside the kitchen sink to retrieve the first-aid box.

I lean down slowly and reach in to the top shelf, closing the fingers of my good hand around the box and dragging it out. The box is heavier than I remember, and I almost drop it. It catches on bottles of washing-up liquid, of bleach and furniture polish, packets of batteries, shoe polish, light bulbs, and they all come tumbling out. An almost empty vodka bottle, hidden behind the rest, falls heavily into view, knocked over like a pin in a bowling alley. I flinch and dismiss the sight. There's turpentine too. Turpentine? Why do I have that? I don't remember. But the vodka, I don't have to question myself about the vodka. I know why that's there.

I walk away. The cream-coloured floor tiles are cold. They're always cold. And I hate the way they feel beneath my bare feet. Slick and smooth; slimy almost. The soles of my feet stick to their shiny surface with every step. A layer of iciness attaching itself to my skin, leaving behind a burning chill. Everything hurts more these days. Maybe that's my fault. Maybe I shouldn't have done it. If I hadn't, everything would be different. Everything would've stayed the same. But I did do it, because I wanted everything to change. And I know I need to stop thinking about it, but I can't. I can't find the switch to turn it all off. Not yet anyway.

My left-hand finds my forehead and as my cool fingertips leave pools of calm against my clammy skin, my elbow connects with the work surface and I hold myself there exhausted, head heavy against the palm of my hand, heat burning through the ruined dressing afresh as I riffle through the open first-aid box on the kitchen worktop with the hand that works properly. I find a new sticking plaster. It's covered in brightly coloured cartoon characters. It's all I have left. It'll have to do. I stare at it until the colours blur into a muddy smear and I'm not really seeing anything anymore. I'm thinking again. Thinking of other things. Of *that* thing. The thing that won't go away. I close my eyes yet still it dances in front of me, a taunting waltz where everything I should never have done whirls and spins and revolves dizzyingly around me. I snap my eyes open and clench my jaw until the muscles hurt, my head shaking in tiny rapid movements from side to side as I tell myself no. Not again. Not today. I return to the table to repair the damage I've done to the bandage.

I look at the clock. Ten minutes have passed and they're still not here. I call again for Ruby and James; louder, more urgently, this time. Hoping my voice carries up the stairs. 'Hurry or we'll be late for school.' As I rip the plaster from its packaging and press it into place, I look at the empty table setting in front of me and I remind myself I should probably eat today.

Chapter Two

I've been here before, not long ago. It's been six months to be precise, but it could easily be six minutes. My grandma's funeral. Everything has changed since then. Six months have passed in the blink of an eye, yet have taken me an age to leave behind. In the days since I was last here, I've come to realise that nothing really stays the same for very long anyway, no matter how much you want it to. No matter how much you try and cling to the things you have, forever is never guaranteed. But as I look around this room, this chapel, I see that nothing much has changed at all. Things here are exactly as they were. Unchanged by emotions, by events, by loss. It's all just as it was. Unlike me. I'm almost unrecognisable now.

The same deep citrus scent of polish embedded in the row upon row of dark wooden pews still fills the air. The coarse blue material that lines the hard, bench-like seats still scratches the palms of my clammy hands and penetrates the fabric of my thin trousers to prickle the skin on the back of my legs. The solid, unyielding backs of the pews still presses uncomfortably against my spine, just like last time. These places, the places where we say farewell to the dead: they weren't meant to be comfortable.

I arrived late, trying hard to put this moment off. The huge double doors at the back of the room were slightly ajar and I tiptoed in, squeezing my small frame through the tiny gap. Met by a wall of suited backs, I realised the chapel was standing-room only and I felt slightly guilty for arriving late.

Pressing my back against the rear wall, I slid discreetly to my left, the cold paintwork tugging at my thin blouse. In the corner, I noticed a few spaces on the back pew and I tucked myself into the shadows out of sight. It seems that nobody wanted these seats. The view to the front isn't all that good from here, but I don't mind. I'm not all that sure I want to see anyway.

It seems nobody saw me arrive either. They are too lost in their thoughts. Acknowledging the tragedy in front of them rather than the woman in the corner. I'm glad I've gone unnoticed. I've never really been much good at sadness. At least not until recently. But lately, I'd let it creep up on me. Maybe it had been creeping up on me for the past few years, if I really think about it. And places like this always make you think about it. It's what they do best, especially where I'm concerned.

I reach out my hand and run my fingertips gently across the surface of the shabby hymn book resting on the little shelf in front of me. I remember its rough leather surface from last time, when I'd held it in my pale, shaking hands in front of my eyes to block out the view of my grandmother's funeral. I remember its yellowing pages. How it smelled damp and old. As I trace my index finger over the smooth gold wording on the hard cover, I wonder how many other hands have held this book. How many have clutched it in sorrow, knuckles turning white as fingertips cling on to something tangible? How many tears have fallen among its pages? How many voices have sung out its words in remembrance? How many have been unable to sing because sorrow has taken their voice away? My mind is full of questions. It's always full of questions.

Since that day six months' ago, I'd often wondered how many people would be at my funeral. I'd always had a morbid fascination about who would see me off on my final journey. What would it be like for me in the end? Who would be there on the grey, drizzling day I had set aside in my mind's eye especially for the occasion? The kind of day that seemed adequately depressing for a slow procession of misery. Would I be one of the solitary ones? The abandoned? Would there simply be a handful of family members, weeping dutifully into soggy tissues shared out with just the right amount of sympathy by obediently grieving distant relatives? Would there be more seats left empty than those filled with the people who were supposed to miss me? Would the words of the celebrant resonate around the cavernous room, finding their way into these empty spaces and echoing there for a while, reminding everybody I was one of the lonely?

Or would I have an army of friends there too? People who cared about me enough in life to come along and witness the sadness of my death? Would I be one of the popular ones? One of those who have standing-room only? Where the mourners are squeezed into every available space, shoulder to shoulder, craning their necks to satisfy their morose interest, trying to get a view of the coffin as it passes slowly by? Sitting in silent judgement about the colour of the flowers, the choice of music, the fact that they had to park miles away in the overspill car park and walk hurriedly through the imaginary drizzle, silk dresses and pristine suits tarnished with the stains of a million raindrops, only to end up standing at the back because they hadn't realised this many people had cared enough about me?

I always hoped I'd be one of the latter. That I wouldn't be left to go alone, but would be surrounded by a crowd, a mournful audience seeing me off to who knows where. But I suppose the fear was always that the journey would be a solitary one, with nobody to watch me go. And would everybody wear black? I'd always hoped not. I'd always hoped people would remember that I was happy once, sparkly even, with dancing in my footsteps and music in my voice, and that in the end they wouldn't mourn my death, but would celebrate that I'd lived. There'd be smiles in their remembrance, laughter even, and it would be like a little part of me would always stay with them. I always did like to see life through rose-tinted spectacles. Once upon a time anyway.

I turn my head towards the ceiling and notice that the weather is very different today to the way I pictured things. There's no grey day. There's no rain. Instead, it's a beautiful afternoon. It's as though spring has arrived early. The sun is streaming into the chapel through the bank of small windows which line the room just beneath ceiling height, carefully placed so as not to allow passers-by the opportunity to peer through and view the proceedings with exaggerated interest, as though watching chimpanzees in a zoo. The sun's rays pierce the glass, casting small, perfect rectangles of bright-yellow light onto the opposite wall, their golden edges blurring to nothing until eventually the light disappears and is replaced by the bland magnolia paintwork. I want to reach out my hand and feel the warmth of those sunbeams. I want to let the light play across my fingers and make butterflies from the shadows.

I look ahead and scan the scene in front of me. A sea of black and grey. An undulating mass of figures shuffling uncomfortably, not knowing where to look. The backs of a hundred heads or more, coughing politely to fill the heavy silence. Mourners pressed up against one another on those rigid wooden seats. Overflowing down the sides of the room and into the tight spaces between the pews and the walls, the warmth from so many people combined with the heat of the radiators making the room stifling, claustrophobic. And yet the corner where I'm sitting remains empty. Apart from me. It's like I've been here all along, part of the furniture and nobody has noticed the difference.

I continue to concentrate my gaze on the congregation, needing to look anywhere but at what's happening at the front of the chapel. There are a myriad of expressions hidden from my eyes, a jumble of emotions playing out on all the faces that I cannot see, and I wonder what they are. Sorrow? Happiness at memories of better times? Relief? Gratitude that this hasn't happened to them? Disbelief? Or simply nothing? Shock removing the ability to feel. But the backs of the heads shelter me from knowing what feelings are being played across the features. Protected from view, as we all are in this almost windowless room.

Suddenly, inappropriately, I think of chimpanzees again. They'd always been my favourite animal in the zoo. I'd stand and watch them for hours if I could, laughing at their antics and marvelling at how similar to humans they were. The thought, as sudden and misplaced as it is, makes me smile. But just as quickly as it arrives, my smile fades and

I wonder when was the last time I'd been to the zoo. Was it with you? I shake my head, frowning, unable to catch the memory.

The temperature in the room rises until the air becomes a heavy, stifling weight pressing against my skin. The cloying scent of perfume, aftershave and stale cigarette smoke clings to the congregation and combines with the artificial citrus fragrance of the cheap polish and the heat of the air to create a thick, suffocating odour. I can imagine the scent. I know how it should feel in my nostrils, strong and oppressive, yet I can't smell it. I draw my eyebrows together and rapidly search the air around me with puzzled eyes, hoping somehow to see evidence of my lost sense. I breathe in, deeper and deeper, but the scent still escapes me. A sense of unease creeps over me. My breath becomes shallow, uneven, erratic. I clasp my hands together and clamp them between my knees to stop them shaking. Everything suddenly feels wrong.

My limbs becoming numb against the solid wood of the narrow bench. I look down at my hands knotted together in my lap, and start twisting the group of four slim silver rings that I always wear stacked on the middle finger of my right-hand. I twist and I twist, round and round and round again, the tiny metallic bands catching the light and sending sharp shards of silver lightning into the darkness of my pupils. But I don't turn away from the brightness and my eyes don't close to its heat. I frown again.

Clamping my hands between my knees again, I lean forwards, straining my neck and swaying from side to side in order to see between the rows of black to catch a glimpse of the front pew. And between the pristine suits and beautiful dresses, I see them. My parents. Arms wound tightly around each other, crumpled together against the backdrop of their grief. I imagine their faces marked with threads of ash white from the salt of their tears, new ones spilling from their eyes and making fresh, stinging paths across reddened skin. I close my eyes tight, not wanting to see, not wanting to know, but their images remain imprinted upon my eyelids.

I look again and next to them I see my brother and sister, one younger than me, one older. My brother is sitting bolt upright, broad shoulders statue-like in his suit jacket. My sister leans against him, her face buried against his strong shoulder. My granda is with them too. Suffering yet another loss in his life. One he probably thought he'd never have to deal with in his old age. And I feel like I've been punched in the stomach. I have no breath left in me. The wretchedness of the scene has taken it away. The heartbreak is palpable and shocking. Yet I can't go to them. I can't be there to comfort them, because this is all my fault.

I move my eyes slowly left and right across the crowded room, picking out people and recognising them all, despite being unable to see their faces. Aunties and uncles, cousins and distant relatives, close friends, work friends, acquaintances. The room is filled with love and loss. Then I see Matthew, the man that I married, his parents too, bodies stooped with sadness, heads hanging in sorrow, and I feel like I am being squeezed. Crushed. The life from me fading away. But I don't see our children and for that I'm thankful. I don't want to see what loss has done to their tiny, innocent faces.

My eyes scan the room a final time and are inexplicably drawn to the row of pews directly opposite mine. At the back of the room. In the corner. In the shadows, just like me. Here, my eyes fall on a face so familiar it makes my soul ache. I see the face I'd tried to forget, once perfect, now ashen and drained. The face that was the beginning of my undoing, of my slow and unexpected unravelling. I see Ben, and everything else in my world stops.

I reach out and cling to the shelf of the pew in front of me with both hands, gripping either side of the old hymnbook to stop my world shifting and turning to liquid. My nose is inches away from its tattered surface. The gold letters bright in my eyes. My hands feel cold. Knuckles and fingertips white. Tendons strained from the effort of holding on. I look down. I focus on the blue carpet, an ocean beneath me, trying to calm myself. My feet begin to tap uncontrollably. I squeeze me eyes closed and clench my jaw. And I realise that I haven't yet seen you among the crowd. My eyes fly open and immediately begin to move frantically among the congregation. I search and I search until the muscles around my eyes hurt from the sheer effort of seeking you out. But as hard as I try, I don't see you. I thought I would. I thought you'd be the one person who'd be here for me. But you're not. And I don't understand. Where are you? Why aren't you here? Where did you go?

All around me tilts and spins. I hear a female voice begin to speak, gentle and soothing. She sounds so far away. Her voice is a tiny, thin sound in the distance and I'm at the bottom of a deep hole. Who is she? I can barely hear what she's saying. Who is that? She's telling the story of my life. Summarising everything about me in a few short sentences, in a few short minutes. Everything that I was, everything that made me, condensed into a stranger's words. And in an instant, I realise this is real. This is happening. And I realise that I was loved. I am not one of the abandoned. I'm not one of the lonely. Maybe I'd got it all wrong.

I feel a sickening lurch as everything seems to move again. In the midst of it all, I somehow find the energy to reach my left-hand to my face and touch my cheek gently with my fingertips. I hold them there for a moment, but I feel nothing. There's no warmth, no sensation of skin against skin. I begin to wonder if I'm even there at all anymore. And then I know with a sudden certainty that I'm not. Not really. I'm not anything anymore. Am I breathing? I'm not sure. Is my heart beating? I can't feel it. Am I gone? I think so, but I don't know. I don't know anything anymore. Maybe I don't need to.

As my world falls out of view, I close my eyes. Images saturate my mind like a flipbook, fleeting moments rushing past, shaping the separate parts of my life into one long story. Page after page after page flashing across my eyelids, faster and faster, scenes merging, becoming muddled. I randomly stop the book on a single page, momentarily freezing that part of my life to look closer at the image. I see myself playing on a swing in the garden of my childhood home, knees muddy and full of the careless bruises picked up by bare summer legs, a million giggles bubbling from my mouth. I move on, flicking through the pages again. This time when I stop it's my wedding day, a pure-white dress against the backdrop of vivid green fields and late-summer mountains covered in purple heather. I see the blue lake and the even bluer sky. Blue to match my husband's eyes. Matthew's eyes. I pause here for a second longer, then I let the pages turn again faster and faster. There are children, my children. The pain of childbirth and the rush of a love purer than any I've ever known. The beauty of their faces. The sparkle in their eyes. The feel of their tiny hands in mine.

Then suddenly there's you. And all at once there's laughter and there are tears and there's love and there's heartbreak, and all at once I can see the best of times and the worst of times and I can remember how it felt to have a racing heart. A heart filled with adoration. With passion. With anger. With hate. I am reliving it all again. Visions of a past I'd hoped to forget hammering my head, rushing at me, surrounding me, closing in on me, squeezing me tighter and tighter, crushing me with memories.

And then I see the bottle. The bottle and the pills. The blade and the blood. The things that brought me here. I see it all again one more time. One more time before I go.

You

Chapter Three

October 2011

The pale-blue light of the late autumn morning filters through thin curtains and settles gently against my eyelids. It rests there briefly, pushing through paper-thin skin as it coaxes me awake. I stir, my light sleep disturbed by the pressing light, and open my eyes slowly, lifting tired, heavy lids, and squinting into the brightness. My eyes feel hot and dry from lack of sleep and I want to rub them, but the air in the room is cold and my arms are reluctant to leave the warmth of the heavy duvet.

Blinking a couple of times, I lie completely still and wait until the room comes into focus. It takes a moment, but then I see her. Just inches away. So close it hurts my eyes to focus on her. Raven hair cascades messily around her face, framing her elfin features perfectly in chaotic, tumbling curls. Huge innocent brown eyes gaze unblinking back at me, the half-smile on her ruby lips alluring, suggesting secrets, untruths. Things she knows that I have yet to find out. I look straight at her, and then I remember where I am.

I close my eyes again and a knowing smile plays across my lips as memories of last night fill my mind. I want to giggle at the thought. At how completely out of the ordinary this is for me. 32-years-old and waking up for the first time in a stranger's bed. I want to laugh out loud and high-five myself. If I'd had it in me to scramble out of bed and jump around the room with excitement I would've done. But tiredness and the stirrings of a hangover keep me where I am. Inside my head though, I'm singing.

I shift slightly and feel the dull ache of my muscles. All the way up my body I can feel a tightness – my legs, my stomach, my arms, my neck. I stretch slowly, tentatively, trying to ease the tension, and my smile widens. It's a good ache because it's last night's ache. I want to giggle all over again as I remember our initial awkwardness. The trembling. Not knowing if we were cold or nervous or just full of mischievous excitement. I remember the first kiss. Hot and urgent. The heat of lips upon lips, of skin against skin, the sweet taste of alcohol and the unfamiliar scent of a stranger's body against mine. The memory makes me smile.

I peer once more into the enormous brown eyes that dominate the pretty face. As my gaze sweeps across her features, I notice how the pale skin at the top of your arm seeps between the gaps in the ink, filling the empty spaces between the black outlines. Completing her. Bringing light to her shade and providing the canvas for her vibrancy. I suppress another giggle. I remember being surprised you had tattoos. I remember telling you your face looked too friendly. I remember you rolling your eyes and feigning annoyance, then grinning widely down at me. I remember thinking that I'd fallen in love with your smile and the way it made your eyes crinkle at the corners right there and then.

I lift my eyes from the inked image of the girl covering your bicep and seek out your face. It's in profile, silhouetted perfectly against the soft light radiating from behind the curtains. You are your own black outline, but the light from behind you fills your empty spaces with darkness and shadow. I can't see your features, but I know what you look like, even without being able to see the details. I can picture the long lashes of your closed eyes resting on your high cheekbones. I can see your small mouth and how it smiles quirkily to one side. I know how it feels to kiss those lips and hold your delicate face, the stubble shadowing your jawline rough beneath my fingers, your green eyes veiled in alcohol and lust. Eyes the same colour as mine, mirroring my thoughts.

I watch the gentle rise and fall of your chest as you breathe slowly in and out, sleep relaxing you, making you unaware of my gaze. I want to reach out and touch you, feel the warmth of your skin against mine. But I stay where I am, not wanting to disturb you. I just want to watch.

You stir and your eyes flicker open. You lie still and my heart begins to pound. I try to take a secret breath to still it, but you hear me drawing in the air slowly and turn your head towards me, sleepy eyes taking me in, blonde dishevelled hair falling over your forehead. I'd remembered your face pretty well, but as I look at it again now, in the light of the morning after, I sing even louder inside. I really can't believe my luck! It just goes to show what can happen when you're in the right place at the right time. Fate. That's what it is. After everything that's happened over the past few months, fate has finally dealt me a winning hand. And now inside I'm dancing.

Involuntarily, my heart slams against my ribcage as I think once again about last night. For a moment I fear it's so loud you'll be able to hear it, and I'm trying so hard to look calm and relaxed on the outside. I don't want you to know what you're already doing to me. But then there's that smile again as you say 'good morning' and I feel a familiar warmth spread across my skin as my cheeks flush. I lower my gaze.

'Hey,' I say quietly, voice quivering as the butterflies in my stomach flutter up into my throat.

'Great night hey?' You reach out to brush a stray strand of hair from my forehead, and my breath instantly catches. Closing my eyes, I silently will my silly racing heart to stay calm.

'Yeah, great night,' I respond, mindlessly repeating your words, heat rising in my cheeks again as I frantically search for something more interesting or funny to say. It eludes me.

I clear my throat and press a shaking hand against the hot skin of my abdomen to stop my stomach somersaulting. For lack of anything better to say, I decide that 'it was nice to meet you' will at least fill the silence.

'I'd say that's an understatement,' you laugh, eyes glinting mischievously, and my legs turn to jelly under the duvet.

I smile shyly back at you, trying to hold your gaze for as long as I can before I have to look away. All the confidence I felt last night is disappearing in the pale morning light, and I feel exposed. Vulnerable almost. Like maybe last night was fuelled only by alcohol and none of this is even real. As if you sense my slight withdrawal, you reach out and gently pull me into your arms, encircling me completely, holding me hard against you, skin against skin again. And I allow myself to relax into you, draping one arm around your waist, tracing patterns across your back with my fingertips. As I run my hand up your long spine and across the cool bare skin of your shoulders, my face nestles against your warm neck and I breathe in your sweet morning scent.

I've known you for fewer than 12 hours, but already I think you're beautiful. Already this is dangerous.

Chapter Four

I met you in a nightclub. The kind that small towns do best. The kind that has ideas above its station and happy-hour promotions on gimmicky drinks only a certain type of person cares about. The kind of drinks that get you wasted, for the kind of people who can't wait to waste away. Binge drinking until their pockets and their bellies are empty. The kind of place where the music is hideous. Where one song jumps clumsily into another, beats mismatched, tempos all wrong, but everybody dances to it anyway because a bedroom DJ pumps his fist into the air, convincing everybody he's the master of his craft. And the bingeing dancers pause for a moment, mid-step, adjusting their movement to a new flow. Drunken misshapes on a heaving dance floor.

I met you here, among the faded beauty of our hometown. In this glass box of glitter balls and UV lights and big ideas and broken hearts, nestled between crumbling Georgian facades with what's left of ancient cobbled streets appearing from beneath the worn asphalt of roads that will never be repaired. We meet here, where these two very different worlds rub shoulders. One brash and bold and desperate to be heard, one looking on sadly, clinging onto delusions of grandeur, of better times, unable to stop the light from its own existence diminishing and vanishing from view.

You know all this already of course, because you were there. And this is where it starts. Here, with Melissa, you and me. The friend, the one-night stand and the girl screwed-up like a sheet of writing paper full of mistakes. The one somebody tossed aside, missing the bin and ending up lying there on the floor, waiting for somebody to find her, to open her up, to unfurl her crumpled pages, to look over her mistakes and decide if she's worth saving. I'm that girl. I'm the one who pretends that none of that is true. The one who thinks she can forget.

Melissa grabs my arm and threads it through hers, linking it tight. The taxi we have clambered out of speeds away into the darkness. We walk unsteadily across the uneven pavement in our heels, being careful not to lose our balance, bare legs in short dresses feeling the cold of the icy October air.

As we approach the kerb, the sound of dance music pulses through the open door of the bar across the road. The town is bursting with witches and devils, goblins and zombies, hideous masks and theatrical make-up. Hallowe'en.

The door closes and the noise subsides, but just hearing it is enough to make us hurry across the road, all but dragging each other along, dodging between passing cars to get inside the warmth of the bar. To get a drink, to dance, to forget. And I need to forget. That's what tonight is all about. Letting go.

***

I haven't known Melissa long, just a couple of years or so, but already she's become a good friend. We met at a mutual friend's birthday party, deliberating over where to start at the buffet. Making small talk about the minute sandwiches, the amazing array of crisps and accompanying dips, the limp salad, there as a token nod towards a healthy option, and bonding over conversations involving the lack of cake. We hit it off straight away. Throwing off our heels to dance to loud, tacky '80s' pop. Seeking out the bar, shoes in hand, to avoid the slow songs and the awful '60s' tracks.

Back then I thought my life was all planned out. A husband, two beautiful children, a fantastic house in a pretty countryside town right beside the river. I thought I was settled and as close to happy as anyone could expect to be. Back then I knew where I was going. Back then I didn't drink too much or smoke cigarettes or stay out late. Back then I didn't put myself first – I put the important people there instead. Back then I didn't know what it meant to be on a downward spiral.

***

I shrug off the unwelcome chill of a memory and bring myself back to the present. Melissa still has my arm jammed through hers, holding it tightly against her body in an almost protective way. It makes me smile inwardly. She's very different from me. Taller, blonde to my dark brown, feistier with a jealous streak, and she never shies from saying what she thinks. Me, I'm much softer I suppose. But still, we get along and we have fun. Lots of it. And fun is what I need right now.

As we reach the bar, I pause, halting Melissa in her tracks.

'What's up?' she asks, concern settling into a frown across her forehead.

'Maybe this isn't such a good idea.' I sigh, suddenly feeling very exposed. 'Maybe it's too soon. Maybe we should just get a takeaway and go back to yours, watch some TV.'

Melissa shakes her head. 'Or *maybe*,' she says, breaking into a wide lipstick-clad smile, 'we should get inside that bar and dance until our feet hurt, like old times.'

I cast a nervous glance over her shoulder to the bar. 'But what if –'

'What if nothing,' she interrupts, squeezing my arm reassuringly. 'Come on Belle, you deserve a bit of fun for once. It's time you gave yourself a break and let your hair down.'

I inhale deeply and agree. The past few months have been hard. More than hard. Sometimes, I wonder how I've managed to come through it all relatively unscathed. But then I wonder if maybe I deserve my scars. Frowning to myself, I shake my head to dispel any negative thoughts.

Tonight is all about forgetting. I feel like I've been holding my breath for months, trying hard not to drown. But now it's time to breathe again.

'Okay, let's go,' I say determinedly. 'But quickly, before I change my mind again!'

Melissa's 'Don't Care' pink lipstick-shaded lips grin again and she pulls me towards the bar without hesitation.

We reach the entrance and Melissa loosens her grip on me to pull hard on the glass door. As it opens the music oozes through the gap like liquid, pooling at our feet and sucking us in. My senses seem heightened. It's a long time since I've been here. As we step through the door, the stale, saccharine smell of alcohol fills my nostrils, the bass notes of the music rattle in my chest and my ears are filled with a mass of jarring sounds: boisterous laughter, the sharp clink of glasses, voices shouting above the music – conversations lost among the rhythms. I stand for a moment taking it in, and as I do, a strange sense of the familiar tiptoes cautiously across me, trying the feeling out first before committing. I turn to Melissa, face beaming, eyes alight. This is me finally feeling like myself again. Finally feeling alive.

Seeing my smile, she steps forward and folds me into her arms, hugging me tight against her shoulder. Her long blonde hair falls across my face and within its softness, I can smell the delicate floral scent of her shampoo – red berries, summer meadows, honey.

'You look amazing,' she says loudly over the music, holding me at arm's length by my shoulders and gazing warmly at me. I feel a lump form in my throat and tears threaten my eyes. I swallow hard, forcing the feeling away.

'Oh, don't say that!' I protest, part joking, part meaning it. 'You'll have me in tears again and I think we've both had enough of that.'

Melissa smiles and squeezes my shoulders gently. 'No more crying, missy,' she says. 'Unless, of course, it's tears of laughter.' She winks at me and we grin. With Melissa, it's easy. I don't have to pretend. I can be strong, I can be weak, I can cry, I can laugh, I can be whoever and however I feel like being at the time. No big deal.

'Okay, okay,' I say, taking a deep breath. 'Tonight is all about laughter and good times. Agreed?'

Melissa widens her blue eyes and nods her head vigorously. She knows all too well the pain I've been through. The battles I've faced. 'Come on,' she says letting her hands drop from my shoulders. 'Let's find a seat.'

As she turns and begins walking in the direction of an empty booth, I look over at the busy bar. We're late tonight, too busy devouring a takeaway and watching trashy TV to get ready, and the place is already crowded. The swarms of impatient customers waiting to be served is two deep, people jostling against one another, drinks being spilt, ten and twenty-pound notes held aloft at the bar staff in the hope of getting served sooner. Inwardly, I roll my eyes. It's been a while.

I grab Melissa gently by the waist and lean in towards her ear. 'You get a seat,' I tell her, 'while I go to the bar for the drinks.' I nod my head sideways, gesturing towards the bar. 'It might take a while, that's all!'

She turns and glances over, following my gaze, and rolls her eyes at the crowded scene. 'No worries, I'll just be over there.' She points to a bank of red upholstered seats against the opposite wall. 'I'll have my usual.'

Melissa takes a seat as I squeeze between the hot bodies and eventually reach the bar. I lean against its surface with both arms, feeling the sticky wetness of sugar and alcohol against my forearms. It takes a few moments, but I catch the barman's eye and lean over as far as I can, standing on tiptoes despite my heels, holding the hem of my short

41

dress to keep it at thigh length while I reach across and shout my order into his ear. He nods his understanding and turns his back on me.

He's distracted by a beautiful young blonde in the far corner. She leans in towards him, flawless skin glowing in the subdued lighting, make-up perfect. She speaks into his ear and he laughs, touching her shoulder gently as she giggles back. Then he kisses her on the cheek before returning to work, and to my drink order. Maybe they know each other. Maybe they're friends or ex-lovers, or maybe they're friends who want to be more. I try to gauge, but the meaning escapes me. Maybe there isn't one to find.

The girl catches me looking at her and I drop my gaze quickly. I sense my face reddening and I curse my childish need to stare and wonder. I straighten my dress some more and immediately question why I decided to wear something so short. I've lost a lot of weight over the past few months and, although I've always been slim, now I'm almost too thin. The black fabric of the dress clings tightly to my small body, accentuating the slightly protruding bones of my hips and hugging my tiny waist. Its one-shoulder cut reveals my slender form and exposes the way my collarbones jut out a little too much.

Self-consciously, I raise a hand to my neck and run my fingers across its surface, the sharpness of the bones harsh beneath my soft skin. I let my fingertips stroke back and forth in the smooth dip between my collarbone and my neck as I look around the bar to see if I recognise any of the faces. I don't. They're all much younger than me. Most people my age are probably at home curled-up with husbands, wives, partners. A tiny pang of sadness stirs somewhere inside, and I take a deep breath to keep it in its place, holding it for a second and then blowing the air out slowly between my lips.

Dropping my arms to my sides, I tug at the hem of my dress again, stretching the fabric further down my thighs. At least my legs still look decent, I think, casting a quick critical eye over them. Long and lean and not too skinny. Not like the rest of me. Smoothing the soft jersey fabric across my stomach and over my hips, I look over at the barman again. He's added blackcurrant to a half-pint glass and now hurriedly fills it with strong, sweet cider before placing it on the bar in front of me and turning away again to add spirits and cola to another glass.

As I wait, my eyes fall on another drink waiting on the bar next to mine. It's not one that I've ordered. I don't recognise it. Suddenly it feels like forever since I've been here. There are two glasses, one inside the other. The one inside is a shot glass filled with a dark liquid, the larger glass holds something clear. I stare at it for a moment, then without thinking I point at it and blurt out 'What's that?!' I turn quickly with inquisitive eyes to look up at the person standing to my left. And all I see is a huge smile. Your smile, with laughter lines that go on for miles. And for a moment I see nothing else. It's so warm and happy and I can't take my eyes off it.

I hear laughter coming from the smile and it brings me back. I focus my attention on your face now instead, and I see smiling eyes set against features that are both delicate and striking. You're about my age, tall and definitely handsome, but not conventionally so, yet I instantly like what I see, immediately warming to you. And I realise I'm smiling right back up at you. Really smiling. Like I mean it.

You laugh again and raise the glass to your mouth, swallowing its contents in one quick gulp before placing the two glasses heavily back on the bar, using the back of your right-hand you wipe your lips, removing traces of the sticky dark liquid. A half-smile. The suggestion of dimples. Then your eyes find mine and they stay there, part serious, part playful. I hold your gaze, eyes never leaving yours as I take a mouthful of the sweet liquid in my glass and let it flow down my throat, spreading its familiar warmth into my stomach. But it's not just the warmth of the alcohol I feel. There's an excitement building too. 'Jagerbomb,' you say, a look of amusement in your eyes. 'One of the quickest ways to intoxication.'

'Oh.' I shrug and laugh. 'That's a new one on me! I think I'll stick with the cider.' I look down at the glass I'm holding to illustrate my point, then from beneath my eyelashes I cast a cursory glance at your hands, feeling hopeful when I see there's no sign of a wedding ring.

'Very wise,' you say, nodding curtly but grinning all the same. 'Stick to what you know.'

I take another sip of my drink. 'It's probably the safest option.' The cider fizzes as it descends behind my ribcage. 'I haven't been out in a while, so I think I'm a little out of practice.'

You hold my gaze again as I smile up at you. 'Yeah, I thought I hadn't seen you in here before. I'm pretty sure I'd have noticed you.'

The barman places the drink I ordered for Melissa in front of me and I put my glass down next to it. Reaching into my small black bag for money, I peel a ten-pound note from a tiny zipped compartment, fumbling to get it out past my house keys, my lipstick, my phone. I hand over the crumpled note and wait for my change. I take it, shoving it quickly back into the bag with shaking hands. I suddenly feel flustered and slightly out of control. Where's Melissa? I stand on tiptoes and crane my neck to see above the crowds, and holding up her drink I beckon her over.

I'm glad when she's by my side and I don't have to deal with this alone. It feels a little alien to be accepting attention again and I begin to doubt whether coming out tonight was such a good idea. She jostles in between me and the bar, pushing me closer to you. Accidentally or intentionally, I can't tell, but now I'm standing so close our arms touch and I can't decide if I like this or if I want to turn and run. You have a bottle of beer in your hand, hanging loosely from your fingers as you lean into the bar and I get the feeling that you're drunk. But you hide it well.

Towering over me, you tug at the sleeves of your navy-coloured jumper, pulling them up your forearms slightly, stretching the fabric tightly over the increasing width of your arm. As you do, the edge of a tattoo is revealed, extending out just below your left cuff. I immediately place my glass back on the bar and, without thinking, reach out and pull the sleeve up some more, exposing the black and grey design. I've always loved tattoos and this one's beautiful. A delicate pattern like lace across your skin in shades of soft grey covers your entire arm, disappearing beneath the fabric of the jumper, which is now pulled up towards your shoulder.

You look down at your exposed arm too, as if seeing it for the first time.

'Do you like it?' you ask, not looking up, taking another mouthful of beer from the bottle hanging loosely in your hand.

My eyes follow the swirling pattern carefully and I nod my head slowly in silent approval, holding your sleeve so you can't pull it down again just yet. The work is refined and subtle, elegant even, yet the design is bold and hypnotic. It really is stunning. I think about the tattoo that I have on my lower back, and a rush of unwelcome memories follows. Three stars in a row down my spine, sparks bursting from each of the five points, surrounded by cascading arcs and sweeping curves following the length of my back. The stars were for my husband and my children, one each. I thought by adorning myself with the permanence of a tattoo I could convince myself, prove to myself, that forever was what I wanted. But the sparks, those bright flashes igniting the space around my stars, they were for somebody else.

Before the memory can take hold, Melissa nudges me, an amused look on her face, eyes flicking between us, inquisitive and filled with the same sense of excitement that I'm feeling. She turns to me and gives me a wide-eyed, raised-eyebrow look to show her approval, then turns to face you, her expression immediately changing to one of cool indifference.

'This is amazing!' I say almost breathlessly, my gaze returning to the artwork on your bare arm. Taking it in once again, following the sweeping soft curves, until they jar with the sharp edges of a geographical sunburst, marvelling at the delicacy of the shading and the intricacy of the inked image. I look up to your face again, and I see that you're watching me with both patience and amusement etched in your eyes. I hold your gaze for a moment longer and smile shyly, lowering my lashes again as I feel the colour rise in my cheeks. There's something about you that's making me turn to liquid inside. It's unexpected and bewildering, but at the same time, I feel energised and alive.

My thumb grazes the warm skin of your upper arm as I adjust my hold on your sleeve, and my heart reacts as though it has been replaced by a caged bird, wings fluttering rapidly behind my ribcage, trying to escape. Instinctively, I jerk my hand away and let it fall clumsily to my side, looking across at Melissa to avoid your gaze. Trying to get some control back. Thankfully, Melissa is unaware of the mini battle I'm currently having with myself, and leans heavily on my shoulder, stretching across me to get a better look at the tattoo in the dim light of the club. I silently thank her for defusing the situation. For giving me time to breathe.

I take another long mouthful of my drink, then another and another in quick succession. Already I feel the alcohol having some effect, and I'm beginning to relax. What if you are single? I allow myself to think. Would I be in with a chance? Would you be interested in me? *Should* you be interested in me? I take the final mouthful, hand it to the barman and order all three of us another round.

And in the moment that follows, when you place your hand at the base of my spine as you thank me for the drink, I decide that I want you and I'm going to have you. If you'll let me.

Chapter Five

The kids smell different. Their hair, their clothes, their skin.
It's not the smell of my house, my home. It's the smell of
somebody else's. They rush past me through the tiny porch
overflowing with too many coats and shoes, knocking
jackets and scarves from the pegs, and they squeeze their
way into the equally tiny living space of my small, cramped
terraced house. I manage to ruffle James's hair as he shoots
past chattering non-stop the way four-year-olds do, and as I
do, I release more of that unfamiliar scent into the air. Ruby
is close behind him, taller, quieter, older by three years, and
I squeeze her shoulders and kiss her head as she pauses next
to me for a second to let me say hello. I run my hands
through her long, golden-brown ponytail letting the soft
strands slip between my fingers as my lips linger for a

moment longer against the top of her head. She smells of coconut. She should smell of strawberries and lavender.

She pulls against my grasp and I release her, turning back to the open front door. The autumn sun is already beginning to set, and the intense late-afternoon glow casts a wide, deep-orange path down the centre of the quiet lane outside. Although I live in the town, the lane is set well back from the main roads and feels relatively isolated. The row of twelve little whitewashed, rickety terraced cottages can easily be missed if you don't know they're hiding at the end of it. And for now, that's just the way I like it.

Matthew stands on the pavement. He doesn't come in. His face is a picture of opposites in the sunset, the left side bathed in fierce orange light, the right lost in shadow. But that's all I see before I look down. We hardly look at each other at all anymore. Can't bear to see what feelings might lie behind each other's eyes. It's been that way since it happened four months ago. When everything fell apart.

He looks up briefly and hands over two small rucksacks, one pink, one blue. The kid's things. Matthew's done his duty this weekend, and now that it's Sunday afternoon it's my turn again. That's the way things have turned out as we feel our way cautiously through our separation, becoming accustomed to our new lives apart. I thought I'd feel relieved. Turns out I mostly just feel sorry and I feel sad.

But today I feel a little differently. Today I feel happy on the inside, and I'm sure it shows on the outside. I can't stop smiling. Everything seems brighter, more vivid. The weight on my shoulders has lifted slightly. I no longer feel like I'm taking the strain of the world and all its problems. Instead, I feel as though my sparkle has really come back. Despite being tired after last night, I feel full of an energy that I don't know how to expel. I feel like the very surface of me is shimmering as though in a heatwave, effervescing, awakened, alive. Because of you.

I take the rucksacks and drop them on the floor at my feet. I can hear James and Ruby in the back garden now, their screams of delight floating through the chill of the October air, warming it with their laughter and little singsong voices, the rhythmic creak of the trampoline joining in the chorus as they jump.

'I'll pick them up from school on Wednesday then,' says Matthew, half asking, half telling me. His voice soft and deep, still heavily accented with an Irish lilt. I used to love listening to that voice. It was one of the things that attracted me to him all those years ago. Back when I was only 19. I nod in agreement and lean heavily against the doorframe, watching him for a moment. He raises his eyes to mine and half-smiles. I smile weakly back before removing my gaze and focusing on a place on the old stone wall just behind him, which lines the length of the lane. Its rough grey surface, darkened with the dampness of autumn, is covered in green and yellow mosses and lichens. Weeds and grasses grow from gaps in the mortar and from the places where the stones no longer fit together neatly. In the summer, the kids loved to climb on the wall and jump down onto the soft patch of grass on the other side. But now it's too slippery, too dangerous, and I won't let them. Not until the warmth of spring arrives again.

'How're things with the new house?' I ask politely.

Matthew left the old house we'd shared a month ago and moved into a large detached house on the other side of the river. It's beautiful and spacious, and nothing like the claustrophobic space I live in now. We're both moving on, and we need to, but while he seems to be able to carry on his life without sacrifice, I'm left to start all over again. Leaving our marriage with nothing and trying to rebuild a new life for myself, by myself. Renting this tiny, damp cottage, driving an old, worn-out car, buying second-hand furniture, still desperately trying to find a job, any job, so that I can afford to live a decent life. While Matthew's moving on, I feel like I'm going backwards.

He shrugs. 'Getting there,' he says with a sigh. 'Your parents have been a great help.'

In a flash, hot anger threatens in my stomach and my insides shake. My parents have helped Matthew almost non-stop since we separated. He became a son to replace me, their daughter. He got all their help, I got none. He got their attention. I was left out in the cold. I'm still left out in the cold. I shake my head in frustration. I don't understand why they're doing this to me.

'I'm sure they have,' I say under my breath, trying to hide the note of resentment in my voice. I can feel my face flushing and my hands begin to tremble. Quickly, I push myself away from the doorframe and take a deep breath to quell the rising anger. It's not his fault, I remind myself: it's theirs. And I guess it's mine too. I shouldn't have been stupid enough to think that I might've mattered more than outdated principles. I should've known.

'Anyway,' I say quickly, looking over my shoulder through the house, 'I'd better go and check on the kids. Wednesday's fine.'

Matthew nods and steps backwards away from the door, hands thrust deeply into the front pockets of his jeans, shoulders pulled up towards his ears, bracing himself against the increasing chill of the afternoon. As he turns away, he takes a beanie hat from the pocket of his khaki-coloured winter jacket and pulls it down low over his head. He raises his hand in a silent goodbye and I close the door to him and the bitter afternoon.

I walk through the house and stand in the tiny kitchen at the back. Looking out onto the small garden, I watch Ruby and James playing happily together, unaware of the falling darkness and the growing cold. I'll have to call them in in a few minutes, I think. But for now, I let them play. I pull myself up onto the worktop by the window and sit gazing at them, swinging my legs from side to side, watching a bundle of bright-pink and of pale-blue bounce up and down over and over again. Tumbling over one another, falling onto their backs in fits of giggles, legs and arms flailing everywhere. The enormity of how much I love them strikes me, and as always, it's shocking in its intensity but not in its reasoning. They are my creation, my world, my reason for carrying on through the past few months. Nothing will ever compare to that.

So many times over the past few months I have questioned myself. I have looked at them and asked myself why I did what I did. If it was worth the pain I saw on their little faces. But now I see their smiles and I hear their laughter and I submerge myself in it, closing my eyes and leaning my forehead against the cool glass of the window, letting their happiness saturate me, flooding my mind and dissolving the negative thoughts that still linger there from time to time. And I let myself think, for the first time in what feels like forever, that maybe now everything's going to be okay.

And my mind turns once again to you. I let it wander back to earlier this morning. Memories of waking up next to you. Of letting myself feel the warmth of another being. Of letting another become a part of me. Of letting somebody else take over me, if only physically and if only for the night. My heart starts racing, and the feeling of tenderness I already have towards you, still a perfect stranger, overwhelms me. I want to relive last night all over again, in all its perfect, unexpected chaos and awkwardness and drunken passion. I open my eyes and an excited smile plays across my lips, because I know I'll see you again. I made sure of that.

Chapter Six

I'm curled-up in bed when the text message finally arrives. It's only 9pm, but I'm exhausted. The previous late night has already wiped me out, but an afternoon spent running around after Ruby and James, making tea, bathing them, making packed lunches, ironing school uniforms and bundling them off to bed has left me worn-out. An unwelcome reminder that I maybe shouldn't burn the candle at both ends, that I should remember where my responsibilities lie.

Still, despite my weariness I can't escape the fact that last night was fantastic. It was just what I needed to raise my spirits, to boost my confidence. I've been trying to read a book before attempting to sleep, some trashy romantic holiday novel, but I can't concentrate. My mind is awash with amazing recollections. They're just little things, but they're important little things. I remember my cheeks aching with the constant laughter. I remember how we caught each other's eyes over and over again. I remember how our hands brushed together sometimes as we talked. How I clung onto you to steady myself as we walked from one bar to another, our friends chatting to one another up ahead, me holding tightly onto you, arm linked through yours, leaning against your shoulder in my less-than-sober state. And I remember how you didn't seem to mind and how I didn't want the night to end and how, when the taxi we'd all piled into pulled up outside your house, you invited me in, not wanting it to end either.

Smiling, I pick up my phone from the small bedside cabinet tucked into the tiny space beneath the window and see an unknown number on the screen. I know instantly it must be you. I'd given you my number this morning just before I left. As I stood on your doorstep in the harsh light of the early afternoon, in last night's dress and dark make-up staining the skin around my eyes, with Melissa waiting patiently for me in her car, I had kissed you awkwardly on the cheek, unsure what would happen next, and asked you to call me sometime. That maybe we could do this again, if you wanted to.

We'd lain in your bed for most of the morning. Hardly saying a word. The atmosphere swaying between lazy affection and disbelief that we'd ended up here. Strangers back at your house, in your bed. And as the morning drew on, the pain in our heads increased, alcohol draining from our systems and leaving its telltale throbbing behind our eyes and sickness in our stomachs. As the clock reached 1pm I'd decided it was probably time to leave. I'd be getting the kids back later. I needed to get home. Get organised. Get showered. So I leave you alone with your hangover, and in Melissa's car on the way home, giggling about what happened, sharing secrets, I try to put on hold all my feelings about last night, because I don't want to let myself get carried away in my rose-tinted world. I don't want to hope that this could be something, only for me to end up hurting like I did before. Because I don't want to hurt ever again. I can't. I won't.

Still, I can't help the flutter of excitement in my stomach as I prop myself up on the deep-purple-coloured pillows of the borrowed bedding and swipe my index finger across the screen. The message flashes up instantly in my palm and I kick my legs up and down vigorously beneath the duvet in pure animated happiness. I curse myself for being so cynical and instantly push the thought to the back of my mind, out of sight where it belongs.

'You've left something behind,' your words say. 'I was thinking you might want to come and get it back sometime?'

Flirty? Or annoyed? My brain instantly plumps for the second option, always putting a downer on things, while my heart argues that of course you're being flirty and this is an open invitation to meet up. It's obvious really, it says. My head doesn't agree and sulks in the corner when I take my heart's side, not wanting any part in this anymore. But really, my heart admonishes, you should be used to this by now. Suck it up: we're on the verge of happiness here.

I pause, looking around the bedroom as I decide how to respond. My gaze falls on the worn grey carpet turned up in the corner by the skirting board, coming away from the floorboards, frayed and tattered and horrible. My double bed, one of the few possessions I salvaged when I left Matthew, takes up almost all the space in here. The air smells damp and old. James and Ruby are squeezed into the other bedroom. Tucked up in bunk beds with little room for anything else. Dark patches of dampened brickwork staining the paint above their beds. This is not where I want to be. This is not where I want to stay. I need to forge a new life for myself, and now is the time to do it. I smile and know I have to seize this opportunity.

My thumbs are poised over the screen keyboard, but I'm not sure what to say. I want to see you again, but I don't know how to ask without sounding too keen, desperate almost. I read your message a second time, and I try on the feeling that maybe you really do want to see me again. And it fits, it definitely fits. If I were standing up, maybe I'd do a little dance, jump around a bit, let the feeling flow. But instead, I lie gazing up at the awful paper lampshade that hangs from the single bulb above my bed and I let my face break into a grin so wide it hurts. My heart and I high-five each other excitedly, while my head sighs and glowers from over in the corner where she sits sullenly biding her time.

I giggle quietly to myself, pulse racing. My plan has worked. I've waited all afternoon for you to find the silver ring I left on your chest of drawers. Crossing my fingers that you would see it and get in touch. And you have. And I'm over the moon, soaring across space like a super-jet pilot, a crazy rocket ship with nowhere else to go but up. But I'm not sure I should let you know that. In fact, I'm pretty sure

I shouldn't. Do I want you to know that I'm dying to see you again already? Or maybe I should tell you. I don't want you to get away after all. I can't have you slipping through my fingers already. But at the same time, I don't want to frighten you away. Moons and rocket ships after less than 24 hours? Maybe not.

I groan and throw my phone down on the bed, burying my face momentarily in the pillows. I need to stop overthinking this and just punch out a reply. So I pick up my phone and respond: 'Thank you for letting me know. I'd wondered where it had gone! Yes, I would really like the ring back and perhaps I could pick it up sometime?' Send. There. Done.

I stare at the screen. Wait. Wait some more. Fingers tapping a nervous, impatient beat on the back of the battered Union Jack phone cover. Come on. This is excruciating. Two whole minutes. Surely that's enough time to read and reply. Five. Six. What is he doing? Eight. This is ridiculous, I'm a grown woman, not a love-struck teenager! I shove the phone roughly underneath my pillow and switch out the light. I'll just wait until the morning. I can do that. He's probably tired and has gone to sleep too. He'll have work tomorrow. It's fine, it's fine.

Two minutes and two beeps later, it's done. We're meeting up again, in a couple of weekends' time. When I don't have Ruby and James. When they're with their dad and I can play at being myself again. I can't remember the last time I felt so happy. I save your number into my phone and let myself bathe in a brief moment of contentment. And then, another thought barges its way in, all pointy elbows and accusing eyes, shoving through the crowd and breaking up the happy party I had going on. 'Don't screw this up, Belle,' it says, blowing a sickly-sweet kiss of reality at me that strikes me hard and square on in the face. 'Do not screw this up.'

Chapter Seven

October gives way to November, and as the daylight hours grow shorter and the nights draw in even further, Matthew decides he wants a divorce. The message comes out of the blue. He says it'll help him to move on. That it'll help close this chapter of his life and let him start a new one. And I understand, of course I do. Since I left, all we've done is skirt around the issue, doing our best to pretend we don't have any big decisions to make about our family. But we do. What's the point of putting it off any longer?

He says he'll pay. I agree. And it's done. Right then the decision is made. And suddenly our story ends. Just like that, the book is closed. A love story stopped midway. A happy ending lost to the harsh truths of real life. There are no fairy tales here.

But then there is you. And there could be a new story, if I'm lucky. I could write another ending. A better one. One that doesn't hurt quite so much as before. And that night, the night Matthew and I leave our tale behind, you call me. And I smile at the sound of your voice. Through the distant sadness, I feel happiness tugging, and I let my smile widen. Because I'm going to see you again. And soon.

Chapter Eight

November 2011

I look good. You told me so. Your eyes, your smile, the way your hands found my waist at every opportunity. It paid off, I think, smiling to myself. All those hours spent in the bath this afternoon, skin turning white and fingertips shrivelling under the mountain of frothy bubbles I disappeared beneath, breathing in their expensive perfume, veiling my skin with the warm scent of vanilla, sweet honey and exotic coconut. A new twist on luxury, or so the girl at the sales counter said. As long as I smell irresistible, I'd joked. She told me you'd love it, so I bought the matching body lotion too. I didn't want to take any chances.

As it turns out, I feel amazing and I'm here with you in this little bar ordering drinks and you look just as beautiful and as I gaze up at you I can't quite believe this is happening and my heart backflips and somersaults out of control when you hand me my drink and lean down to plant a kiss gently on my lips and everything just feels so incredible, and happiness and excitement and exhilaration rush at me all at once and spin me around and around until I'm dizzy and giggling and on the verge of loving life once more.

Then the glass hits my face. I didn't see it coming and at first, I don't feel the pain from the force of the blow to my jaw. The tumbler falls to the floor and shatters at my feet, the sound lost among the loud music, shards of glass catching the light like poisonous glitter. I taste blood. Then the agony hits me, delayed, but no less intense. The side of my face is burning. The inside of my mouth a metallic cocktail of bloody warmth against my tongue.

And through my shock I see her, an apparition, blurry through a haze of disbelief and irrepressible tears. A shadow watching me from the sidelines of my past, a vague shape who tiptoed in, bided its time, inched ever closer from the back of my mind until it is right in front of me and I can't decide if it's real or my imagination goading me, making me crazy.

But it is her, and I feel sick. Vision distorts. Images lost in the periphery to wavering blackness, its edges creeping inwards obscuring my sight. Bright sparks flicker and float on the threshold of an incoherent space. Her face among the blackness filled with a wild mix of satisfaction and pure hatred; the smile on her lips at odds with the inferno in her eyes. And I am suddenly petrified. This is not how it's supposed to happen. This isn't fair. Why now? Why now?

I stagger backwards into you, legs giving way. Pain blasting the side of my head as the loud music around me dulls to a muted, meaningless thud. People disappear from view as everything crashes inwards. Then I feel your arms around me, and you're holding my head tightly against your chest, my mouth oozing blood and staining your shirt in bright-red seeping circles. I can hear shouting and I feel bodies jostling against mine as the chaos continues around me. Your voice reaches my ears in muffled waves as I'm crushed against you and I hear shreds of conversation, fragments of a past coming back to haunt me.

'That was well deserved … you don't know … find out what she did … she doesn't give a fuck about anyone but herself.'

And all I can do is close my eyes to everything that is happening, cling onto you and hope with all my heart that it all goes away.

Seconds turn into minutes, and through the commotion, you take my head in your hands and hold me gently away from you. Everything around me fades into the distance as I try to focus only on you, and try to ignore the look of confusion and concern in your eyes. Somebody hands you a towel and you take it with uncertain hands. My face must be a mess. Fresh blood trickling from my lips, running in tiny rivers to join the already dried and darkened stains on my cheeks and chin. You try to give the towel to me, try to get me to clean myself up, but I can't let go of you. I hold on tight to the shirt at your waist, bunching the fabric between my clenched fists, scared that if I let go either I'll fall or you'll run. So, I hold onto you and I won't let you go. And you understand, pressing the towel to my broken skin gently, turning the white cotton blood-red. Just like your shirt.

Just like the towel and the bathroom and a 17-year old's blood on the floor.

At least she's gone. In those desperate minutes, when I wished it all away, she left. I don't need to see her satisfied smile and burning eyes anymore. So now you take me home. The night cut short. Our first date ending in the worst possible way.

You hail a taxi and help me climb in gingerly, sliding in gently beside me and pulling me close to you, wrapping your arms around me and placing a hand carefully against the side of my head, holding me against you to stop me shaking. My head rests against your chest and I can hear the racing of your heart, punching a confused rhythm against your ribcage.

Rain is falling outside in a fine mist and as the taxi pulls away from the kerb I hear the rhythmic squeak of the wipers against the windscreen. My eyes gaze out of the window, though I see nothing but the smear of raindrops as the headlights of passing cars turn them into tiny yellow globes against the glass. As the taxi speeds up, orange streetlights cast a strobing glow across your shirt where your arm lies across your chest, your hand never leaving its gentle resting place against my cheek. Your fingers weave their way through my hair and you stroke my head backwards and forwards, backwards and forwards with your fingertips. And the windscreen wipers continue to whine in their measured way, the streetlights pulse by with mesmerising regularity, and your fingers dance across my scalp, backwards and forwards, backwards and forwards as my eyes slowly close.

You close the front door having settled the taxi fare and turn to me. I sit on the edge of your sofa, stooped over, arms wound around myself, hair hanging limply across my face. If I reached out to touch it, I know it would feel sticky because I can smell the sweetness of the alcohol that drenched me as the glass made contact with my face. I look up at you from beneath the dark strands and you don't move. You stand by the door, looking at me without expression. I look at your shirt, stained red and ruined, and I shuffle uncomfortably, not sure what to do or say. Endless seconds pass and not a word is spoken. Then you walk right past me and head into the kitchen. I try to follow you with my gaze, but turning my head sends a jolt of pain through my jaw and I put my head in my hands instead.

When you return you have whisky and you hold the glass out to me wordlessly. I look up at you but I still can't read what your face is telling me. So I take the glass hesitantly and press it to my swollen lips, sipping the liquid slowly. You have a glass of your own and you knock back the measure quickly, wincing as it hits the back of your throat, never taking your eyes off me. I look straight back at you and do the same, the heat of the drink quickly spreading down my throat and across my chest.

'What now?' You ask into the silence, placing your glass heavily on the coffee table in front of me.

I shake my head and shrug, looking down at my glass and swirling the remains of the whisky around and around, watching it coat the sides in syrupy waves.

'I don't know,' I say. My voice is thick and it's difficult to talk through the pain in my mouth and the sting in my fattened lips. 'I should explain. I'm so sorry, I…' my voice cracks and tears threaten my eyes. I take a deep breath and reach towards the coffee table, placing my glass beside yours. I put my head in my hands and try again, talking to the carpet, too ashamed to raise my head and look at you.

'I don't know what happened. I didn't expect to ever see her again. I thought it was over. I…I…' Words tumble out of me and I know I'm not making sense. I let the breath I've been holding escape slowly between my bruised lips, shoulders falling as the air leaves my lungs. 'I thought everything was over now,' I say through the sigh, more to myself than to you.

I look up and when I catch your gaze, I want to tell you everything, but I'm not sure what will happen next if I do. Before my resolve completely disappears, and while I still have some trace of courage left, I inhale sharply, about to begin again, but you take a sudden step towards me shaking your head and I jump slightly at the unexpected movement.

'Not tonight,' you say softly, crouching down and pushing my hair away from my eyes. You look directly at me, holding my face gently in your palms, and I stare back at you, wondering if you can see the fear and uncertainty in my eyes as clearly as I can see the guarded judgement in yours. You run your hands down my arms, raising goosebumps across my skin, and circle your fingers around my wrists. 'Not tonight,' you say again.

You pull me carefully to my feet and, feeling dizzy and light-headed, I lean into you to steady myself. You wait a moment, hands resting at the base of my back, the heat from your palms penetrating the fabric of my dress, spreading over my hips and upwards to my waist. My head rests against your shoulder and I can see the pulse in your neck. I raise a hand and hold my fingers against it, lightly touching the skin there, feeling the beat of you pressing against my fingertips, slowly at first then quicker, more urgent. I stroke the skin of your neck in hesitant uncertain circles, softly tracing the line of your jaw down to your chin and back again.

You inhale deeply and press me hard against you, the pressure of your hands on my lower back strong and insistent. Something stirs inside me, my stomach jumps and twists, a flicker of electricity as my own pulse accelerates to match yours. I tilt my head upwards and press my swollen lips against the heat of your neck, suddenly wanting nothing but to feel your skin against mine.

You draw in another sharp breath and bend to scoop me up in your arms as if I'm nothing, as if I'm a feather and you're the breeze. Somewhere on the periphery, I feel pain, dull and distant, across my jaw, down my neck and through my shoulders. But another feeling is taking over, and the aching sensation blends into the background, becoming something I almost can't place for the moment.

Upstairs in your bedroom, where just two short weeks ago we lay carefree and reckless, you now lower me onto your bed tenderly and carefully, as though I'm fragile and delicate. As though I might break at any moment. As though I'm already broken. Yet my fragile heart beats hard and fast, and my breath quickens as you lay over me and place a line of gentle kisses along the curve of my neck and across my exposed shoulder. I arch my back, pressing my body against yours, crushing myself against you despite the pain I know exists somewhere outside this bubble.

And then you're undressing me. Tugging my dress from my shoulders and letting it fall to my waist, running your fingers over my stomach, pulling the dress free from my hips, down my legs and discarding it on the floor, drinking me in with your eyes. And I fumble with the belt of your jeans in the dark, finding the zip but then switching and wrenching your shirt over your head as you kick your jeans off.

My fingers find the muscles of your back and I cling on to you, feeling the strength in your shoulders and tracing every protrusion of your long spine as you kiss me hard, your fingers burning paths across me, my skin savouring every move you make as you take my bruised and shaken body and relieve all the hurt. As my pain and awareness finally dissolve, melting away into the heat as we give ourselves up to each other again, I don't allow myself to wonder what's going to happen next. I can't think beyond now, this moment with you. I know I can't pretend; I can't hide. There's no escaping my past. I can't make it not exist.

Because it does exist and it's always going to be there. But for now, if only for now, it's forgotten.

***

I wake and it's pitch black, but I know instantly where I am. I'm turned away from you, but I can feel the weight of your arm across my waist, the warmth from your steady breathing on the back of my neck and in my hair. I can feel the length of your body pressed tightly against mine, and you feel so inviting, but I'm so, so cold. The shock of the attack, and the sadness at what I know has to happen next, drains all my heat away.

I open my mouth to lick my parched lips, but the action sends a heatwave of pain through my jaw. A whimper escapes involuntarily and I reach out for your hand, taking it in mine and gripping it tightly, swallowing hard and squeezing my eyes shut to stop the tears. I haven't cried yet. I won't let her win. But I'm not sure how much longer I can pretend.

I feel you stir at my touch and you pull me closer into you, planting a soft kiss on the back of my head, resting your cheek there, stroking the back of my neck with your free hand.

'You okay?' you ask into the darkness.

I try so hard to be brave. I try so, so hard. I nod, scared if I speak, I'll break down. But I break down anyway, my body shaking as I cry silently into the blackness. And as I cry, you turn me carefully towards you. You run your thumb slowly across my swollen lips, kissing my bruised face gently. And you kiss away my tears with such tenderness that it makes me want to cry all the more.

You didn't ask again. Even though you wanted to, you didn't ask why. But I have to tell you. I have to tell you what I've done. And I know that when I do, when you know the truth about me, I'll need to hold onto you so tightly, because I don't want you to go. I need you to stay so, so much.

Chapter Nine

November 2011

It continues to rain the following day, lashing loudly against the living-room window, pushing hard against the panes as though trying to get in. But you turn up the sound on the TV to drown out the storm and hug me in closer. It is late-afternoon, and the sky is dark; heavy clouds refusing to give way to the crisp autumn day on the other side, leaving the day grey and surly instead. In contrast, your living-room is cast in the warm golden glow of the table lamp, and the bright flames dancing eagerly in the fireplace throw animated shadows across the carpet. I'm curled-up in your arms on the sofa, cocooned among you and the duvet you've dragged from your bed upstairs. I feel safe.

I'd woken late that morning to find you looking at me. Lying silently beside me, the heavy light of the grey morning barely illuminating the room, your face muted among the blue shadows. I'd half-smiled at you through my sleepiness, exhaustion still clinging to me from the previous night. My eyes were swollen and red from crying, and they were stinging with every movement they made. Without speaking, you'd leaned forwards and kissed my eyelids, your lips cool against their troubled heat, and I'd smiled again, but the ache across my mouth and jaw had quickly turned the smile into a wince.

'Come here.' You'd frowned along with me and pulled me towards you protectively. 'I can take you home if you'd like me to,' you'd told me gently as I'd pressed my aching body against yours and buried my head into your neck, finding the warmth of your skin soothing. 'Or, you know, Belle, you can stay here with me too. For a little while longer, until you feel better. But only if you want to. It's up to you.' You'd kissed the top of my head with such tenderness my heart almost broke. I didn't deserve this kindness.

'I'd love to stay,' I'd managed to whisper. The last thing I wanted to be right then was alone. I'd felt safe there in your embrace. Protected.

But what if you start asking questions? I was instantly on edge. What if you wanted to know why? I'd pulled away from you slightly, needing space to breathe while the brief feeling of relief at being wanted by you was quickly replaced by fear.

A surge of panicked energy coursed through my veins, causing my limbs to shake and my breath to become too shallow. Too fast. What if, when I tell you what happened, you send me away? The room began to spin. What if, when you find out, you don't want to know me anymore? Nausea. I retch.

'Shit, are you okay, Belle?' you ask. 'Let me get you some water.'

You're bound to question everything; I know you are. You're bound to ask. And I'll have to answer you, somehow.

You'd found some tracksuit pants and a hooded top and laid them on the bed for me, both of us laughing, knowing the clothes would drown me. But I was so grateful for your kindness and understanding. You had such a calm, gentle air about you, and right then I wanted to be drawn inside that and to be held there forever, to calm the whirlwind of my own life that keeps chasing me persistently. A stubborn tempest I can't seem to shake off.

You'd taken a towel into the bathroom for me and started the shower, telling me I'd feel better once I was cleaned up. And I'd suddenly wondered how I must look: battered, bruised, bedraggled. Lost and frail, perching precariously on the edge of a bridge known as the truth, about to hurl myself off.

When I'd entered the bathroom, I was naked and the mirror hanging over the sink was steamed up from the heat of the shower so I couldn't see my reflection clearly, just blurred lines and hazy shapes. Vague and indistinct. I'd reached my hand out slowly towards the glass and rubbed my palm across its cold surface, clearing away the fog and revealing the shock of my reflection. I'd visibly flinched, jolting away from myself and averting my eyes momentarily.

All along my jaw a bruise was forming beneath the redness and the swelling there. Grey-blue to match the stormy sky, its edges bleeding upwards across my cheek. My chin and neck were laced in ribbons of blood, dark-red slurs across my skin, scabbed and peeling, pooling in the hollow of my collarbone in a dried-up well. Lips, swollen and edged in the deep crimson of dried blood – a stark hue smeared across the pale skin of my right cheek, fading into the grey bruising at my jaw. Eyes so bloated they barely opened, their whites tinted pink and crisscrossed by a web of tiny bright-red veins. Salty stains left telltale rivers down my cheeks and their remnants hurt my eyes. My hair hung in dull, lank knots around my face.

And yet you hadn't said a word. You hadn't let me know how this was, how bad I'd looked, how utterly defeated. You just took it all in your stride and I'd wondered what I did to deserve that. I'd stepped into the shower and let the heat wash away both the evidence and the memory of last night. I'd used your shampoo and ran my fingers through my hair, tugging at the knots to loosen them, letting the suds dissolve the grime and the stickiness and the alcohol. Then I'd turned towards the flow of the water and let it rain down over my face. And it hurt, it really hurt, but I'd let it keep washing away, washing away, until everything was gone.

**

And now it's late-afternoon and I'm here with you, curled-up and warm in your arms. You'd brought me breakfast cereal after my shower and for lunch you'd made us sandwiches, waiting patiently while I broke mine into small pieces and pushed them through my lips, chewing slowly and carefully through the stiffness in my jaw. For the rest of the day, we've watched TV. Films mostly. Flicking from one channel to the next. I let you choose what to watch, partly because you keep the remote, but mostly because I'm just happy to be close to you and I don't really care about anything else.

But halfway through one of the films, without warning, you mute the sound and look down at me curled around you. My head rests on your shoulder, my legs are drawn up across your lap and my arms circle your waist tightly. But you pull away from me slightly and remove your arm from my shoulder, shuffling around so that I have to move too until we're facing each other. You tip your head to one side, a curious, questioning look in your eyes. You've been thinking, and I know what's coming. And I hate this, because if last night hadn't happened, you'd never have needed to know.

'Who are you?' you ask. 'What did you do?'

Ebony

Chapter Ten

Amy stands in the corner of the playground clutching a jam-jar tightly to her chest. Her head is pointing downwards, her chin disappears into the top of her fluffy blue jumper, but her eyes look up, peering through a fringe of thick dark hair that I can already tell she likes to hide behind. I like that jumper. It's a pretty colour and it looks all new and soft. I bet her mummy let her choose it. I bet they went to town together, to all the shops, and I bet her mummy bought her whatever she wanted. Clothes and shoes and sweets and colouring books and that nail polish that smells of strawberries and pretty sparkly hair clips and that new My Little Pony that comes with a stable and a little ginger cat. I bet she did. Not like my mummy who goes shopping all by herself and chooses everything for me, or who makes me wear horrible jumpers she's knitted herself and that everyone laughs at because she's not really all that good at knitting. I bet her mummy would never do that. I bet she'd never pretend to be able to knit.

I watch her as I crouch down and remove a smear of mud from my new black patent-leather shoes. I lick my finger and rub the stain away roughly. Rub, rub, rub. Mummy won't be happy if I get these new shoes dirty. She just bought them all ready for me going back to school today. I can see myself in them and they need to stay that way. That's what she told me. So I rub and rub until the mud's gone and all that's left is my reflection in the shiny black and a dirty index finger. I wipe it on my white knee socks and tut at the brown fingerprint it leaves behind. Mummy didn't tell me to keep my socks clean though, so I'm sure it'll be okay.

I look across the playground again and wonder who that girl is and what she looks like underneath all her dark hair. I imagine that she has bright-blue eyes to match her jumper and rosy-pink cheeks like a pretty flower and ruby-red lips just like Snow White. She's one of my favourite princesses, Snow White, because she's beautiful and kind and she helps everybody, and I think that's really nice. But there was one time that I think she ate an apple, which was bad for her and that was really sad, and also a bit mean of somebody to give that to such a nice person. But then the handsome prince came along and saved her and they lived happily ever after. That's how it always ends. I like that ending. It's my favourite.

I stand and pick up my skipping rope and decide to go and say hello. I'm not at all sure where she came from, but she looks a bit sad standing there by herself. Maybe she can play my game with me if there's time. I look at my watch, the one Mummy bought me to help me learn how to tell the time, and I think it says twenty minutes past two, so that means there's only ten minutes left until Mrs Robinson blows the whistle. I think. I walk over to her anyway, dragging the skipping rope along behind me so that the wooden ends scrape and scratch across the tarmac and bounce off my ankles, probably giving me even more bruises. Mummy tells me off for being so clumsy and not watching where I'm going. But I can't help it if I've got so many things to do and I can't concentrate on them all at once. Yesterday I fell up the garden step because I was chasing a butterfly and didn't see where I was putting my feet until it was too late and I tripped. I fell into the red flowers that Mummy had just planted and squashed them all flat. Mummy didn't like that. I had to go to my room.

I run my hand across the back of my legs and remember how hot and red they felt yesterday after Mummy had told me off for ruining the garden. I twist round to look again, lifting my dress up a little bit so I can see better. They look okay today, no naughty red bits, just normal skin with one old yellow bruise on my thigh. This is my favourite dress. Mummy let me wear it today because it's my first day back at school and I really, really wanted to. But after today she says I need to keep it for best. It's dark-green and soft with a shiny gold belt, and I like the way the material feels all velvety against my fingers. It's a dress just like one Princess Diana wore once and she's an actual real-life princess, not just a fairytale one. I tried to change my name to Diana once and told everybody to call me that instead of my real name, but Mummy told me not to be so silly and that if I wasn't going to be sensible then she'd take the dress back to the shop. So I stopped.

As I get closer to the new girl, she lifts her head up a bit and her hair falls away from her face. It's really, really long hair. It goes all the way down her back and touches her bottom! I almost had hair that long once, but I got chewing gum stuck in it and Mummy made me get it all cut off and now it's really short. The ends tickle my chin all the time and I wish it was long again. Mummy says it'll grow, but I don't know how when the hairdresser just keeps cutting it all off. How am I meant to have plaits again if my hair never grows further than my chin? I suppose Princess Diana doesn't have plaits because her hair's short too, so maybe it's okay. With her hair away from her face, I can see I was almost right about her. She has pink cheeks and almost ruby-coloured lips and her face is so white it looks like the milk in the bottle that's on our kitchen table at breakfast time. And she has no freckles. Not one single one. I've got loads all over my nose. I wish I didn't. Princesses don't have freckles. They have faces like hers. But her eyes aren't blue, they're brown. I'm a little bit disappointed about that, but then I think her eyes look like chocolate buttons and I like those, so it's okay. My eyes are green, which is nice, but it's still not blue. I'd like shiny blue eyes like Cinderella. Shiny blue eyes and yellow hair like Cinderella and Princess Diana, My little brother and big sister have blue eyes and it makes me cross that I didn't get them too. For some reason, I was missed out. Somebody forgot. Or maybe they just ran out.

I stop staring and say, 'Hello, what's your name? I'm Isobel. Do you want to play? I know a good game. What's that you're holding? Can I see?'

She clutches the jam-jar even tighter to her jumper and puts her head down again so I can't see her almost Snow White face anymore. Then she tells me that she's called Amy. But I can hardly hear her because she just seems to whisper instead of talking properly and the words get lost in her jumper. If we're going to be friends, I'm going to have to get Amy to talk a bit louder, because otherwise my ears will probably get fed up of trying so hard to hear her all the time and then I won't be able to be her friend anymore.

'What's that, Amy?' I ask, dropping my skipping rope to the ground and stepping a little bit closer, pointing to the jam-jar.

'Caterpillars,' she says, stepping away from me until her back is up against the fence. She looks a little bit worried, like I'm going to grab the caterpillar jar and run away with it. But that's just silly because why would I want a jar of caterpillars? Unless they were like those yummy jelly sweeties and then I'd want the full jar. But then, they're actually jelly worms, I think.

'Caterpillars? Why do you have caterpillars? Ewww!' I scrunch my nose and pull my best 'urgh' face. Caterpillars are horrible squiggly things that eat all my Mummy's orange flowers and put big holes all over the place in all the leaves. Why would anybody want those?

'I'm growing butterflies,' she says quietly to the ground, and she sounds a little bit sad. And then I feel sad for making her feel sad when I didn't mean to.

'You're *growing* butterflies?' I need to double-check that I heard her properly, because I'm not sure how anybody grows a butterfly in a jam-jar.

Butterflies are my most favourite thing because they are just so pretty and their fluttery wings look like somebody painted a lovely colourful pattern onto them to make them look extra special. But just on one side, then they folded them up and pressed them together so the pattern ended up on the other wing too, all matching and exactly the same. I make butterflies like that on paper with loads of splodges of messy paint. My daddy showed me how when it rained for hours and hours one day.

Amy nods and slowly holds out the jam-jar for me to look at. I bend down and push my nose right up against the glass, but I can't see anything except for some brown leaves and bits of grass and it all looks a bit soggy.

'Where are they then?'

She holds the jar up to the light and twizzles it around a bit until she finds what she's looking for. 'There,' she says all proud, pressing her finger against the side of the jar so hard the end of it bends back and goes all white. 'See?'

But I don't.

'Where?' I ask again. I'm getting a bit fed up now because I can't see anything and I think she's just making fun of me. Trying to make me look silly.

'There,' Amy says, tap-tapping on the glass. 'Right there.'

I screw up my eyes, but there are no squiggly creatures in there that I can see. I look at Amy over the top of the jar and sigh loudly, like I've heard Mummy do when she's had enough of everything. 'There's nothing there is there? You're just making it up.' I bend to pick up my skipping rope. 'Well I'm bored now; I'm going to play.'

Her chocolate-button eyes suddenly go all huge on her milk-bottle face. They look all sparkly, the way eyes get when people are sad, and I feel bad all over again for making her upset. So, I put my skipping rope back down and shrug at her, shoving my hands into my coat pocket and looking away like I've seen people do when they're fed up. I find an apple I'd forgotten about crammed in my pocket, and I take a big bite, hoping Amy didn't poison it while I wasn't looking.

'You'd better show me then,' I say impatiently, between the chunks of lovely crunchy apple. Mummy would tell me off for talking with my mouth full, but Mummy's not here so she'll never know.

'Look, here,' she says, holding the jar out again slowly and pointing at the same place. 'See that brown thing hanging there? It looks like a little leaf on that piece of grass. See it?'

I look again and that's when I see it: a brown, lumpy thing that looks like a scrunched-up, crispy autumn leaf. I love autumn leaves, especially when there are piles of them on the pavement outside my house and I can jump in them and hear a zillion crunchy, crackling noises when they get squashed underneath my wellies. It's one of the best sounds *ever*, like when the waves hit the stony beach at Seamill and they're all white and foamy, like the top of Daddy's beer is sometimes, and then they go backwards again and pull all the pebbles with them, and the noise is like somebody saying 'shhhhhh' really loudly. Sometimes, when we visit there, I wish I could stay and listen to that noise forever.

When I see the brown thing she's pointing at, I nod hard, but I'm really confused. It's a brown thing, not a caterpillar, and *definitely* not a butterfly. I knew she wasn't telling me the truth.

That's not a caterpillar Amy!' I say, rolling my eyes at her and tutting my loudest. 'Don't you even know what a caterpillar is? It's a green thing that wriggles, a bit like a green worm, but it eats all the plants you put in your garden. That thing there is not one of those.'

Amy nods slowly at me, eyes still wide, as though I'm the silliest girl she's ever met. 'But it *is* Isobel. It's inside there. Inside that brown thing is a caterpillar, but it's busy turning into a butterfly just now.'

Now my eyes are wide too because I think she must be telling me naughty lies. Butterflies do not belong in horrible brown cases inside jam jars in my school playground. They are meant to be looking all pretty on flowers and sitting in the sunshine and fluttering about in the garden. I think *Amy's* the one being silly.

'It's a chrysalis,' she's explaining in her whispery voice that sounds like the wind blew most of it away. 'Caterpillars make them when they're ready to turn into a butterfly. They live inside there for a little while, getting everything ready, and then when they feel like everything is looking all nice and pretty and just right, they come out, just a teensy bit at a time. And when they do, they're not little caterpillars anymore, they're beautiful fluttery butterflies.' She says this last part like it's the happiest ending in the world, and I believe her.

'Just like Cinderella when the Fairy Godmother makes her beautiful,' I gasp. 'Just like a real proper fairytale.'

Amy nods at me really fast so that her fringe bobs in and out of her eyes, like a curtain at the theatre going up and down, and a clean soapy smell comes floating off her. Suddenly I have an exciting thought. 'I'm seven in a few weeks,' I say, stretching my head up and making my neck all long so I look as tall as I can. 'Next month. Do you think there'll be butterflies by then? I'd like lots of beautiful jam-jar butterflies for my birthday. That would be the best present *ever!*'

I jump up and down a little bit at the thought. A jam-jar full of pretty birthday butterflies I could keep beside my bed and feed lovely colourful flowers to so that they wouldn't get hungry. And they could keep me company when I'm sent to my room and can't watch the TV. That'd be perfect! But Amy looks at me like I'm not making any sense at all and tucks the jar back in her jumper out of sight. 'Oh, you don't get to keep them,' she says quietly. 'You have to let them go.'

You

Chapter Eleven

It's Boxing Night in the pub and I'm trying to get your attention. I'm trying hard because I've been so, so stupid. I should never have said it. I didn't mean to upset you, but I have and now I really want to make it better. But you won't look at me. You look over me and around me, but not at me. I can't meet your gaze because you tower above me, and I begin to feel like maybe this is pointless. I stand on tiptoes, leaning against the bar for balance, stretching my spine as far as I can to try and reach your level. But I can't.

'I'm sorry,' I say insistently, looking up at you again, searching your face for clues. 'It was just a silly comment. I didn't mean it, honestly, I didn't.'

But still, you ignore me.

I place my hand gently on your arm and shake my head, looking up at you with eyes I know are wide and pleading and confused. But you pull your arm away from my touch and turn your back, ordering a drink from the barman. I feel stupid. And I feel nervous.

I don't know where all this has come from. One minute we were having fun with friends, the next minute this. One throwaway comment I'd made in a fit of giggles saw you forcing your chair back from the table so hard that it fell over. The laughter stopped immediately and the atmosphere turned quickly to one of tension. I looked at Melissa, eyes wide and uncertain, who looked nervously between you and me. I turned to you and started to speak. I wanted to ask what was wrong, but I heard you swear under your breath and then I could only watch as you walked away. Melissa had shrugged and picked up her drink, concentrating very hard on stirring the cubes of ice around and around with her straw.

I looked across the table at the others, two of your good friends from school, and they stared blankly back at me, saying nothing. I sighed heavily, realising this was up to me to fix, and suddenly I felt embarrassed and slightly awkward in front of your friends. I felt the heat rising in my cheeks as I stood slowly, unsure of what I was meant to do, but knowing that I would have to do something. I looked to Melissa, who shrugged her shoulders again and nodded her head in your direction. I knew that I was expected to go to you.

So now I've followed you to the bar and I'm beginning to wonder why, because you're acting like I'm not here. And I am. I fucking am! You pay the barman for your drink and take a sip, and even though you make no attempt to move away, you ignore me still. And suddenly I've had enough. I slam my hand down hard on the bar, the action immediately stinging my palm and sending prickling ripples of pain up my arm. I clench my fist, knuckles white, and I stare hard at you, daring you to ignore me again.

'For God's sake, will you just fucking speak to me.' I slam my hand down again, my fist this time, so hard that it makes the three discarded, half-pint glasses at my elbow jump and rattle.

Still no response and I'm really angry now. 'Fucking. Look. At. Me.' I demand through clenched teeth. Jaw clamped tight. Adrenaline making me brave.

It's only then that you turn slowly around and look directly at me, straight into my eyes. And for the most fleeting of seconds that look tells me I'm the most despicable being you've ever laid eyes on. Words die in my mouth and I feel like I've run straight into a brick wall, my breath catching in my throat as I hit the hard surface of your stare. But almost as soon as it arrived, the look is gone and your features soften.

'Don't say those things,' you tell me, quietly and matter-of-factly. 'I don't want to hear you speak that way. You should know not to say things like that.'

I swallow hard and look at the floor, heart racing, blood pumping hard in my veins, coursing through them with a curious mixture of apprehension and anger. I want to tell you that I didn't mean anything by it. That it was a meaningless comment, a casual gesture made in the flow of conversation. But I don't, because I'm still knocked out from your gaze. Suddenly I feel like you're right and I'm wrong and the anger that rose so quickly inside me retreats. And instead of speaking up, I promise you that I won't ever say those things again. I don't want to ever upset you; I only want to make you smile. I won't ever compliment another man on his outfit again. It was wrong of me. And I'm sorry. Really, I am.

You step towards me then, beer bottle in hand, and put your arms around me. You press a kiss hard against the top of my head, and I feel the cold glass of the bottle against my shoulder.

'It's okay,' you say. 'It's okay. I forgive you.'

Then you steer me back to the table, free hand firm against the nape of my neck, and you carry on as if nothing has happened. It's all forgotten in an instant. So, I take my lead from you and do the same. I shrug it off like it was nothing. Laughter returning, drinks flowing. But I'm on edge, and that feeling stays with me for the rest of the night. Because I can't forget that momentary blaze in your eyes. I can't forget how it made me shrink to nothing inside.

Ebony

Chapter Twelve

December 1985

I knew something bad would happen when she wasn't here.

Amy's gone away for Christmas to somewhere. I don't know where. She didn't look very happy about it when she told me. Said she had to see some people on Christmas Day that she didn't really want to. She thought they didn't like her very much because they never wanted to talk to her, and the place they lived was always full of other people that she didn't know who kept getting in the way. She said they were always sad too, these other people. Always crying and talking to each other in tiny whispery voices. I think that must be how Amy ended up with a voice that sounded like a wispy breeze.

When she was telling me she had to go away for a while, her cry-baby eyes got even more cry-baby and actually cried, and I don't think I've ever seen her cry for real. Except for that time when she was running too fast in the playground and tripped over her own shoes. She scraped her knee really badly and I had to sit with her in the classroom while Mrs Johnston put some ointment on that smelled so strong it made my eyes water and my head hurt. T-something she said it was called. T-see-something I think. Anyway, it was awful and I really wanted to go outside to get away from it, but Amy was so upset and so sad and said her knee was really hurting her, so I stayed and just kept taking big breaths and holding them for as long as I could to stop the smelly stuff getting up my nose and into my eyes. It made Amy laugh, really laugh lots and lots, and she forgot all about her cut knee. So I did it for longer than I really needed to, because after a while the nasty smell didn't smell so bad after all, and I probably could've just stopped the Holding-My-Breath game. But doing it stopped Amy crying, so I carried on until I was dizzy.

On the last day of school before the Christmas holidays, Amy had given me a Christmas card she'd made from a piece of cereal packet folded in half. I know it was a cereal packet because on the inside I could see half of a photograph of cornflakes with her scribbly writing smudged all over the top. She said her Mummy had got cross with her for getting glue on the kitchen table while she was sticking on the stars all around her drawing of baby Jesus, and she got sent to her room so she didn't get to finish it.

So, baby Jesus is half coloured in, his blanket isn't coloured in at all, and he looks a little bit pale if I'm honest. I'd have done his cheeks all pink and chubby, and made his blanket lovely and blue because he's a boy and boys should have blue everything. Not like Richard in my class. He wears pink jumpers sometimes and it makes me giggle a little bit. I bet he's got one of those mummies who buys him everything and doesn't let him choose either, just like I do. Because what boy would choose pink? Looking at the card Amy handed me, I'd have made baby Jesus's manger a little bit bigger too, because he looks a bit like a giant baby in there, and if it was real life there's no way he'd have fitted into it and the innkeeper would've had to think of a whole new place to put him, like a hotel with a bunk bed or something, and that would've changed the whole story of Christmas.

I don't tell Amy any of this though. Instead, I say it's okay because that happens to me too. I get sent to my room *all* the time, and it's so *boring*. That's why I always draw pictures, to pass the time. Amy said she reads books. Her mummy tells her not to and says she has to just sit on the bed quietly and think about what she's done. But Amy says that it only takes about five minutes to do that – maybe eight if she really stretches it out and thinks about some other stuff too, so afterwards she reads her book. She's not meant to, she says, but who's going to know? And when she hears somebody coming up the stairs, she hides the book underneath her pillow so that they don't see. I think that's a really, really good idea, and I must remember to try that the next time Mummy tells me not to do something. I might be too scared though, I think, but I don't tell Amy that.

As well as being sent to her room, Amy gets red legs like me. Sometimes her mummy makes her come to school in itchy scratchy tights to hide the naughty red marks. Amy says her mummy tells her it's so that nobody asks how they got there and she won't need to explain about her eczema. I ask Amy what 'x-zeema' is because I've never heard that word before in all my life and she says she's not sure, but that it must be another word for when mummies smack you for being naughty. So now I think that all mummies must be the same and that makes me feel better.

Maybe 'x-zeema' is a bit like 'x-rays'. They're something to do with your skin and bones, aren't they? I remember my big sister getting a special picture taken of her insides by a machine that can see right through your skin and into your bony, bloody bits! I'm not sure what was wrong with her, but I think that something was poorly on the inside somewhere, and it wasn't just a cut knee or something. She's okay now though. I remember how we all hoorayed when the doctor told us...

I'd be feeling in a hooray mood right now if Mummy hadn't made beef stew for tea. I hate beef stew, and I especially hate how the carrots are all soggy and mushy, and the beef bits get all chewy and then she puts big squishy dumplings on the top and it feels like eating big balls of fluff and they make me gag. But it's Christmas Eve, so I eat it all up because Santa won't come if I don't. That's what Mummy said, and Daddy nodded so it must be true. So I put big mouthfuls in and try to swallow them so that it's all over and done with quickly. But the mouthfuls are too big and my throat won't let them passed, and so I have to chew and chew and chew to get it all smaller, and my tongue just wants to spit everything out because it doesn't like the nasty taste.

I have to hold it there inside my mouth though until I can swallow it, but it makes my eyes water and everything goes all blurry from the tears and I feel a little bit sick. And now my tummy feels funny because of it, but I daren't tell Mummy, because then Santa might hear me complaining and he won't stop at our house. He'll miss us out because I'm being silly, and he'll go right on to next door instead, which wouldn't really be very fair because they're really old and they probably only need things like new slippers and a woolly hat, and then it'd be all my fault if nobody in my house got any presents.

So to stop me thinking about my sore tummy, I'm sitting on the floor in front of the fire making snowflakes. I saw them doing it on Blue Peter the other day and they looked so pretty, so I'm making some and I'm going to ask Daddy to put them in the window so that everybody passing by can see them, and I might make an extra special big one for Amy and one for Santa too. I don't think Amy watches Blue Peter, so she probably won't know how to make them, and she'll love it so much if I give one to her because she likes pretty things and she'll like it even more because I made her it and we're the most best friends *ever*.

I hold the piece of white paper flat against the brown and orange swirly carpet and fold it up carefully loads and loads of times until it's a really small triangle. Then I cut out little holes all around the edges, which is really tough and sometimes I have to ask Daddy to help me. Then it's the best part, where I unfold it and once it's all opened out it looks just like a beautiful snowflake. It's like real, proper magic right in front of your eyes. It looks really easy to do, but actually you have to be really, really careful and you can only make a good snowflake if you do it properly. My little brother does *not* do it properly. He can't fold straight or cut out the right shapes or anything. His snowflakes look like scrunched-up bits of waste paper. My sister doesn't even want to make any because she's too busy watching Alice in Wonderland on TV, so mine are definitely the best.

I can hear a song in the background about a very merry unbirthday, but I'm just too busy at the minute to watch the film properly. I'm at a really important bit, the middle of the snowflake. Daddy showed me that if you cut this bit out in just the right shape, you get a teensy star in the middle of your snowflake when you open it all out and it looks even more brilliant. So I really take my time, biting at the tip of my tongue and squeezing my left eye shut so I can concentrate on getting the shape just right. Bit by bit, carefully … carefully …

The scissors are whipped from my hand and fly across the room, hitting the sideboard that stands against the opposite wall, before falling to the floor and sliding under Daddy's armchair beside the fire. The almost-finished paper snowflake is still held up in my hand in front of me, waiting for me to cut out the little triangle that will make the pretty star shape that will make my snowflake look extra special. For a few tiny seconds, I'm not sure what's happened. Then Daddy's eyes look past me from his seat in the armchair in the corner to somebody standing behind, and that's when I hear her voice.

'For goodness sake, Isobel, can you just stop that!'

Mummy.

I look at Daddy because I'm a little bit confused about what it is that I need to stop and maybe he can help, but his eyes are fixed on Mummy and he doesn't look at me at all.

'Stop with all the noise,' she carries on. 'The constant annoying squeaking of those scissors is driving me mad. Why do you always have to make such a commotion, such a din? Why can't you just sit quietly like everybody else and stop being such a nuisance? I've had enough!'

I turn to tell her that I am being quiet and that I'm sorry the scissors made a noise, but she's not looking at me, she's looking at the floor all around me, at all the tiny pieces of white paper that I've cut out to make my snowflakes. Her neck and her cheeks suddenly start to go all red and I worry that her head is filling up with something nasty.

'And look at all this mess.' She's still looking at the paper-strewn floor, but she's shouting at me now. 'Honestly, sometimes I think this house would be a lot better off if it were just your brother and sister who lived here with us and we didn't have to constantly run around after you.'

My eyes suddenly feel all hot and wet and I look down at my knees so that nobody sees. Mummy would just ask me why I'm crying anyway, and Daddy would snuggle me on his knee if Mummy would let him. But she won't. So it's easier if nobody notices.

'This is ridiculous.' Mummy still hasn't finished. 'I've got enough to do on Christmas Eve without you adding to it. Get this cleared up right now and then get out of my sight. I've had enough of you today. *Enough.*'

At the sound of her loud shouting, I start to crawl about the floor picking up all the little paper cuttings and scrunching them into my hand. Mummy stands over me, watching. Even though I can't see her, I can feel her looking at me, her horrible 'your-fault' stare goes right through the Christmassy red dress I'm wearing and starts poking me in the back, like the naughty boys at school do when they want to get on all the girls' nerves.

Poke, poke, poke. Go away! Poke, poke.

The bits of paper look like confetti from a princess wedding and it makes me extra sad to have to put them into the bin. As I clear up, I look at Daddy and he just nods quietly at me as I carry on scuttling about the carpet on my hands and knees picking up every last piece I can find. The more I do it, the hotter I feel. My tummy starts to go all funny, like it's fizzing and the bubbles want to get out so that they can fizz even bigger and even louder. They go all down my legs, making them feel all foamy and shaky inside my bones, and my hands get all damp and slippery and I think my heart wants to run a race because it goes all boomy under my skin until I feel like I want to burst.

And then I do.

'I hate stupid Christmas anyway and I hate stupid snowflakes and I HATE YOU,' I shout at Mummy, sitting back on my heels and using all the breath I have inside, face burning, skin prickling with anger.

After the words fall out of my mouth I stay where I am on the floor, shaking, because I'm not sure how what I said has found its way out of my mouth and into the living-room with us all sitting there to hear it. I didn't mean for them to jump out. They're meant to stay inside where nobody else can find them. That's where they usually are. But now I've let them get out somehow and they've gone and told everybody a secret, and I know I've done a really, really bad thing by the way everybody is scowling at me. Even Daddy looks upset with me.

I wait a split second, longer then before anything else can go wrong, I jump up and run as fast as my shivery legs will let me, dodging past Mummy before she can catch me and rushing out of the living-room door towards the stairs. I go up to my room without even being told, hoping that Santa forgives me because I don't really hate Christmas, it was just that stupid fizzy feeling that made me say it. As I run up the stairs, I can feel Mummy's eyes on me again, and I wonder for a moment if stares can leave bruises too.

You

Chapter Thirteen

January arrives in its usual sluggish way, lacklustre and grey, dragging its feet like a stubborn teenager who doesn't want to get out of bed. The short days become tedious while we wait, not so patiently, for the sunshine and warmth of early spring. I can't wait to see those tiny pinpricks of golden-brown freckles sprinkled across the noses of Ruby and James again. Can't wait for lazy afternoons in our little back garden, sitting with my face to the sun, head back, eyes closed and listening to the perfect sounds of their laughter as they race happily around.

I look forward to those long summer walks we take along the river, where we stop to paddle in the cool, clear water, or to skim stones across its surface. James is the best at this by far, so Ruby and I leave him to it as he busies himself searching the little riverside beach for smooth flat pebbles, and we lay together on the grassy bank, occasionally looking up to his cries of 'Mum, watch this!' and 'Did you see that one? It went for miles!' And Ruby and I laugh at his excitement before getting back to making daisy chains, or looking for animal shapes in the white summer clouds floating far above us across the pale-blue sky, or just lying in comfortable silence, each of us lost in our thoughts.

When we've finished playing by the water, we call in for ice creams at the little café in the narrow street that runs adjacent to the river. Vanilla with chocolate sauce and a million coloured sprinkles. Wiping sticky hands as the ice cream melts faster than we can eat it in the early evening warmth and covers our fingers. Then we finally walk slowly home, as the sun hangs low and fierce in the sky before disappearing behind the spire of the church in the centre of town, our shadows long on the ground, like giants. And as we cross the bridge to take the path home, we throw our empty wafer cornets to the ducks, laughing because none of us likes eating them. I smile at the memory, and at the thought that, this year, you'll be a part of it too.

For now though, summer seems a long way off as the rain pours heavily down, icy filaments lingering in the air as they fall from the fabric of saturated clouds. Arctic velvet so close to the earth it drapes elegantly across the tops of the trees, its grey-blue softness hanging in molten threads from naked branches, pooling into fluid folds on the ground at my feet. I pull my coat tightly around me against the onslaught of the weather and rush back to the car after dropping off Ruby and James with Matthew for the weekend. Fat, cold drops of rain blow inside my hood, prickling my scalp and turning the wind-whipped strands of hair around my face into chaotic spirals.

I pull the car door open hard against the force of the growing storm and climb inside. It's early Friday afternoon and I'm already late setting off to your house, Ruby insistent on showing me a model she made last week of a castle using toilet-roll tubes and cereal boxes before allowing me to leave. It's a princess castle, she tells me. Just like the one she's going to live in when she's older. I smile and kiss the top of her head, breathing in the clean, innocent scent of her, and remember the tragedy of my own childhood dreams. And I remember to let her keep them, those big dreams of hers, for as long as possible. Until the very last minute, when life will inevitably show her otherwise.

I hope you're not too mad about me being late. If I drive a little faster than normal I shouldn't be more than ten minutes late, but then I remember the traffic will be heavy through town now, workers leaving their jobs to go home for the night and shelter from the winter as she throws her weight around outside, looking for the next party to crash.

I turn to throw my phone onto the passenger seat and as I do my eyes linger on the weekend bag sitting there, packed and ready for a couple of days with you. And then I see him, in a blindingly bright flash behind my eyes. I jump backwards in my seat, my knee-jerk reaction still being to back away, and my skin prickles at the memory. He said we'd be okay. He said we'd be fine. He said I wouldn't need much, not at first. We'd sort it all out later, there'd be plenty of time for that. Details didn't matter, he said. Details could be worked out eventually, but for now, just be there, he said. Be there with him. And he was right. Nothing had really mattered much anymore. Just him. Just Ben. There was no room for anyone else.

I feel a dull pain begin behind my eyes and I press my thumb and forefinger against my closed lids to stop the memory growing and spilling out in glistening rivers across my cheeks. My breath hangs heavy in the damp air inside the car and the windows are slowly becoming laced in a silvery-white film. I shove the key in the ignition and start the engine, trying my best to shake off the nagging memory that is sitting just behind my eyes, flickering on and off like a slideshow, scene after scene after scene of him. Sepia-toned. A fading recollection. Some long-forgotten passage in a well-loved book, or at least trying to be.

The pretence of 'long-forgotten' wanes with every passing day, stretching and straining, weakening, pulled from all directions, pulled out of shape until it can't be recognised as anything much anymore and the whole thing falls apart. Snapping, tearing, ripping open right down the very centre until everything spills out like dirty water. I remember every little thing about him. Ben. And about how he tore me apart too.

The engine revs, windscreen wipers spring into action, the radio screams a coarse, cat-like vocal that scrapes against my eardrums like sandpaper on brick. I pull my sleeve down over my hand and lean across the steering wheel to clear the glass. The noise is too loud. I don't recognise the song. My head hurts in time to the beat, so I switch off the radio and lean against the headrest, massaging my temples and letting out a long sigh into the quiet. Gazing out of the window through the grey and the rain at Matthew's perfect house, I imagine them all inside, settling down to watch TV together or playing board games or drawing pictures. In the house I should've had, living the life I wanted. The life I wanted until I didn't anymore.

Silence surrounds me, holding me close, and I let my eyes drift closed. Playing out against my eyelids I see the warm red brick, the cosy porch, the large front garden with the bright-green lawn and room for James's football nets, the colourful pots by the front door, empty now but full of tulips and daffodils in springtime. Birds in the trees, the puppy Matthew says they'll get running around haphazardly on the grass, chasing a ball, Ruby and James throwing him sticks. Butterflies clumsily fluttering by on the breeze.

Butterflies.

Ebony.

My eyes snap open. The rain comes sharply into focus, pounding loudly on the windows and scratching at the roof, wind buffeting the car from side to side, whistling through the tiny gaps around the door and reaching its feathery fingertips into all the minute spaces, my spaces, picking everything up and blowing best-laid plans into frenzied circles until they get stuck high up in the trees where nobody can ever reach them; a familiar chaos riding on the coattails of an emerging past.

Shaking, I force the clutch to the floor, jam the car into reverse and release the handbrake. Tyres spin on the wet road as I accelerate too quickly, desperate to get away. I barely miss the gateposts at the end of the driveway, and almost hit a passing car as I pull out hastily into the street. Why can't everybody just leave me alone? Why do they keep coming back? We're done now. All of us. We're done now.

***

Your palm connects hard with the side of my face and the instant stinging heat brings tears to my eyes. All around me I see flashing pinpricks of white, a hideous polka-dot pattern like a sick dot-to-dot outlining the agony of the blow to my cheek. The stinging turns into a million biting insects that crawl across my face spreading their hot venom under my skin. I'm disorientated. I didn't have time to stop it. I couldn't stop it. I didn't know. Where did it come from? Where? The sound from the TV is muffled and distant, my earlobe throbbing with a fresh wave of pain where your fingertips caught the skin there. I turn to look at you but I can't see through the tears and the stars. I try to focus on them but they move around and make me dizzy and I don't want to chase them.

You swoop down in front of me from your seat beside me on the sofa. Crouching on the floor, grabbing my wrists in your fists and holding me hard, holding me in my place, keeping me hostage. Your face is inches from mine, so close I'm breathing your air. Eyes alight, that look of disgust coursing through the green and burning into me. Fingers tightening around my wrists, my pulse pounding against your fingertips as sweat rises to the surface and pricks the skin of my armpits. I feel it run in a thin trickle down my ribcage, soaking into the fabric of my T-shirt. My heart reacts, thundering in my ears, the sound pressing hard against my eardrums, my ribs jumping against my skin as it threatens to break out of its cage.

I swallow hard. My throat is parched and thick with fear, closing in on itself. I force saliva down again, the action almost painful, but my stomach contracts and forces it back up into my throat. The back of my neck is damp with fear. My mind working overtime, spinning and searching through a million different scenarios and finding no sense in any of them; nothing that connects. I'm urgently hunting down all the words I know, trying to put them into an order that will make all this better, but they crash into one another and run away, and hide behind things like panic and dread, stealing away my phrases and leaving me speechless.

You tilt your head to one side and inch closer to me, teeth clenched, the muscle in your jaw twitching with the effort of controlling yourself, eyes never leaving mine. When you speak, the words grate harshly as they slide over your clenched teeth and punctuate the space between us like gunshots in a quiet neighbourhood; shocking and out of place.

'You fucking bitch,' you say, gripping my wrists harder until my hands begin to heat up, skin reddening and raging beneath your fingers.

A tear escapes from my eye and I shake my head rapidly from side to side to stop it. I don't know what I've done. All understanding vanishes with the embrace we shared a moment ago. My head on your shoulder savouring the warmth of you as the relentless storm continues outside. Your fingertips lazily playing with my hair; your breath skimming my cheek and prickling my skin with goosebumps; the film on TV; the actor. How I tell you I've always loved him. The crack of your hand against my face.

'Not only did you have the nerve to get here late, now you're telling me that you love him?' you rage. 'You fucking *love* him? This guy right in front of me.' You stab a finger towards the TV. 'I should've known I couldn't trust a girl like you.'

You let go of my wrists now, throwing my hands back down into my lap as if suddenly repulsed by them, rocking back on your heels and shooting me the look of loathing I've seen so many times before. And just like all those times, I wither beneath your gaze, curling up inside like a flower closing its petals to the darkness, putting myself away inside a box and waiting for you to let me out again.

'No, really, that's not what I meant,' I whisper, dropping my gaze to the floor, unworthy of looking at you, unable to trust my voice to speak louder without breaking down. 'I'm sorry I said that. I didn't mean it the way it sounded.' My own voice sounds miles away, like this is happening to somebody else in another town. Not me, not here, not now.

'What was that, Belle?' you sneer. 'I didn't hear you.' You lean forwards again, hands resting either side of me on the sofa, thumbs pressed hard against my thighs, blue-green veins in your forearms bulging and biceps twitching as you push yourself up to standing.

'I'm sorry,' I say, louder this time. Voice cracking, wincing as I wait for another blow. 'I didn't mean it the way it sounded. I…I don't love him. I just meant, well, just that he's a good actor, that's all.' I look up at you towering above me, your face unreadable in the shade as the lamp behind you throws your features into shadow. 'Please don't be cross with me. Please. I really am so sorry.'

You reach out and grab my wrist again, and I cry out as you drag me to standing, bracing myself for another onslaught. But you pull me into you and circle your arms around me, holding me gently against you, kissing the crown of my head, fingers drawing barely-there circles at the nape of my neck. My head rests against your chest, the fabric of your T-shirt rough against the raw tenderness of my cheek, the remnants of pain replaced by tingling heat.

'Shhhhh,' you say gently. 'It's okay, it's okay. I forgive you. I forgive you.'

I cling on to you and nod my head as silent tears fall.

Chapter Fourteen

'All I asked was that you think about meeting the kids. Is it really too much to even consider? They're a big part of my life – no, a huge part of my life. In fact, they are my life. Come on, you need to be reasonable here! What's wrong with you? What? Did you expect to be able to see me but have nothing to do with them? Seriously?! Well, that's just ridiculous. *You're* ridiculous.

'No, I won't just leave it. This is important! I won't let you push Ruby and James aside in all of this. You want me, well you have to have them too. You don't get to pick and choose. It's that simple. And the fact that we're even having this discussion is fucking insane!

'I mean, do you even live in the real world? What sort of a person are you? No, don't answer that, you're crazy. You're clearly crazy. And you're driving me crazy too. Look at me. Pacing around like a lunatic while you sit there like some sort of dictator. All I'm asking is that you meet them. How can you not even consider it? Not even think about it? I'm beginning to wonder why I'm even bothering with you now. What's the fucking point? Really, what's the –'

'Oh, of course you want me to leave. It's easier that way isn't it, rather than actually having to deal with a problem? If we just don't talk about it, it'll just go away. Isn't that what you think? Well, I'll tell you something, this won't go away. But me, as for me … yeah, maybe I just might.

'Oh, that's right, walk away. Don't worry, I'm going. This whole thing's a waste of time anyway. I'm going. Just leave me alone.'

Chapter Fifteen

I love days like today. Lazy days, bedroom days, the kind of days that follow a hectic week. Where lying in bed all day is finally an option, and where staying in your pyjamas is a must. The kind of days that say 'hey, you deserve a break, so switch off your alarm clock and have one on me.' Those sorts of days are definitely my favourite, because they're so rare.

In the background, a Saturday-morning cookery programme is on TV. I think they're making some sort of breakfast muffin or something. There are bananas and apples and what look like blueberries being mixed into a huge bowl of golden batter, while the merits of using honey instead of sugar are being discussed with some unrecognisable celebrity studio guests. But I'm not really paying much attention.

Your head is resting on my chest, rising and falling a fraction in time with my steady breathing. Beneath the warmth of the duvet, I gently follow the undulations of your spine with my fingernails, pressing just hard enough to leave a pale, scratched out path in their wake, making you wriggle and smile in quiet pleasure, and I nuzzle your head closer into me. As the monotonous chatter of the TV blends into the background, I listen to the excited chattering of Ruby telling me all about her plans for the rest of the weekend and all the things she's going to do with her cousins.

I wish she and James were here, but I have to make do with hearing her on the other end of a mobile phone. It's Matthew's weekend with the children and they're away visiting family, hence the lazy day, hence why I'm still in bed at almost noon. If Ruby and James were with me, I'd have been woken at 6.30am, 7am if I was particularly lucky, by James bounding in, arms full of as many soft toys as he could carry, squirming under the covers next to me with the singsong sound of his little voice in my ears. First, he'd wish me good morning Mum, then almost without taking a breath he would plunge headlong into the thoughts, questions and observations only a four-year-old would find appropriate at such an early hour. But his enthusiasm for everything fills me with joy and I listen patiently, answering his questions when he pauses just enough to let me.

Ruby would follow later, sleepily peeking her head around my bedroom door, rubbing the sleep from her eyes and asking if she can climb into my bed for a little while too. And me and James would scoot over to make room for her, and we'd lie there for a few minutes longer, me in the middle, my children on either side, playing I Spy and Twenty Questions and talking about what we were going to do that day. I'd make a mountain beneath the covers with my knees and James would carry out expeditions to the top with his teddy bear, giggling at our cheering as his teddy reached the summit. And Ruby would lie quietly with her head resting on my shoulder, occasionally giggling at her little brother. Our little man. I love our little morning ritual. I miss it when they're not here. I miss them.

Ruby tells me her dad is calling her so she'd better go. I say my goodbyes, return the phone to the bedside table and sigh, the sounds of my daughter's happy voice filling my head. I stretch out my legs and wriggle my toes to bring life back to my lazy limbs, and I lean forwards to place a kiss on the top of your head.

'What shall we do today?' I ask, and then laugh. 'Well, with what's left of it!'

Shuffling up in the bed until you're level with me, you roll on top of me, arms either side of my head holding your weight just above me.

'Well that's the thing isn't it?' you say, a playful glint in those bright emerald eyes of yours. 'We might as well stay right here. There's not much point getting up now, the day's almost done after all.'

I giggle and squirm beneath you. 'We should do something,' I protest. 'It's probably a really nice day out there. Not that we'd know, given that neither of us have even looked outside.'

'That's because what's inside is far more interesting,' you reply, a mischievous half-smile touching your lips as you press yourself against me.

I laugh again and shake my head affectionately at you. "You're terrible,' I say in mock anger. 'But you may have a valid point.'

Your laughter fills the room unexpectedly, and it's a beautiful sound. In it, I can hear proper joy and happiness, as though this is a brief moment of total abandon for you. It passes in an instant, but in that moment I realise what has just happened is so rare and that's why it was unexpected. I realise that you hardly ever laugh, not truly. Not like you mean it. Not like just now. The laughter reaches your eyes and they sparkle green, with flecks of gold I've never seen before. They crinkle at the outer corners, the way they did on the night I first met you, and the laughter lines open long crevices across your cheeks. And they're beautiful. You're beautiful.

'I love you,' I say quietly.

It just comes out, as unexpectedly as your laugh. I just say it. Without thought, without anxiety. I say it because I mean it. And your face becomes suddenly serious as you look right at me, right into me, and suddenly I can feel my face flushing, the heat in my cheeks burning bright under your gaze.

Then you kiss me. Slowly, excruciatingly but exquisitely slowly. You kiss me but you don't respond. You don't say you love me too.

Chapter Sixteen

'No, I'm not having a go at you at all. All I'm saying is that maybe it would've been nice to hear it said back to me, that's all. When a girl tells her boyfriend she loves him, I guess she kind of hopes to hear it said back to her. But hey, I guess I'm wrong.

'Well, of course, I'm a little bit sad and disappointed. I'm not going to pretend I'm not. But can we please not have an argument about it? Please? Not today. Not over this. We've had such a lovely morning, please don't spoil it by taking this too far. I was just trying to let you know how I feel.

'Yes, it would've been nice if you'd said 'I love you too', but you didn't. So, you know, end of story. Forget it. Let's just leave it for now and enjoy the rest of the evening. It really doesn't matter.

'I'm pressuring you? What do you mean? I'm sorry, what? Pressuring you to say 'I love you'? No, no I'm not. It would just have been nice to hear it, that's all I'm saying. But okay then, fine. You won't hear those words escape my lips again until you decide that maybe you love me and you say it to me. Then I'll reply. Is that okay with you? Now, can we just let this go? I feel shitty enough about it as it is, without going over and over it. Will you pass me the remote and I'll see what's on?

'Oh I'm sorry, please will you pass me the remote? Jesus Christ, there's no pleasing you is there? Seriously, I'd just like to forget this conversation and watch some TV, so if you would possibly hand me the remote…please.

'Why did you do that? Jesus Christ, what was that for?'

Chapter Seventeen

March 2012

There's a slight warmth in the air as we walk hand in hand along the promenade one late-afternoon. The sun is regaining some of its ferocity after the coolness of the winter rays, and I can feel its faint heat nudging against my face, hinting at what's to come in the weeks ahead. Spring and summer and all that goes along with them are most definitely on their way. My stomach eagerly fizzes at the thought of picnics in the park, boat trips on the lake, long lazy afternoons in the garden, barbecues, walks in the countryside. All the things the warmer weather brings and, this time, all with you.

I smile. Perfect days have passed since I told you I loved you. When we argued afterwards. When you threw the TV remote at me in anger. When you bruised my face.

It was an accident. I know that. I was as much to blame as you. Pushing the subject of love. I shouldn't have. I realise I can't force you to love me, and I know that I've just got to be patient until you decide you feel the same. Until then, I've decided not to broach the subject again. The bruise at my right temple has faded now anyway. It's gone.

I spend my days happily with Ruby and James at home in our little house, and I always look forward to seeing you when they stay with Matthew. Time with their dad means time for me with you. And mostly this works.

But I miss them so much, and more often than not I find myself wishing that all the people I care about could be together all at once. That I didn't have to split myself in two or three or four. That I could just be one and have everybody here with me. But for you, it's too soon, and I understand that. For me it's hard. It's really hard.

Compared to last summer though, I have high hopes for this one. Last summer was bittersweet. I was alone for the first time since I was a teenager and for the first time, I had nobody to lean on. I spent most of my time feeling lost, and when I wasn't lost, I was stuck. It was as though my life had fallen into quicksand and was desperately trying to drag itself out, kicking and screaming, pulling harder and harder against a relentless grip, trying to break free. I remember how nothing seemed to work no matter how hard I tried, and I stayed there, stuck in that place, for what felt like an eternity. And the more I struggled, the more I got sucked in, the tighter the grip became, and the more tiring the fight became.

I feel an icy cloud begin to press hard against the warmth of the happy place I've found, trying its best to invade the space with its dense, impenetrable grey. The cloud is heavy with my name. It reminds me it was all my fault. My fault that I lost everything.

Not now, not today, I say determinedly to myself as I breathe out a long, slow breath, chasing away the clouds and painting the smile back onto my face. This summer you'll be here, I remind myself. This summer I won't be alone, and I can't wait for everything good that's going to come our way.

Right now, I feel free. Right now, with the fresh air blowing gently over the top of the breaking waves on the shoreline below, its saltiness kissing my face and tugging at my hair, with my hand in yours, fingers entwined, the warmth of your palm pressing into mine, with the heat of the sun, with the rushing sound of the sea, with you by my side; with all this, I feel alive and I feel happy and I feel again. And just to feel again makes me smile.

The long coastal path we walk along snakes away from us, bending to the right and tucking itself behind a small hill so vividly green against the bright-blue sky it almost hurts my eyes. Everything is radiant and amazing and beautiful. I raise my face to the sun and close my eyes, breathing in the sharp, zingy air around me, listening again to the waves breaking gently on the pebbled beach, seagulls calling to one another somewhere overhead, their cries carried out to sea on the gentle breeze, and another smile plays across my lips. Today everything is perfect.

I open my eyes and catch you looking down at me, the sun behind you casting a bright halo of gold around your darkened edges. You hold my gaze for a second before letting go of my hand and taking my face between your palms, tenderly stroking the pad of your thumb along the points of my cheekbones, fingers woven deeply into my hair. Slowly you lean towards me and place the lightest of kisses on my lips, our skin barely touching, lingering there as I close my eyes again, mouths hardly touching, but touching just enough. I slip my arms around your waist and pull you closer, breathing in the scent of you. Cologne and mint and the traces of salt picked up on the breeze. And that breeze tiptoes around us and goosebumps rise up on my skin as my hands find their way beneath your T-shirt and across the smooth, warm skin of your back.

You draw in a sharp breath as my fingertips float across you and you press yourself closer to me, pulling my head towards yours and kissing me harder, over and over and over again. My hands move quickly up your spine and find your shoulders, and I hold on to you so tightly, feeling the sharpness of your shoulder blades and collarbone beneath my hands as I kiss you back. The sea, the sounds, the breeze, they all pale into the distance as it becomes only me and you. Right here, right now, there's nothing else and nobody else.

When you pull away, I feel dazed and giddy and I stare at you with eyes full of feeling. Full of love. You're still holding my head in your hands, and I lean into them like a cat that can't get enough of being caressed, pushing my right cheek further into your palm, needing, demanding, pleading with you to never let go. You smile down at me and as you plant a quick, playful kiss against my nose I think again how beautiful you are and how lucky I am to have found you.

Before I have time to think, you wriggle free of my grasp and start running backwards away from me, a huge grin on your face.

'Last one to the top of that hill buys all the drinks tonight,' you shout, laughing as you turn and sprint towards the bright-green mound ahead of us.

'Hey!' I shout back. 'That's not fair, you didn't give me a chance.' And bursting into fits of giggles I run as fast as I can, chasing you up the hill.

I catch up with you when we're almost at the top. Breathless, heart pounding, legs shaking from the exertion, I reach out and grab the hem of your T-shirt in my fist. You wrestle me playfully to the ground, both of us laughing between exhausted breaths, and I don't have the energy to resist you. Sitting on top of me, straddling me, you pin my arms above my head. The grass feels warm beneath me and it gently tickles the skin of my upper arms. The sun glows behind you again, casting your face in shadow while the whole world lights up behind.

You loosen your grip on my arms, and my hands reach up into those shadows to caress your darkened face. I trace the outline of your smile, and I mirror it with my own. I run my thumbs along your cheekbones before pulling you towards me, kissing you softly, holding your face in my palms, wanting to keep you there forever.

You smile against my kisses.

'Looks like you're buying the drinks tonight then,' you tease and I laugh into the warmth of your neck.

'Looks like I am,' I say, punching you playfully in the shoulder. 'Though I still don't think it was a fair race. You took advantage. I wasn't prepared!'

'You love me really,' you laugh, rolling off me and lying by my side on the grass, the words slipping innocently from your lips. And as your fingers find mine and we link them together, as you rest your head against mine and we lie looking up into the clear sky on this beautiful day in March, my heart becomes alive again. Just for a split second it's not simply beating. It swells and it heats up and it quivers and it makes way for that feeling we both know can cause so much pain.

'I do,' I reply quietly, a sudden seriousness replacing the playfulness of a moment ago. The early spring air holding a new weight. My breath catching in my throat because I'm not sure how you'll respond. 'You know I do.'

'I think maybe I do too,' you say, speaking to the sky, almost as if you're thinking out loud. And I do nothing but squeeze your hand tighter, to let you know that that's enough for me. If there's love, then we'll be all right.

Ebony

Chapter Eighteen

Ebony's dark hair hangs in a ponytail reaching almost to her waist. It's been that way forever, glossy like melted chocolate, but Ebony herself is new. I stand behind her as she sits at the kitchen table. I am leaning against the doorframe of the open back door, and I watch her hair flowing in a steady stream from the crown of her head, dripping onto her shoulders in thick rivulets and flooding across her narrow back, the ends swaying seductively just above the place where her waist tapers to almost nothing inside her jeans. Sometimes, when the light is right, you can find strands of pure gold in there, but on a normal day, like today, the dark brown hides the gold and keeps the secret safe, and today, only the lacquered sheen of cocoa silk remains.

I imagine its familiar scent as she raises a hand and flicks the strands around to rest across her right shoulder. As she twirls the ends around and around her index finger, I can almost see the scent of clean linen rising like a dense aura around her. An aroma of purity now laced with nicotine.

I pull my jacket tighter and hug it close, taking a long drag on my cigarette and letting the smoke roll softly over my tongue and into the back of my throat, its presence like a comforting old friend. My crutch as well as my rebellion. I lean my head against the doorframe and let the dizzy, light-headedness wash over me for the split second it takes these days before the head-rush is over, and I exhale the thick, warm smoke in one long breath out of the door and into the cold night air. The white plume makes mesmerising curlicues on the icy breeze, spinning in a mini vortex until they fade into the darkness and merge with the night. I watch them go and let the scent of tobacco and chemicals settle themselves into the white fake fur of my coat.

I throw the stub onto the paving slabs outside the door and grind it into the ground with my heel. The toes of my boots are all scuffed. Black leather scraped away, the graze gaping open like a tan-coloured scream framed in tiny threads of peeled-away blackness. I did it on purpose, of course. Who wants perfect shoes anyway? The thought makes me smile inwardly. I did. I wanted them. When I was little. When I didn't know any better. When I rescued Ebony from loneliness.

I kick the crushed cigarette butt under the shrubbery beside the back door and close it against the late winter night, a little shiver rolling across my skin as the tail end of the breeze kisses my neck. I turn back into the kitchen and into its warmth, the room bathed in the yellow glow of the two strip lights overhead. The house is free from grown-up conversations, devoid of skulking adults, empty of parents and their restrictions. It's just us this weekend.

'Thank God for that,' Ebony says, not lifting her head from writing feverishly, black fountain pen scratching out incoherent scribbles on the lined notepad. 'I was fucking freezing.' The bones of her spine push insistently against the black cotton of her T-shirt, like the curve of one of those slinky toys falling down the stairs. Poetry and lyrics, that was Ebony. Poetry, lyrics and reading. Always and forever.

I shrug off my coat and sling it across the back of one of the dining chairs before sitting down heavily opposite her and crossing my legs on the tabletop.

'Needs must,' I say, matter-of-factly, picking up a bottle of bright-pink alcopop and taking a swig. It's warm and it's vile and I force it down. 'I'll kill Matty for this though. It's all his fault.'

Ebony looks at me and smiles. 'He didn't force you to try it,' she says, eyes glittering with amusement. 'But it does suit you. Very Courtney Love.' She winks and the air around us resonates with the sound of our giggles, as we clink matching bottles together and throw back another sickly-sweet pink mouthful.

I think of the times it was just Matty and me. Before I let Ebony in, and before Dan came along almost from out of nowhere. Matty, with his bright-blue eyes and unruly hair that he tucked behind his ear whenever he played guitar. We would sit together in music class, the only class at school I attended without Ebony because her parents hadn't allowed her to study the subject at exam level. It wasn't academic enough, they'd said. Too creative. Too arty. Too obscure. To me and Matty, that was its attraction.

'Plus,' I say, withering slightly as the aftertaste of the grapefruit and vodka stings my mouth, 'my mum hates me for it, so that's another bonus.'

Ebony puts down her pen and looks at me carefully, her eyes all melted chocolate just like her hair, warm and beautiful. Swirling whirlpools of sweetness in which to get lost. Not like mine. My eyes get greener as my hair gets blacker, that's what Ebony says. Piercing. Like a kaleidoscope with a hundred shades of green colliding and creating sparks. She told me they have the power to keep people away because they don't understand what they see. Everyone except Daniel, that is. My beautiful Dan. He looked into my eyes this one time and then couldn't look away again.

'You and your mum,' Ebony says softly, reaching across the table and taking my hand in hers. 'You should talk, maybe.'

I sigh and let my feet drop from the table. 'About what exactly?' I ask, leaning forward and putting my forehead where my feet had been. I'm tired of this conversation. We have it all the time. Every time my mum gets annoyed with me for doing something wrong and I retaliate. We've talked about it over and over, ever since we noticed that I never get it right: the hole in my tights when my nine-year-old self fell in the playground playing chase, the poor test result in maths, being picked for a lower class for science, how my

English assignment only got an A and not the A* that was predicted, the stripe of red oil paint left across the carpet when my paintbrush fell from the table onto the dining-room floor while I was 'painting stupid pictures', the guitar lessons my parents paid for only for me to decide I wanted to be a drummer instead, the blue streaks in my hair last summer, the time I came home from town with seven new earrings throbbing in my right earlobe, the packet of cigarettes she found stuffed at the bottom of my underwear drawer, the night I had one too many fizzy vodka drinks at Matty's house when his parents were away and I let him bite me. He kissed me too, but that was before Ebony, so it was allowed.

And then there's Dan. She hates him. Hates him for all the reasons that I like him. For his bright-red hair, dyed the colour of a pillar box; for his love of music and art; for the way he talks like poetry and she doesn't understand; for his little-boy-lost nature and the way he sometimes disappears inside his own head for long moments. She says he's an 'odd boy'. A 'drifter'. I say Dan's my boy and he's sticking around no matter what she says.

Okay, so maybe I don't help myself. But if she's going to hate me anyway, I might as well give her some more reasons.

'Like, you should ask her what you're meant to have done,' Ebony suggests, and I roll my eyes like she's wasting my time and hers. 'I mean, apart from the obvious things lately,' she carries on in her quiet, gentle way. 'Before that. When you were just little.'

'I was born,' I answer, stealing my hand back from her grasp and rubbing my eyes. 'That's what happened, Ebony. No other reason I can think of.'

Ebony picks up her pen again and begins absentmindedly doodling on the page around her poem. One shape flowing into the next, curling and twisting together, hearts emerging from spirals, stars exploding from corkscrew swirls, butterflies intertwined among stylised stems, their wings trapped behind broken hearts and crooked lines.

The silence hurts my ears.

'So anyway,' I say, the sound suddenly too loud in the quiet kitchen, 'I got you something.'

I pick up my bag from the floor and rummage around in it. I made the bag myself. Patchwork in all the colours I could find, sewn together with scarlet thread and fastened with a silver filigree star button. Patterned and plain, rough and smooth, silky and coarse. Soft velvet against crude denim, delicate flowers against harsh stripes. Jarring and chaotic. I'm not sure it was planned like that, it just turned out that way. My fingers find what I'm looking for and I hold it out to Ebony.

'Happy birthday,' I say. 'For yesterday.'

She puts down her pen and grins widely, taking the pale-pink gossamer pouch from my hand and pulling gently at the tiny drawstrings that pinch the top together. Her pale, thin fingers dive into the opening and bring out a delicate silver necklace, the chain draping gracefully across her stubby, ragged fingernails, ruby coated and bitten down to bleeding point day after day after day.

A shimmering silver E is suspended from the links, quivering in the air as she holds it up to the light and watches it catch the honeyed glow of the fluorescent strip bulbs overhead, reflecting into her eyes. A tiny silver butterfly hangs from the chain next to it, delicate, shiny wings fluttering against the E and making a tinkling sound, like coins jostling in your hand.

'Because you're sixteen,' I say, grabbing her arm and shaking it excitedly. 'And because now this makes it real.'

She gasps and her eyes gleam with that familiar luminous glaze, tears, threatening but never appearing, like the ghosts in stories around a campfire – you want to believe in them, but they never quite surface from the rumours. For a second she disappears from view and instead, in front of me, is a scared and timid little six-year-old standing in the corner of the playground, still in vivid technicolour after all this time. Still here a lifetime later.

She's different now though. Amy disappeared a long time ago. She got lost somewhere among the discovery of cigarettes and boys. When sex and smoking took over our playground games, when the jam-jar butterflies were replaced by loud music and six strings, when we stopped building dens and started staying in our rooms, when we got good at keeping secrets and even better at telling lies. That's when we knew everything had changed. That's when we knew we'd never be the same again.

That's also when she stopped eating. A few months back, when the band happened. When Matty and Dan happened. When she said that I was perfectly skinny and she was monstrously fat. When Matty looked at me that way one time, and she locked herself in her room for days, refusing to come out because her face was ugly, her hips too wide, her thighs too big. We didn't see her for a week after that, and when we did, when she walked into school that Monday morning, head down, face hidden, burgundy velvet coat hanging loosely from her newly narrowed shoulders, she was slightly more fragile than before. Skin a little tighter across bone. A little more translucent. A little more not there.

I probably should have noticed her fading then. I didn't. Instead, I hugged her and dragged her to band practice when our lessons were over. Instead we all – Dan and Matty and me - made a big fuss of her, told her how much we'd missed her, put her bass guitar in her hands and taught her the song we'd been working on. I played out the rhythm until the drumsticks carved rivets into my palms and my hands blistered and bled, the guitar riffs repeating over and over like a needle stuck on scratched vinyl, the lyrics, not quite there yet, but the idea sketched out roughly in a few scribbled notes on the back of a tattered copy of Romeo and Juliet. We played until she got it. Until she smiled. Until she forgot everything else.

She wanted to go home alone after that, and I let her. I saw the chocolate bars in her bag. I saw the packets of crisps, the biscuits. I saw the sadness, that whimpering child, huddle tightly up against her again now that the distraction of practice was over, wrapping its greyness around her like a scratchy woollen blanket, resting heavy on her limbs, covering her face, leaving a rash. Claustrophobic and smothering. But I pretended I didn't see. I pretended everything was as it should be. Instead, I let her go, and then I let Dan have sex with me in my bedroom while my parents were still at work and my brother and sister watched TV downstairs. And while we fumbled around, while Dan lurched and swayed above me, I stared at the ceiling and saw her image play out across the swirling white emulsion, stuttering against the brushstrokes as she sat on her bed and ate and ate and ate. I watched as she left the room and came back a ghost.

That was the day we changed her name. Because we were rock stars. Because Amy or Amie or Ami didn't fit. Because Ebony sounded better. Because she was the story of Snow White in a person, with skin as white as snow, lips as red as blood and hair almost as black as ebony. Dan said I should've taken that name for myself since my hair was actually black, but I already had a princess name so I let Amy take that one for herself. My Isobel became Isabelle became Belle, some sort of beauty-among-beasts idea of Dan's. And I wore a tiara to prove the point.

That was the day we emerged from our chrysalis. That was the day we wanted to belong to something. That was the day we should've seen it coming. But we missed it. I always miss it. I'm always looking the other way.

***

Ebony puts down her pen and walks over to the kitchen drawer. When she turns back, she's holding up a pair of scissors and looking at me with an excitement I haven't seen in her for a while.

'Let's complete the transformation,' she grins, raising an eyebrow so that it disappears into the curtain of chocolate strands covering her forehead.

'Ebony,' I say with mock restraint. 'What are you thinking?'

She takes a hairband from her wrist and pulls the chocolate waterfall into a low ponytail which hangs the length of her spine, perfectly smooth, perfectly central, perfectly placed. Then she holds the scissors out to me.

'Cut my hair,' she orders. 'Here, right above this hairband. Cut it all off.'

I take the scissors. 'Are you sure? That's, like, most of your hair. All this long, gorgeous, shiny —'

'Belle,' she interrupts, slight impatience in her voice dampened by the impish gleam in her eyes, 'just do it.'

So, I do. I cut her hair right where she says I should, as she stands in the middle of the kitchen. Lifting it away from her neck, my fingertips grazing the protruding bones of her spine and leaving behind a sprinkling of goosebumps on her downy skin. I saw the scissors backwards and forwards across the ponytail, ripping through the strands, until it's holding on to Ebony by a thread, until it comes free and I'm left with the ponytail in my fist like a hideous cheerleader's pom-pom, some sort of gruesome trophy. I swallow hard and suddenly I really want another cigarette.

She shakes what is left of her hair and it falls perfectly, skimming her jaw, dipping into the shadow her chin casts across her neck, tucking itself around her delicate face and clinging to her jawline in a smooth, silken curve. She turns to face at me, her big eyes gazing out from beneath her thick fringe, and she looks fragile and she looks beautiful. And I remember the day I found her, all alone in the playground, scared and unsure. The day I saved her.

Without speaking I hold the ponytail up loosely in my fingertips as a silent question.

'Bin it,' she says softly, as if she knows what I'm thinking. 'I'm gone now.'

Ben

Chapter Nineteen

He was always going to leave. Or rather, I was always going to walk away from him because he would give me no choice. The only question, of course, would be when? It didn't cross my mind though. Not then. Not when I was driving to his place with nothing but a few essential things thrown into a hold-all slung casually onto the passenger seat beside me. Nor did it as I was getting dizzy from his enthusiastic welcome, when he picked me up as though I was as light as a feather and spun me around and around until my legs flailed out behind me and I was giggling like a little girl.

I didn't think about it as he was searching the kitchen drawer for a knife. When the best he could find was a Swiss Army version which he used to saw roughly back and forth through the yellow and red sponge and jam layers of his birthday cake. When his fingers were strawberry sticky and I licked the sweet mixture from their tips. When I sang him an overenthusiastic 'happy birthday', and planted a kiss hard on his lips. Not once did I think about the end.

Neither did I as he carried me upstairs that night and made love to me on the antique bed, dark wood creaking warmly as he laid me down on the old lumpy mattress, the dark of the night peering in through the bare window and the stars glinting like glitter-ball fragments through the gaps in the trees beyond the glass.

It sounds romantic, and I suppose it was. For a little while. On this farm in the middle of nowhere, where we'd been thrown together like some tragic fairytale.

I'd always wanted a fairytale.

But one day he would leave. Or I would. Because everything ends eventually. Or at least that's what I've come to learn.

You

Chapter Twenty

'Please, please don't.

'I'm sorry I didn't have the money. I thought I did. I thought I had some in my purse. I'm sorry, I'm sorry. Really, I am. Please, put the glass down. Please. I promise I'll pay for the pizza next time. I'll make sure I have the money. I will. I'll buy an extra-large one to make-up for it, and I'll get some drinks too. Whatever you want. Honestly, I will. Just tell me what you want and I'll get it for you. Just please, please, just put the glass down.'

Chapter Twenty-One

April 2012

The glass smashes against the wall behind my head and I scream. I squeeze my eyes shut so tightly they hurt and clench my jaw so hard I almost bite through my tongue. Immediately, the adrenaline surges through me and I feel sick. Bile rises in my throat, acrid and stinging, and I swallow it down hard. I can smell the sharp scent of red wine weaving its way around me, escaping from the pile of shattered glass on the carpet, the alcohol running down the wall in blood-red rivers. I want to run, but I can't move. I'm frozen. My limbs are paralysed. I want to cover my face with my hands, but they're clenched tightly against my sides, clinging onto the fabric of my jeans, knuckles white with tension.

I'm trying to figure out what just happened. Trying desperately to make sense of the tangle of events in my head. Saturday night at your house. I suggested ordering pizza, but when it arrived and I opened my purse to get the money, the purse was empty. I thought I had at least a twenty-pound note in there, but remembered too late I'd stopped for petrol earlier and used the note to pay for it.

All you had to do was pay for the pizza because I didn't have the money. Was that really what caused all this? I'd apologised, over and over again, but I knew it was futile. I knew the damage had been done. I knew because you'd looked at me like that. Like I was disgusting. Like I made you sick. And I knew then, as I shrivelled to nothing inside, that something bad was about to happen.

The door slammed behind the delivery boy and the pizza boxes hit it soon after, their contents sliding down the doorframe as you flung them in silent rage. I stood still in that silence, because I knew I should be scared. I watched the orange stain glide down the white door. Watched the pizza slide into a soggy heap on the doormat. Watched you, in slow motion, as you turned towards me, fists curled into tight balls at your side, jaw set, darkness in your eyes.

'You fucking bitch!' Your words cracked like thunder through the heavy silence. My whole body tensed at the sound, muscles gripping tightly to sinew, sinew clinging to bone. 'Fucking *parasite*!' Rage spilled from your lips as you strode towards me, long legs closing the gap between us in a split second.

'Take, take, take, that's all you ever fucking do!' Beads of spit flew from your mouth and landed on my face. I flinched, every part of me vibrating with terrified energy. You leaned in closer, slowly, slowly until your face was almost touching mine. 'Thieving little whore!'

The words hit me with such force the pain was almost physical. A whimper escaped my lips. The hollow sound of a wounded animal being kicked into submission.

You inhaled deeply then, taking a step back from me. 'You're like a disease.' Your voice was quieter, dangerously calm as you seemed to contemplate the tears burning hot paths down my cheeks. 'An *infection*.' A sneer crossed your lips as you delighted in my fear.

My eyes stung and my throat burned with the effort of holding back the sobs, I silently willed myself not to break down. And I silently willed you not to hurt me anymore.

But my silence seemed to anger you further, and you reached out to me, gripping the top of my arms tightly, your fingers gouging out deep crevasses in my skin.

'Got nothing to say, you worthless piece of shit?' You gripped harder, jaw clenched, eyes burning with hatred.

I flinched again, but still said nothing, and this angered you more. You squeezed and squeezed until I cried out in pain until the sobs came in never-ending waves, and your vile words covered me in sticky black tar, burning me, settling into my skin like scars. I gasped for breath, struggling for air against the sobs until I was choking on my own fear.

And when I thought it was never going to end, you stopped, the silence ringing in my ears, hanging heavy all around. A silence filled not with calm, but with menace. A silence vibrating with fury. Quiet and contained. Your eyes – those beautiful green eyes, eyes that I love, eyes that crinkle at the corners when you smile – full of loathing, never leaving mine as you slowly let go of my arms. I didn't want to move, but I was trembling. Physically shaking. Stuttered spasms involuntarily running the length of my body. I tasted vomit once more in the back of my throat as my stomach twisted and rose, threatening to lose control.

My head filled with air, silver stars pricking my vision, my neck unable to hold my head steady. I felt drunk, unstable. I needed to sit down before I fell. But I stayed where I was, using all the strength I had to return your look, praying you didn't see the fear inside scrabbling to get out.

You stepped back then, moving away from me towards the table, picking up one of the glasses of wine I'd poured for us earlier. And now that there was space between us again, I'd let my shoulders drop the tiniest fraction, loosened my grip on my jeans, stretched my aching fingers ever so slowly, frightened that the smallest movement, the smallest interruption, would make you angry again. I let the air escape from my lungs in a long, slow breath, concentrating on pushing it all out and inhaling a fresh breath, clean air to replace the nightmare I'd just exhaled. I focussed on the rise and fall of my ribcage, urging my heart to slow its pace and my body to stop shaking.

'I'm sorry,' I whispered as you turned your back to me.

Big mistake. You freeze and I see the fist of your free hand forming at your side again, fingers twitching, finding their place, settling into a familiar grasp.

'You're sorry?' you asked, sarcasm dripping from you, still facing away from me. 'You're *sorry*?'

I bit down hard on my bottom lip and wrapped my arms around my waist. Bracing myself. Waiting for another blow. You straightened to your full height and turned slowly. 'You're always fucking sorry.'

You spat the last words out as though the taste made you sick.

'I'll make you feel sorry,' you said, swirling the wine slowly around in the glass. Smiling to yourself. A small, chilling curve on your lips which didn't reach your eyes. Then you looked at me over the rim of the glass.

'Do you want me to make you feel sorry?' you asked, staring at the wine and the dizzying whirlpool you'd created in the glass. Transfixed. Lost for a moment.

I shook my head hard and fast, fresh tears welling up in my eyes as I backed away from you. Step after step until my feet hit the skirting board and I couldn't go any further. I looked over towards the front door and wondered if I could run, just run away, far, far away from here and from you. But my feet were rooted to the spot, and as I turned back you were looking at me. Looking into me. Looking through me.

You raised the glass slowly above your head and in a moment of pure panic and dread I knew you were going to throw it.

'Please. Please don't' I pleaded. 'I'm sorry I didn't have the money…'

But no amount of begging made a difference. You hurled the glass at me. It missed and hit the wall to the left of where I stood. I felt the air move against my face, and the collision of glass and plaster rang sharply in my ears. I tried to decide if this was a mistake, or if you did it on purpose to scare me – missed me to give me a warning. But whatever the reason, it was done. You had done this.

And now I'm screaming, screaming, screaming. I'm terrified of you.

Chapter Twenty-Two

'Don't cry. Please don't cry. It's okay. I'm okay. It can be fixed. It can all be fixed.

'I love you. Don't worry. I love you.'

Chapter Twenty-Three

May 2012

James sits among a pile of wrapping paper in the middle of the living-room floor, grinning up at me wider than I think I've ever seen him grin. His excitement is infectious and I smile back at him from the sofa, Ruby lying beside me, head on my lap, her hair a tumble of golden-brown waves across my legs. She's giggling at her brother as he proudly shows off his latest birthday present before tossing it to one side and quickly moving on to open the next one.

Five today. My little boy is five. And as I look at him, smooth skin tanned and sprinkled with tiny freckles across his nose, big brown eyes wide and sparkling, hair sticking out at all angles from his sleepy head, I feel such pride, such love, and such sorrow. Because despite everything, despite everything he's seen, everything he's been through, he still loves me unconditionally. Still trusts me implicitly. And looking at my beautiful boy I know I don't want to ever let him down again. Ruby too. Her gentle soul and peaceful nature deserve nothing less.

I run my fingers over Ruby's head and through her soft hair and she wriggles and squirms, half laughing, half telling me off for tickling her.

'I'm sorry.' I smile and kiss the top of her head. 'Who wants breakfast now that James has finished opening his presents?'

I'm greeted with two loud cries of 'Meeeeeeeeeeeee!' so I gently slide from beneath Ruby, leaving her sprawled on the sofa, and I head into the kitchen.

'Bacon sandwiches for the birthday boy and his sister?' I ask, knowing the answer.

Again, two voices shout in unison 'yes please!' and, checking the clock, I smile to myself again. Still only 7am and we've already been up for ages. James was so excited though and I couldn't be angry at his 6am wake-up call today, running into my bedroom shouting 'Mummy, Mummy, I'm five, I'm FIVE!', Ruby following slowly behind, rubbing her eyes complaining that it must still be the middle of the night. Any other day I'd have sent them back to bed, but this morning was special and I couldn't wait to see the happiness on his face when he saw all his presents.

I listen to their excited chattering as I set the frying pan on the hob and begin to cook the bacon. The smell soon wafts through the tiny kitchen and into the living-room, reminding me suddenly of Matthew and a week spent in Cornwall, long before we were married or had children. When things were still exciting, still fresh.

I close my eyes for a moment and picture the little fisherman's cottage and outhouses that had been converted into a cosy bed and breakfast. The whitewashed exterior nestled against the cobalt-blue sky, window boxes full of colourful flowers, bright-yellow curtains hanging in the windows, the horseshoe above the door holding all the luck. I remember how the window of our tiny bedroom faced out onto the little harbour. How the boats rested happily there, sometimes on the slick chocolate-brown mud left by the receding tide, sometimes bobbing contentedly on the water.

I remember the way the light was so different down there. So crisp and clean. It had a quality and clarity all of its own, making the colours brighter and more vivid than I'd ever seen them anywhere else. I remember the taste of salt arriving on the sea mist each evening. How it settled against my lips and in my hair. How we lay on the beach through the day in each other's arms, needing nothing more than the warmth of the sun and each other, and how we drank cider in the small local pub in the evenings, tucking ourselves away in a corner, lost in our own little world.

We'd wake-up every morning to the scent of freshly baked bread and bacon cooking in the kitchen below, and we'd sit at a table by the window in the little dining-room, looking out at the sea, deciding what we were going to do that day over hot sweet coffee and glasses of orange juice. Everything seemed clearer then. I knew where I was, where I was headed, what I wanted. Despite Ebony, I tell myself. Despite all that.

I open my eyes as I smell the bacon beginning to burn. I quickly turn off the gas and remove the pan from the heat. Another time, another place, another life. It all feels so long ago now.

I cover slices of bread in butter and tomato sauce and quickly assemble the sandwiches, plating them up onto pink and blue plates accordingly. As I take them into the living-room, I check my phone – which is lying on the worktop – for what must be the hundredth time this morning. Still nothing. No messages last night and none this morning. I'd hoped you'd reply. I was stupid to think you would. I should have known better. I shake the irritation from my mind and hand the sandwiches over to James and Ruby. You are not the most important thing today.

They've switched on the TV and are half-watching cartoons, half rifling through all the presents that are strewn in messy piles across the floor.

'I think this is my favourite one Mum,' James says, holding up a Spiderman figure. 'Or maybe this one,' he says, picking up a football. 'But I really like this one too!' he cries, dropping the others and holding up a magic set. Ruby tuts loudly and he starts giggling, which sets all of us off. And I think this must be the most beautiful sound in the world.

I let them eat the sandwiches sitting on the sofa this morning rather than at the table, and we all squeeze on, me in the middle, them either side. And we eat in companionable silence, watching Saturday-morning cartoons, James wiping his hands on his pyjama bottoms and spilling tomato sauce down his top, Ruby doing my job of telling him to go and get a napkin, and me smiling at just how in love with the both of them I am. For a moment, the snapshot is perfect.

My phone beeps, the ping of a message arriving, and I leap from the sofa to see who it's from. I feel stupid that my heart is racing in the hope it's you. And I feel even more stupid when I pick up my phone up from the worktop and see it's not. It's a message from Matthew asking me to wish James a happy birthday and to tell me he'll pick him up at 3pm to take him for a birthday tea.

'Hey James,' I shout into the living-room. 'Daddy says happy birthday to his big five-year-old boy and he's looking forward to seeing you for your birthday tea later.' My voice sounds too happy, forced, but I know he won't notice. I don't want James to go away today. Ruby either. I want to keep them both here with me, but I know I can't. I lost the right to be selfish a long time ago.

James turns and smiles, giving me a thumbs up and mumbling something through a mouthful of sandwich. He turns back to the TV.

I type out a quick reply to Matthew and throw the phone back down onto the worktop. It slides across the surface and clatters into the frying pan before falling to the floor. I curse under my breath and press my fingertips against my eyelids in a gesture of mild despair. I can feel frustration beginning to rise up inside of me, that all too familiar sensation of impatience, anger and desperation clambering over one another, and I want to stamp down hard on the phone, to crush it so I won't have to wonder if you'll reply anymore.

But instead, I bend to pick it up and I scroll through the messages until I find the one I sent you last night.

Message sent 19:03.

'*Hey. You know it's James's birthday tomorrow? Well, I'd really like it if you'd come over in the morning. It'd be the perfect time to meet him and Ruby. I know I mentioned it the other day, but you didn't really say either way. You don't need to bring a present or anything, just you being here would be lovely. He's so excited already! Anyway, let me know xxx*'

But still no reply. I put the phone in the pocket of my dressing gown and look out of the kitchen window into the garden. I watch the birds swooping in and out, landing on the feeders the kids hung out for them on the lower branches of the trees, and greedily eating the nuts and seeds. The grass needs cutting, I think, and the garden needs weeding, and it could probably do with a few more plants and flowers about the place to brighten it up. But I'm not quite there yet. I wish I were. I wish I were one of those people content to potter about in their garden, doing odd jobs around the house, finding satisfaction in the little things.

I know something is wrong. I know that. We both know that. After that night a few weeks' ago, after you'd crumpled, after I'd held you tight despite fear taking over me like a red-hot fever, after I'd cleared up the broken glass and wiped the deep-burgundy stains from the walls, we both knew. And I'm trying to understand, I really am, but it's harder than I thought. So much harder than I thought. And now I have to stay in the kitchen a little longer than I needed to, because I can feel tears begin to well up in my eyes and I feel such a fool. I'm the girl I said I'd never be. The girl who can't leave.

***

My parents arrive at noon, James excitedly answering the door, chattering to his grandparents before they'd even gotten inside the house. I hear the 'happy birthdays', the exclamations of how tall James has become now that he's turned five, Ruby pointing out all of James's presents and proudly proclaiming how he liked the present she'd chosen for him the best. I listen to all the commotion from the kitchen, but I don't leave my place at the sink washing-up the breakfast dishes, and my parents don't come in to say hello. That's just the way it is now. We don't do the family thing these days. It's in the past, a forgotten tradition. Like maypole dancing or lacemaking or getting an orange in your Christmas stocking where the presents should be. It hardly happens anymore.

I listen to the chattering and the laughter in the background as I finish washing the dishes. I pick out words like 'wonderful' and 'fantastic' and 'wow' and I wish I could remember what all those things mean. I've forgotten how to relate to the wow and the wonderful. They seem a long way away. I feel like I should know what they mean, but it eludes me right now. What I can do is act like I know what they mean. I know how to smile and nod and agree and charm everyone into believing in the fantastic. Sometimes it gets tiring, but for the most part, I pull it off. I've had to really. It's either that or go under, and I damn well refuse to sink. I'll find that elusive happiness one day. Until then, what is it they say? Fake it until you make it. That's it. Just fake it. Easy.

I've made washing the dishes last as long as I'm able, scrubbing hard at imaginary food, so to stall for time I decide to dry them and put them away. Waiting. For what I don't know. Maybe to give my parents the benefit of the doubt, to see if they'll surprise me by actually acknowledging my presence. So I busy myself in the kitchen with things that don't need doing; finding stubborn stains on the hob and crumbs to sweep up from the floor, and I really must get those sticky fingerprints off the fridge door and maybe I should put the kettle on and make some cups of tea, you know, try being friendly, give them a chance. Maybe if I make the first move, if I show willing, maybe they will too. Maybe. But quicksand appears in my head and the thought gets stuck there, sinking lower and lower until I can't really see it anymore and it doesn't quite materialise into action. I'm not there yet. I'm a long way from there.

Seeing that my waiting changes nothing, I throw the tea towel down on the worktop. One end falls into the sink and I watch the water from the bowl soak into the material, climbing the fabric slowly and steadily, turning the bright-green dark. I watch it for a moment, this saturation, until the fabric can't take any more and the darkness stops spreading and the shades of green blur in front of my eyes. There's only so much anything can take, I think. Even tea towels.

I leave it where it is, it's soaked now anyway so there's not much point trying to save it, and I take a deep breath ready to join the rest of my family as James opens yet more presents. My parents talk to me through him: 'What time's Daddy picking you up?', 'Did you wake Mummy early today?', 'Did Mummy spend all night wrapping your presents ready for you to open this morning?', 'Did Mummy manage to go to her friend's birthday party last Tuesday night?'

No Mummy didn't because you wouldn't babysit for her. You refused, remember? But I keep my mouth shut.

The day continues in a stream of forced politeness and awkward silences. James is too excited to notice, and Ruby is too excited that James is excited to notice either. But I do, and so do they. We light the candles on James's huge chocolate cake, piled high with Maltesers and Flakes and white chocolate buttons just like he'd asked, and sing 'Happy Birthday' at the tops of our voices. We light the candles five or six times because blowing candles out and making wishes is the best part about cakes, according to Ruby. James just wants to eat it and keeps poking his stubby index finger into the fudge icing, scooping a chunk out and quickly hiding it inside his mouth, against his cheek, sucking the evidence from his finger before anybody can stop him. Not that we would. Birthday boys get privileges.

I go cold on the inside then as a name suddenly sweeps in and skitters across my mind, like a pebble skimming across the surface of a lake, sending ripples out from its centre. Concentric circles getting bigger and bigger, colliding and pushing against each other, their edges blurring and fading as they reach the shore. Ben. Birthday boy Ben. He had a cake too. Last May. He was too old for it, but I thought it would make everything seem normal and right.

'Not now, not now, not now,' I say, completely to myself. Or at least I think it is. The voice sounds a little loud. 'Stay away!' I imagine myself being firm because it's insistent now. 'You're not welcome here, especially not today.'

Did I speak that out loud?

I look across at my parents to check their reactions, doubting myself. My Mum is busy lighting candles 'just one more time' with Ruby, and my dad sits at the small dining table with James on his lap, looking on, waiting patiently as though nothing has happened. They haven't noticed. I guess that means I didn't say anything then. Unless they just ignored me, which is a distinct possibility.

James squirms from his granda's lap as the flames leap into life and nudges his nose closer to the cake, the orange glow of the candles dancing in his chocolate-brown eyes. Chocolate-cake eyes.

Orange chocolate eyes. Chocolate-button eyes. Like Ebony.

I plaster a big smile on my face, to prove more to myself than anyone else that I'm fine, just fine, as James lowers his mouth towards the five little flames in front of him and blows hard, covering the cake in melted candle wax and droplets of saliva and who knows what else. He grins up at me, dimples delving deep into his little cheeks, and asks if we can eat it now, so I go into the kitchen for a knife.

Ben didn't have a knife, interrupts my memory again. Not a proper one. Not for cutting cakes. But he'd get one, he said. A good one. Nothing cheap. For now, he had a Swiss Army knife he'd found. But that would do, he said. It would work just as well.

A knife through a cake covered in chocolate-button eyes.

The psychedelic image shimmers in front of my face. 'Let's not do this now,' I say again through gritted teeth as I rifle through the drawer for the cake slice I know I have in there. And I know that this time what I say isn't completely to myself, because I need to speak it out loud now, because

I'm obviously not listening to myself and because I need to hear it better. I'm so maddeningly infuriating. Nobody hears though, apart from me, I'm pretty sure of that. They're all too busy singing 'Happy Birthday' again.

I try to focus on the party and what I'm meant to be doing, but my mind taps on my shoulder again, harder this time. Its long spindly fingers punching out a dull thud against my shoulder blade. Tap-tap-tap. Hey. Tap. Tap. Hey, hey. Tap-tap-tap. It won't stop until I listen. I pause, my hand resting on the knife, and sigh. Okay, I'm waiting. What it is? My memory joins in and together they're tapping all along my spine, and they're kicking the backs of my knees and making my legs twitch, and one of them stands on my foot until I get pins and needles, prickling right across the sole, while the other takes my free hand and curls my fingers into a fist. And all the while they're whispering sweet nothings in my ear: 'It was your fault…it's always your fault…you make them do it…you're not good enough…you never were…never, ever, ever were.'

I squeeze my eyes shut, grab the knife and slam the drawer to scare the memories away, quickly heading back to the living-room. If I carry on, if I just carry on, everything will be fine. I pass my phone lying beside the toaster and I can't help but pick it up and check it again. Even though I haven't heard it sing with a message, even though I know there's still nothing from you, impulse, habit, makes me check it anyway. And still, there's nothing. Just as I thought. And now I want to put the phone in the toaster, because I should've stamped it to smithereens earlier. Then I wouldn't have looked at it again and it wouldn't have made me feel sad and angry when I saw there was actually nothing to see. I want to put it in there and melt it, turn it to mush, so I don't keep doing this to myself. Instead, I open the cutlery drawer, shove it roughly to the back and slam it shut. There. Better. Out of sight, out of mind.

Does that ever really work for anybody, I wonder as I press the blade of the knife into the spongy flesh of the cake and carve it into neat slices, all the same size so it's equal. Fair. It's always best that way. Because out of sight makes my mind go crazy, I think.

I transfer the slices of cake onto plates and hand them round. Ruby politely eats hers with a spoon, taking her time over each tiny mouthful. Swallowing it all before taking another. James picks up his cake with both hands and shoves as much of it into his mouth as he can. Fudge icing squidging out between his little fists and smearing his cheeks, fingertips lost in the sponge.

'James!' I exclaim, laughing. 'Take your time. We don't want poorly tummies from cake overload on your birthday.'

See, you can be normal, some distant part of my mind pipes up.

He grins at me with a mouth full of gooey chocolate and says something I don't understand because the words are muffled and lost behind the cake blockage. Then he carries on chewing, swallows hard, and crams the final handful in, palm open wide, pushing the last crumbs into his mouth. Ruby giggles at his hamster cheeks and asks him if he's saving some of that for later. And we all laugh, my parents and me too, and for a moment it's like we are all joined together. All here at the same time and everything else is forgotten. But as the laughter dies down and we return to quietly eating what's left of our own cake slices, I remember that we're not all together. Not anymore. Not since I let them down a year ago.

I clear the plates to punctuate the silence. The sound of crockery clattering harshly through the quiet makes my ears ring, but it's a welcome noise over the sighs of my mother and the sound of my father humming an unrecognisable tune to fill the space.

'Well, I suppose we should go then,' my father says as the silence stretches. 'You kids will be off to your daddy's soon and me and Grandma have a few things to do at home this afternoon, so…' He leaves the sentence hanging in mid-air, unfinished. I know they don't have anything in particular to do at home, at least nothing that would mean they have to leave right now. But we understand one another without the need for unnecessary explanations. I know why they have to leave, for the very reason I'm banging noisily around in the kitchen, finding things to do, ways to fill the air with something other than conversation. I know it's because we have nothing to say to each other anymore.

Out of sight makes my mind go crazy, I think again as I pass the cutlery drawer and remember my phone incarcerated in there. Still silent. Still no electronic rings or pings or metallic vibrations against the knives and forks to signal that you care. The thought tumbles over and over in my mind, making my limbs shake and my blood boil and causing me to swallow the constant lump of sadness in my throat. Biting back the tears.

And as if to prove that point, you find me later curled-up on the floor, crying silently into the silent living-room of my deafeningly silent house. The same place I've been for hours, since James and Ruby left. Since my parents left, because I'm really not worth sticking around for when I'm just their daughter and not mother to their grandchildren. So you find me there, by the front door, where I'd closed it behind me and slid to the floor in a blur of useless tears. Because what was the point in trying to pretend I was okay now that everybody had left me? And why are you even here anyway? You're too late. Too late for everything.

Chapter Twenty-Four

'The least you could have done was reply to my message last night. Let me know if you were going to be here. I spent all night and all morning wondering. But I guess I know now, because it's over, the party's finished and you're still not here and you still haven't answered my texts or calls. This was really important to me. It mattered. It mattered a lot. You knew that. I don't know what to say to you anymore, I really don't. Why do you do this to me? Why?

'Why...why didn't you come? I needed you. I, I needed you. I really did. Really, really did. And you...you...you didn't reply. You just left me there, wondering, like it didn't matter. But it *did* matter. So much. It mattered so much. And now. Now...well now everybody's gone and left me and you're too late and...and...I don't know what to do. I just don't know what to do or what I've done or why any of this happens anymore. What have I done? Tell me what and why and how I can change everything I've ever, ever, ever done to make it all better again. And tell me why, why you…you didn't come. You just didn't come.

'Don't say you're sorry. Please don't. Please. I don't want to hear sorry. It doesn't change anything. It doesn't…it doesn't make a difference. You still…You…you still weren't here, and I needed you here. I needed you and you didn't come. You didn't come. I needed you and you didn't come. I always need people and they don't come. They go, they just go, like…like it doesn't matter. Like I don't matter. I never matter. Never, ever, ever. Why did you stay away? Why? No text, no…no phone call. Nothing. It's not fair, it's not fair.'

Chapter Twenty-Five

May 2012

When I wake-up, the grey-blue light of early evening is nudging against the bedroom window, and from where I lie, I can see the sky is blemished with steely grey clouds, their edges gilded orange as the sun sets. I have no idea what time it is. At a guess, I'd say around 8pm, but I'm not sure.

My throat is raw and my eyes are hot. Without looking in a mirror I know they are swollen and red from my near hysteria earlier. I hate that. I thought those days were gone. I thought things were going to be better from now on. I thought I had a hold on everything. But my grip seems to be slipping. I can feel my fingers being prised apart by a hundred different things. Like vultures circling, waiting to take what they can from me. Everything is loosening. I'm getting tired. But I don't want to let go. I don't want to fall.

Because if I fall, I'm not sure I'll be able to get back up again. So, it's best to keep holding on, keep the vultures at bay, ignore my tired arms and hands and heart and just keep going.

I feel you behind me, the curve of your body matching mine. Pressed up against me, solid and safe, like a fortress. Your arm is draped across my waist and you're holding my hand, stroking your thumb along my wrist, backwards and forwards, backwards and forwards. I watch until the skin beneath your touch becomes numb and I shift my hand slightly so your thumb caresses a different part.

'Hey,' you say, gently pulling me in towards you some more. 'You're awake.'

I vaguely remember you carrying me up the stairs earlier, scraping me off the floor, something messy and pathetic.

Am I becoming Ebony?

We're lying on my bed on top of the covers. The pillow is wet beneath my head, I'm guessing from tears, and my neck aches from tension or lying awkwardly or both. The arm I'm lying on tingles with pins and needles, so I shift my weight to free it. I turn my head slowly to face you and try to smile. At the sight of my swollen eyes and blotchy face, you frown and the look of concern in your eyes makes mine fill up all over again.

'I'm sorry,' I begin. 'I didn't mean to get so upset. I just...I...I...I just get a bit sad sometimes.' I don't know what else to say or how else to explain it. Because that's what it is. Sadness. Just sadness. But it's okay, because happiness is just around the corner. I know it is. It has to be. After all this time, it has to be.

'Shhh,' you say, leaning forwards and placing warm kisses on my hot eyelids. 'It's okay, it's okay. I'm here now. You don't need to be sad anymore.'

'But why didn't you come sooner? Why didn't you call?' I swallow hard against my dry throat. 'I just got so confused and you made me feel so...'

'...Shhh,' you say again. 'Shhh. None of that matters now. Don't think about it anymore.' You kiss my forehead gently, whispering words against my skin. 'You'll only upset yourself again, and I don't want my baby upset.'

I close my eyes against the soothing warmth of your breath as it dances across my forehead each time you exhale, and I let myself relax into you. Muscles softening and moulding themselves into a new shape. Your shape. And I start to think that maybe you're right after all, maybe it doesn't matter anymore that you weren't here sooner. Not really. Because it's only me that missed you. Not Ruby, not James. And anyway, you're here now. You're beside me, just like I wanted. And for today at least I don't think you're going to hurt me. Because today the man I fell in love with is here, and that's what counts.

You tuck your hand under my shoulder and pull me round so I'm facing you properly. Chest to chest, hip to hip, eye to eye. You smooth a rogue strand of hair behind my ear and rest your hand against my cheek, looking at me with a gaze I can't seem to read. I press my face into your palm, nuzzling hard into you like I can't get close enough, and I close my eyes again, letting the heat emanating from you soothe everything inside that aches.

Your lips skim mine, barely touching me, just hinting at something more. I inhale sharply. It's enough to ignite a spark. Deep down beneath the weight of past woes and almost lost in the darkness of my loneliness, something glows and the dim light fights its way to the surface until it is almost close enough to touch, intensifying with every movement until it catches fire as I reach out to you, hands holding your face, pulling you towards me, holding you there, not letting you go, our mouths seeking each other out, drowning out the earlier sadness in hard, urgent kisses. Your hands find the waistband of my jeans as I feel the need in you hot up against me. And when we are skin against skin, when I feel you deep inside of me, everything melts away. Everything liquefies and evaporates in the explosion of us.

And I forget that you're the reason for it all. I forget that you did this to me. I don't see you slowly dragging me under.

Chapter Twenty-Six

'We can't keep going on like this. I don't know what I've done to deserve this…this anger. I don't understand, I don't understand any of it. I'm sorry for upsetting you, I really am. I'm sorry for whatever it is I've done. So, so sorry. If you would just tell me what I said I can make it right, really I can. It's just I'm…I'm trying to help you, but I can't. Not on my own. I can't do it for you, you have to understand that. I can't make everything better on my own. Especially when I don't know what's wrong. Just tell me. Why can't you tell me?

'Look, I can't do this anymore, I really can't. I'm walking on eggshells every single day, all the time, worried I'll say the wrong thing or do the wrong thing and you'll get upset. Like now. Like you always do. And I've got no idea what it is, because you always explode out of the blue at me and I hate it. Awful shitty things happen when you get upset, and if I'm being really honest, you...you scare me. I'm scared of you sometimes, really, really scared.

'No, I'm not saying I'm leaving. I don't...I don't really know what I'm saying. Just that something needs to change, because we can't keep going on like this. Look at my wrist. Look at it! There are fingerprints on there, *your* fingerprints. And why? Why? Because I had to leave here earlier and look after Ruby instead of seeing you? Is that it? She was sick, fucking sick and you know Matthew couldn't get away from work early to collect her from school. You know that! She's my daughter, I can't just abandon her! And anyway, I'm here now. I came back as soon as I could to see you, but now all you want to do is argue!

'No, that's not true at all, they're not more important than you, you're all equally important to me. But they depend on me, they're little children for God's sake. You're a fully-grown man, you can do without me for five minutes, can't you?

'Is that it? Is that what's wrong? You're *jealous*?! Tell me because I don't know. I never know. And I fucking love you, but unless you get help, unless this changes...unless you change...I'm sorry, but I can't live like this anymore.

'I need to go now. I have to go home. I can't stay here tonight. I don't want to. No...no...tonight you can't make me stay. Not after this. You can't keep hurting me like this, you just can't.'

Chapter Twenty-Seven

June 2012

The pills sit on the dining table in my living-room. I've taken two from the pack and placed them there with a glass of water. For when you're ready. And I hope with all my heart that you'll be ready soon, because I can feel everything's about to break. Nothing this fragile can last. Nothing this delicate that balances on a knife edge every single day can stay that way without somebody eventually looking over their shoulder to take in the alternative view, and then falling and feeling that sharp edge cut through everything they thought they loved. I don't want to come undone, don't want to let you down or let you go. But holding it together for you, and for me, is making me ache.

I tell myself there are reasons why. I can think up a hundred reasons why. Why I deserved the slaps across the face, or the crippling blows to my kidneys or last night's subtle but tight warning grip to my wrist to remind me of my place, or the screams and the insults and how I'm not good enough, how everything I do is wrong, how you despise me, how you love me, how you want me to go, how you want me to stay.

And the remedy is there. Right there inside those two white pills.

Housebound for days. That's what did it in the end. The summer showed her face in all her glory, pouring out the sunlight and heat for endless days and long balmy nights, as the smiles arrived on people's faces and stayed there, as the coconut scent of sunscreen filled the air and ice creams melted over a hundred clammy hands. Watching you as you lay alone and refused to leave your bed.

I'd spent endless afternoons in the park and weekends at the beach with Ruby and James, making the most of the early-summer. Climbing trees, rolling on our sides down grassy banks until we were dizzy, paddling in the icy-cold river and the much milder sea, building sandcastles and sitting back as the tide rushed in around them, listening to Ruby and James's giggles and squeals as the waves eventually toppled the castle into the sea. We'd looked in rock pools and found tiny crabs and sea anemones and millions of barnacles clinging tightly to slippery sandstone rocks. We'd searched the beach for driftwood and used it to draw masterpieces on the smooth terracotta sand.

We'd play until the sun set and the air turned cool. On calm evenings at the beach, when the sea barely moved and the orange slash of the sunset reflected on the water, we would skim stones across its surface until we could barely see and it was time to go home. All this we did without you. Ruby and James and me. They don't ask who you are anymore, this man who makes Mummy smile and cry in equal measure, and I don't tell them, because I'm realising that I don't really know you at all.

So, I don't ask you to come anymore. I've learned not to. Because you won't give in, no matter how much I beg and plead, you won't change your mind. Instead, you blame me for being pushy, for not understanding, for wanting my children more than I want you. You blame me for making you sad and angry, for making you do bad things, making you say nasty things, for making you the way you are. And maybe you're right. Maybe I want too much, need too much, think too much, feel too much. And maybe I pretend to do none of these things. Maybe I'm good at that, being two people at once.

I'm coming to realise that while I might grind my negatives into the ground like the dirty stub of a cigarette so I can focus on making you happy, I have never completely put the embers out. Instead, those negatives have carried on smouldering long after I've left them behind, blissfully oblivious to the trail of black smoke I have still circling my ankles as they follow me back towards you, laughing to themselves because they know I can't help you as long as their stench continues to cling to me. The aura of my past. Those things I did that won't ever go away.

Chapter Twenty-Eight

July 2012

You're sleeping on the sofa beneath the window, curled-up into a tight ball like a child, arms hugging your knees, your head to one side, breathing slow and deep into the cushion you're resting on. It's a beautiful day outside, the last of what's been another surprisingly hot month, and the mid-morning sun shines through the glass, dancing happily across your skin, turning your cheeks a pale-pink with its warmth, lighting you up, making you golden, glowing for you because we both know you can't find it inside you anymore to shine for yourself. For now, it's lost somewhere beneath the weight of a million other things. A weight that presses down on you and makes you a harsher, crueller version of yourself. A weight that sharpens all your edges and makes you impossible to touch.

I pause and gaze at you from my place by the front door. Right now, those edges are softer. All your angles are gone and you look peaceful. There's no frown on your face. Your features are smoothed out, relaxed, not creased and puckered with tension. Your hands rest loosely against your legs, not taut, not clenching and unclenching into angry fists like they do when the sadness takes hold. I stay where I am just looking at you. Not wanting to move because I don't want to disturb you from this rare moment of calm. This moment where you're a blank space, where your mind is empty, vacant, like a fresh sheet of paper ready to start a new story. This moment where you look more beautiful than I remember. I can see your face, just you, without the contortions of disgust, of hate, of fear. Tears prick the corners of my eyes. I wish it could always be like this for you. Why can't I make everything better instead of always making it worse?

Today I'd let myself into your house without knocking, because I didn't want to wake you if you were sleeping. I know better than to do that now. I made that mistake a few days ago, and the lesson afterwards was enough. Usually, you don't like me letting myself in. I always have to knock. Even if you're home and the door is unlocked, you hate it when I just walk straight in 'like it's my own place'. So, I've learned to knock and I've learned to wait until you allow me in. I've learned to let you keep control of everything, because it's easier that way.

So, when I called round to see you a couple of days ago, I did the same thing I always have. I knocked on the door, and I waited and waited. And I knocked again. And waited. And waited some more. Until eventually you answered it, face grey, body sagging with fatigue, eyes barely open. But through the swollen, sleep-deprived slashes, I saw them blazing with anger. Anger that bubbled and simmered beneath your breath for a split second before erupting like lava, scorching and scratching itself into my skin as a torrent of fury flew from your mouth and out on to the street.

'Poor little princess can't even let herself in.' The words form a snarl on your lips.

I open my mouth to explain, but my mind knows better than to retaliate and I don't find the words.

'You think you're something special, don't you? You think I actually want you here.' You laugh menacingly. 'I don't want you here, Belle. Nobody wants you. You're a fucking leech, draining the life out of everybody. You're a waste of space. Don't you fucking get that?' You pause for breath, and as a sneer curls at the corners of your mouth I feel my legs begin to weaken and my breath quicken as panic descends in a suffocating blanket. 'Everyone hates you. Everyone. I hate you, your family hates you, your friends fucking hate you.' Another pause as you prepare your final blow. 'And one day Belle, one day, your kids will hate you too when they find out you're nothing but a lowlife, filthy whore.'

The words rained down on me, hot and brutal, tormenting me, tearing me apart, breaking my heart.

I'd felt the sudden burn of your hand gripping my wrist, pulling me roughly inside with a strength you must have unlocked from somewhere outside of your lethargy, because my feet lifted from the ground and I stumbled on the step at your front door, twisting my ankle and biting down hard on my lip to stop me from crying out in pain as you slammed the door shut behind me, so hard that it thundered and rattled in the frame. A closed door so that nobody could see what your storm would do to me.

It took a little extra work the next day to cover the bruising you left across my jaw. A little extra concealer, a touch more foundation, powder applied tenderly over the painful blue-grey cloud that polluted my face. But I got rid of the marks in the end. I erased as best I could the remnants of your rage, the evidence of your fist, until I could almost believe it hadn't happened. Then I'd taken a couple of paracetamols to ease the pain I felt whenever I moved my mouth to speak, and now nobody else would ever know that yesterday had even happened. I'm thankful that when we see each other Ruby and James are with Matthew for the weekend at least. These are the times I'm glad this arrangement doesn't involve them. There's only so many times I could trip and fall, or walk into a door when I wasn't looking.

I move my jaw side to side subconsciously as I remember that afternoon. I remember leaving almost as soon as I'd arrived. Running back to my car parked out in the street, face hidden, tucked into the collar of my leather jacket, ashamed. Driving home through a sea of hot tears, unable to see the road clearly, the pain in my face so intense I thought I was broken. Hands shaking on the steering wheel, corners taken too sharply and too fast as I fled home, losing the ability to control even the smallest of movements beneath the black, suffocating mass of shock that had its hands around my throat and its heart in my stomach.

The throbbing that day was so loud inside my head that I imagined my jaw was pulsing in and out, in and out, like a visible heartbeat beating a fearful rhythm for everybody to hear. 'Look at this girl,' it said. 'Poor, poor girl. She let it happen again. When will she learn? When will she learn?' And then: 'Help this poor girl. Help her. Because she can't help herself. Not anymore. She's that girl now. She's that girl.'

For the most part, the pain has gone, but the stiffness is still there, and beneath my make-up – the paint I use to camouflage reality from my own skewed, rose-tinted viewpoint – the blue is beginning to turn yellow.

I'm a chameleon, I think. I can adapt. Look for me and you won't find me.

You stir, eyes moving rapidly beneath your eyelids, eyebrows knitting together as a frown flits across your face. Then you're still again. Are you dreaming? I wonder. The demons are never far from your door. I wipe my own sadness away from my eyes with the back of my hand. The doctor said this would happen, I remind myself. The increased anger, the tiredness cruelly paired with insomnia just to really kick you while you're down. The nausea that grips you constantly, that makes you not want to eat, that makes you hurl the food I've cooked for you back at me because it's not what you want.

You don't want anything, then you want something, but it's not right, nothing is right. Nothing I do or say or don't do or don't say is right. None of it is okay. But the doctor told us this, and anyway it's just for a little while. Until your body gets used to it. Gets used to those white pills. Those magic beans. Jack and the Beanstalk sorcery. So, for a little while, however long it takes, I'll stand here and I'll take it all. Because what else can I do? You need me. I can help make it all better, I know I can. I'm not going to leave you when you need me most. I'll never do that again. Not after Ebony. Not after that.

When I look back over the past few months and really think about it, I've always known there was something wrong. Something in the quiet anger that simmers just below your surface. In the sadness that clings to you like a frightened child. In the way you want me and don't want me at the same time. The way you love me, but then in the blink of an eye hate me so completely I feel like my insides are blackened by the fire you breathe into me, my very core poisoned by the venom that leaves your lips. Something in the way you hold me, after all that, like I'm the most precious thing in the world to you. And you make me believe that the bad things won't happen anymore. And I do believe you, until the next time.

A car passes on the road outside and the sound tumbles loudly through the open front door into your living-room, rumbling around in the silence. I wince and turn quickly to shut it out, but I'm too late. You jump a little at the sound of the engine and slowly open your eyes. I stay where I am and instinctively tense up, waiting for the bad things to start again, but you lie still, staring straight ahead, saying nothing.

'Hey,' I whisper eventually, walking over to the sofa and crouching down beside you. Your eyes meet mine and I want to reach out and stroke your hair, but I daren't touch you. Not yet.

I put my keys down carefully on the coffee table and notice the blister pack of pills lying next to a half-empty glass of water and a magazine still in its plastic wrapping. I remember you can't concentrate long enough to read these days; instead, you stare at the TV or into blank space for what seems like hours. I wonder how long this 'little while' the doctor told us about is going to last.

Your hand reaches out to me and rests limply against my bent knee. I take it between both my palms and squeeze gently, smiling at you, hoping this is a good sign.

'Hey,' you say, and smile back sleepily, eyes rimmed red.

They're still there, those crinkles around your eyes. The ones that reach almost all the way across your cheeks, the laughter lines I noticed when we first met all those months ago. But that's all that's left of the smile I fell in love with. Now, the light has gone behind your eyes, the glint, the mischief, the things that made you, you. The white oblongs of chemicals in the blister pack on the table behind me have taken those things away, yet still, the bad things break through, clawing at you like insatiable demons, always wanting more. And I hate them. I hate them for taking you from me. Hurry up 'little while' I think. Hurry up and go away.

Through a half-smile, you lock eyes with me and blow a long stream of warm air through your nose, the sigh skimming the back of my hand as I watch your shoulders sag. You sit up slowly, long legs curled beneath you on the sofa, one hand still in mine, the other rubbing your eyes, thumb and middle finger moving upwards slowly to press hard against your temples as you pause, head resting against your fingertips.

'I let myself in,' I say quietly, stroking the rough skin of your hand in mine, sliding my fingers between yours and interlocking them in a loose hold. 'I hope you don't mind. It's just that, after the other day, well…well, I thought…'

'It's fine,' you snap back, pulling your hand roughly from mine. 'For God's sake, why do you always have to bring everything back up again? Can't you just forget it for once? Just let it go.'

'I'm sorry, I didn't mean –'

Your head snaps up then and you lock eyes with me again, only this time they're not sleepy and resigned, they're ablaze with emerald fire. And you're moving quickly now. Your feet uncurling from under your body and reaching down to the floor quicker than your tiredness should allow, and suddenly you're standing, looming over me while I'm still crouching beside the sofa, knees and ankles beginning to ache from the awkward position I'm in. Only I'm not just crouching down now, I'm cowering. Waiting. Preparing myself for what's coming next.

'On and on and on, all the fucking time,' you're saying, more to yourself than to me. I stay where I am, down on the floor, staring hard at the carpet, its beige and cream dots swimming and dancing in front of my eyes as though they're playing a game. Catch me if you can. Stars begin to shimmer along the edges of everything as adrenaline makes the room come into sharp focus. Sounds scrape across my eardrums as the world becomes crystal-clear, a spotlight trained on this room, on this moment, on me. And suddenly it's too loud and too bright and too hot, and the muscles in my limbs become taut, flexed, ready to run. I dig my fingertips into the worn pile of the carpet in an attempt to steady myself, still not daring to speak as you continue your monologue, taking the spotlight away from me as you take centre stage.

'Little Miss Happy, Little Miss I'll Make Everything Okay. Little Miss Getting On My *Fucking Nerves*!'

You lean down towards me then with a sudden jerking movement, your face so close to mine I can feel my skin begin to prickle as the cloying warmth from yours bridges the tiny gap between us. I don't move. Those last words shoot from your mouth like a choking ball of repulsion that's finally been coughed up and spat out. I feel them ricocheting off the side of my face, tangled up in your hot breath, and landing with a thud at my feet, ready for me to pick up and take with me later. Ready to join the others like shackles, following me relentlessly as I drag them behind me, their taunts rising with every step and every rattle of the chain that binds them to me.

The room feels stifling now. The heat of the sun is amplified as it beams through the window, slashing a hot stripe of yellow across my cheek, along the length of my body and stretching down to the floor. Its bright-yellow light carves a path along the carpet, a yellow brick road, a fairy path, a happy colour turned bad as the heat rises and the pinpricks of light I can see around the edges of everything glimmer more intensely. Their colour turns from blue to silver to gold to black and back again, like Christmas lights, flickering, wavering, turning everything into a halo of white noise.

'I don't want your help,' you're saying, pacing the floor unsteadily. I steal a glance at you as you turn your back to me and head towards the kitchen, watching as you stumble, flinching as you swear, spitting more words out as though they taste bitter on your tongue. For a moment I wonder if you're drunk. Maybe it's not water in the glass on the coffee table but something much harder and stronger. I wonder if I can grab the glass and taste what's in it. But I daren't move.

'When will you get that through your pretty, dumb head?' You carry on, voice muffled in the confines of another room. 'I want you to leave me alone. Just leave me alone! I was fine until you came along. Totally fine. But no, you had to barge into my life and ruin it with your stupid fucking ideas and your let's-play-happy-fucking-families attitude and your constant pretence that life is some amazing fucking wonderland. But do you know what?'

You've reached the far end of the kitchen now and you pause there for a moment, leaning heavily against the wall, palms and forehead against the black tiles. I watch you warily, not sure if I should answer, but feeling like I should.

'No,' I say quietly. 'Tell me, please tell me what's wrong. I just –'

'You just what?' you sneer, cutting me off and spinning around, stalking back towards me, stronger now, with purpose. 'You just want to 'help me'?' You mimic the sound of a whining child's voice, tilting your head to one side and staring hard at me. I shrink back into myself and suddenly I feel stupid, like everything I've ever tried to do was foolish. Stupid for allowing myself to think that I could save you, that I could right all my wrongs. Stupid for letting my fantasies run away with me. Because really, you're right, I'm nothing at all.

I look at you, wide-eyed, like a rabbit in headlights, and watch a slow smile spread across your lips. A smile that doesn't reach your eyes, doesn't come close.

'Life isn't a wonderland, Belle,' you say, softer now. 'Life is a nightmare that carries on going, even when you're awake. It doesn't just like to screw with your head while you're sleeping, if you can even get to sleep in the first place. Oh no, it likes to really fuck you up while you're awake too.' Your fists clench. That telltale sign. Your voice starts to rise as the vein in your neck rises too, pushing hard against your skin, the contained rage frantically trying to escape.

'Do you have any idea what it's like? Really? Do you? You say you do. You tell me this and that and feed me your bullshit stories and your apologies and your 'poor me' tales of fucking woe. But you haven't got a fucking clue, have you? Not a clue. You, in your perfect little world with your perfect little life. A little princess, a stupid little princess.'

You lean towards me then, crouching down beside me, tracing a line across my cheek with your fingertips, running them gently down my neck and across my collarbone. I swallow hard and fight the urge to retch as your fingers rest in the little well at the base of my throat, their gentle, barely-there pressure enough to provoke a gagging reflex within me, and I have to clamp my teeth together hard to keep it at bay. Suddenly your hand moves and you clench the back of my neck, pulling me roughly towards you, holding me close to your face, your lips brushing against my ear, your breath hot and stale.

'But you're not a perfect little princess, are you?' you whisper through gritted teeth. 'You're a stupid little bitch. You're nothing but a cheap whore.'

You reach out, grab the tumbler on the coffee table and throw it at the wall as if to punctuate this last word with the repulsive shatter of glass. I scream, and fire ignites in the pit of my stomach, so immediate and intense I can't stop it. It takes hold of every nasty word you've ever spoken to me and feeds off the pain of their memory, fuelled by anger and every ounce of me that you stole and took for yourself. The flames get higher and higher, licking hungrily at my insides, burning brighter with every vile story they recall. I wrench your hand from my neck, fingernails digging into your flesh, drawing blood, and I spin around to face you. I want to hurt you. I want to hurt you like you've hurt me.

'I do know how it feels you fucking monster!' I scream, as my fist smashes into the side of your face, pain exploding in my knuckles, blistering heat running up my arm, searing through every nerve ending, violent and raw.

You're blind-sided and for a tiny but excruciating moment, nothing happens. Time stands still. Seconds pass in slow motion, taking an eternity to tick from one moment to the next. I feel as though I'm underwater, struggling against a current but moving nowhere, sounds muffled and sluggish somewhere far away, like nothing has any meaning anymore. I need to leave. I need to get away.

An involuntary sound leaves my lips, a sudden, anguished cry, and I'm breathless, as though somebody has taken a knife to me and has twisted it into my very core, leaving me with no sound. A blow to my stomach, heat spreading through me, radiating from where your fist made contact with my ribcage. I crumple onto my side on the carpet, my back pressed up hard against the sofa. Trapped. The clarity of earlier retreats rapidly and nausea takes its place. I vomit in my mouth and instantly swallow it back down again, bitterness stinging my throat, insides churning, and I heave again, fear spilling from my lips and puddling against the side of my face where I lay.

In a blind panic, I turn onto my stomach, the pain from my ribs sending brutal stabbing spasms through me with every sluggish move I make. The stench of vomit on my skin and clothes clawing at my nostrils, daring me to throw up again as I begin to crawl towards the door. If I stay close to the ground, I tell myself in a desperate attempt at rational thought, it'll be safer. That's what they say isn't it, in emergency situations? 'Get down!' But you dart towards me, grabbing my ankles to stop me moving, and suddenly I'm dragged off my knees, your fingers digging harshly into the soft spaces between my broken ribs.

Pain sears through my spine and into the back of my head as you smash me against the wall, my head snapping backwards and striking the brickwork with a dull crunch. Images melt before me, turning to liquid and running off the page, leaving behind a blank space filled with an eternity of nothing. And then your hands are on my throat, your fingers easily circling my neck, tightening their grip, squeezing, crushing me bit by bit. I flail blindly in front of me with a vague intent to scratch your face, to claw at your skin, your eyes, anything I can make contact. But my efforts are worthless, feeble and weak, as you squeeze my neck harder and harder.

I try to reach my toes to touch the floor, to ease the pressure on my neck, stretching as much as I can until it hurts and I feel as though my muscles are going to snap. But it's no good, I can barely touch the ground. The tip of my boots only just graze the carpet and I can't gain purchase.

I can't reach, I can't reach, I can't reach.

Panic engulfs me then like a fire burning out of control. I can't get enough air into my lungs. I'm sucking it in but nothing is getting through. My vision distorts further, the movie I'm watching becoming black and white, the edges disappearing somewhere around the corner out of sight, the picture becoming less and less clear. White noise and snowflakes. This isn't happening to me, this isn't happening.

'Please,' I manage, voice strangled, desperate, barely audible. 'I…I love…you…'

But you don't stop, and I realise this is my punishment. Suddenly, it all becomes clear. This is no less than I deserve. For everything I've done wrong, for the hearts I've broken, for the people I tried to save and couldn't, for the people I stopped trying for, for the times I was never good enough and for all the things I should've said when I had the chance.

For the things I could've stopped before they started. This is where it ends. This is the price I pay.

My throat burns, raw from the effort of trying to find air, so I decide to stop trying altogether. I hold what's left of my breath and let my eyes close. At least if I'm going to die here, I think, I'll decide when. You won't have the final word. You'll never have the final word. So, I stop breathing and I let your fingers crush my windpipe as darkness closes in, until there's nothing but black, black, black pressing up against me, trying to get in.

'Fuck you!' you snarl through gritted teeth. The sound echoes around the emptiness in my head, faded and watery, a stream running over rocks, diluted, interrupted, frail at the edges.

Pressure releases. I fall to the floor, crumpling like a rag doll into a wretched heap before being thrown roughly onto my back. Air, sharp and harsh, suddenly comes crashing into my lungs, forcing its way into my throat, pushing out my ribcage, filling the dying spaces inside me as hot stale breath after involuntary breath is devoured hungrily by my oxygen-starved body.

Darkness recedes, the ebb and flow of the inky blackness retreats as my consciousness holds on by its fingertips, clawing its way slowly back into view. Your lips are on mine, my heavy head clasped between your palms as your bear down on me, your breath bringing me back, back to this place, back to you, right back to where I don't want to be. And I'm coughing and retching and wrenching more huge gulps of air into my lungs as I step away from the edge and back towards you, struggling and writhing, with a sudden rush of energy, to get you off me. The surge of electricity running through me fuelled by a fear so pure and raw that I'm unable to control it.

I flail blindly on my back, mind struggling against the incoherent weight of semi-consciousness, and I somehow manage to land a feeble punch against the right-hand side of your face. It's not enough. I grab at whatever I can touch, tearing at the skin of your cheeks and jaw, pulling at your hair, dragging your head down until you are level with me. Holding you there, inches away from me until I force my eyelids open through the dense fog of fear, and that's when I finally see you. Your face red from exertion and rage, the beads of sweat glistening across your forehead and top lip, the blood trickling from the gouges in your cheeks where my fingernails made their claim, and your blank eyes staring right back at me. Dead eyes with nothing behind them but a vacant soul. And I scream and scream with complete and all-encompassing terror.

Ebony

Chapter Twenty-Nine

August 1996

Ebony lies wasting away in a hospital bed. I sit on a dirty green armchair beside her, flicking through a magazine, bored. Waiting for her to hurry up and get on with dying if that's what she insists on doing, because I've got other stuff to do. The armchair isn't fooling anyone. It wants to be leather, wishes it was, but in reality, the faded and peeling vinyl proves it's some cheap, mass-produced wannabe. Like the 'in' girls at school. Carbon copies of one other. Duplicates, triplicates, reflections upon reflections in a mirror. All black-cherry lipstick and choppy layers. All the same. All fitting neatly into their little boxes like perfect pigeon-holed pretties. Everything I despise.

It's not even comfortable, this chair. Its high back is forcing my head forwards, making my neck and my back ache, the points of the springs pushing against the fakery of the material, prodding into the length of my thighs, making my legs ache too. I keep shifting position to stop the numbness in my neck spreading across my shoulders and to keep the springs from piercing through the chair, through my skin and into my flesh, pinning me here, unable to move without ripping myself to shreds like in some horror film. Although this may already be a horror film that I'm in, I think, looking across at what's left of the body in the bed beside me.

I arch my back to stretch my spine and I feel my T-shirt sticking to me. It's hot in here, so hot. My legs stick to the shitty chair, short skirt doing little to stop the perspiration forming on the backs of my thighs and leaving a slick residue on the poor, disillusioned plastic. My feet melt into pools of salty sweetness inside my boots and I just want to go home and wash it all away. I feel disgusting. The stale heat, the sickness that hangs in the stifling air making its way into my lungs with every inhale and clinging on there, never quite making it back out again on the warmth of my breath. Heavy silence competing for space with the illness that already saturates the room. The machines and their faint buzzing and beeping and hissing and wheezing and the tubes and the wires and the clock on the wall and its constant tick-tocking. The silence is suddenly an explosion of sound and it's unbearable.

I angle the fan at Ebony's bedside towards me, letting ribbons of cooler air flutter through my hair and tie themselves in knots. It doesn't help. Warm air grabs at my sweat-dampened face and pretends to try and cool me for a moment, before finding a comfortable spot and sitting crossed legged across my forehead instead, too hot to move anymore, laughing at me lazily as its heat clambers into my hairline and settles across my temples, my skin protesting, prickling beneath the sting of slowly spreading perspiration. I fold up my magazine and fan my face with it, moving the warm air around in sweeping strokes, creating miniature gusts with articles about music festivals I can only dream of attending and stories about dead rock stars. Back and forth, back and forth, tick-tock, tick-tock, tick-tock.

The draught I've made stirs the dulled-down chocolate fringe that is plastered to Ebony's forehead. Delicate strands of hair escape and lift on the man-made breeze, reaching out to touch the air, dancing on the tiny storm until they settle themselves once more when the storm has passed. But Ebony doesn't move. She stares unseeing at the ceiling, eyes glazed and milky, paper-thin skin coated in a deathly blue sheen, hair in lank clumps at her ears, her forearms cross-hatched with fine silver slashes, the skin etched by the scars of a careless artist. Everything is either sunken in or poking sharply out. She's all edges and angles, and they're all wrong. It's hideous to look at.

I turn away, unfold the magazine and flick through its pages again. The glossy paper sticks to my damp fingertips and leaves faint ink stains in the grooves of my skin. Rainbow fingerprints. Unintentional art. I wipe them on my thigh and leave a rainbow smear there too. Red, blue and green smudges bleeding into one another like a multi-coloured bruise. Colour among the intentional grey and beige tones of the hospital room. Calming, they say; deathly, I disagree.

Suddenly, I'm thirsty. My mouth dry, throat catching and sticking to itself sharply whenever I swallow. I reach down and rummage for a drink in the bag dumped at my feet. The patchwork one. The one I made. The one I can't throw away despite its frayed edges and undone seams, because it belongs to us. To Ebony, Matty, Dan and me. Because it tells our story inside each one of those mismatched fabric squares. Our lives scribbled and etched in permanent marker across the patchwork over the months and years, in the hearts and the arrows and the song lyrics and the book quotes and the lines from films and the private jokes and the badges and the pins and the bands we love. And in the broken heart where Dan used to be.

I push the thought away and tip my bag upside down looking for a can of cola, shaking it until the contents tumble out and loudly litter the blue-grey linoleum, the weight of the thick air scattering momentarily as the sound of coins, cassettes and my Walkman puncture holes in it like sudden rapid fire. No cola though. I must've left it on the worktop in the kitchen at home before I left. I pick up the coins and count them into my palm – five, six-seven, eight, nine-ten. Ten pence. Mother would've been proud right there. Ten years later and I've finally got it. No, wait, there's another five. There, almost hidden under the bedside cabinet. I fish it out with my thumb and forefinger and shake off the dust. That's fifteen pence, all I have left after I'd paid my bus fare. Shit. Not enough for a can from the vending machine.

I look around and swallow hard again, my tongue sticking to the roof of my mouth. There's a jug of stagnant water on the cabinet and I stand to pour it reluctantly into what I hope is a clean glass, too parched to care.

'You don't mind, do you?' I ask Ebony with more than a hint of sarcasm as I choke it back quickly and spit it straight out again as soon as it hits my throat. It's warm and metallic and tastes like the air feels.

'For fuck's sake!' I slam the glass down onto the cabinet, the sound ricocheting off the walls angrily and firing offshoots into every corner of the room. More bullets to rip holes in the silence. I run my hands through my hair and pace the floor before something akin to a scream wants to break out of me. I force the energy instead into quick, staccato footsteps. From the chair to the door and back again. To the window and its view over the car park, back to the chair, to the painting of the seaside on the wall, hung a little too low and skewed a little to one side so that it grates ever so slightly on your nerves. The waves crash like huge white monsters onto a yellow beach beneath a cobalt sky. It's easy to miss the solitary figure standing on the sand.

Back to the chair again where I slump, defeated. I squeeze my eyes shut and breathe in as far as I can until my ribs hurt and my lungs are full and the air can't stay there any longer and instead comes pouring back out in a hot rush of frustration. I'm angry. I don't want to be here. I want to run away. To hide. To be the solitary figure on the beach where I can't see her anymore. But there's nobody else to stay with her on these long hot afternoons. Nobody else wants to. Her parents busy at work, trying to stay afloat. No brothers or sisters. Just me. And so I sit and I think about it all over again. And I remember why I hate her.

You

Chapter Thirty

Salt hung in the air that afternoon like an old friend, gathering me into its embrace as I'd climbed slowly out of the car. The wind had whipped my hair across my face, dancing around me in 'look at me' swirls, picking up her skirts and performing graceful twists and dizzying turns across the cliff-top, the rise and fall of the waltz showering me in the seaside's briny sweet scent. She continued gliding across my back in tiptoed gusts while I'd leaned, bent double, against the side of the car and thrown up over and over and over again, ruining the beautiful ball-gown of the breeze. Salt and vomit in the clarity of the coastal light like crystals on my skin. The bitter sting of both only just enough to remind me that I was still alive.

My legs had given way then. I was exhausted. The remnants of my energy consumed by the running away, the drive here, the devastating need to get away. All a terrifying blur. Crawling through a putrid mess of bile on your carpet. Your front door just out of reach. Fingertips stretching, knuckles about to pop as they grazed the handle above my head. Your hand around my ankle pulling me back again. My kick. The crunch of bone as my foot found your face. Your scream. And then I was running through the beautiful summer's day. Running, running, running. Tears streaming. Throat burning. Stomach throbbing. To the car. To the splutter of the engine as the key found the ignition. To the screech of tyres spinning on hot asphalt. The scrape and grind of the gears. Hands gripping the wheel. Driving with cataracts over my eyes, to this place. The only place I could think to go. Seamill.

I'd fallen to my knees then on the coarse, damp grass – stomach empty, pained and crumpled up from the sickness – and had lain down among the pink flower heads of thrift and the bare bones of the scabby lips flower, staring unseeing at the sky, hoping that darkness might fall on me right there on the cliff-top and stop the cruel ache that had become me. I wanted to sleep, wanted to drift off, wanted to stay drifted for the longest time, until nobody missed me anymore and I didn't need to return. I looked for the darkness in the purity of the blue as the edges of everything turned hazy and soft and shimmered in the afternoon light.

Memories of my childhood trickled into the gaps between the violence that filled my head. Oozing like caramel, syrupy like honey, sour as citrus. 'Don't touch that,' Mother would say, slapping my hand away from the white petals that bloomed at the end of black skeleton stems. 'It'll give you scabby lips.' But I didn't listen. How could that be true? How? So, one day I'd touched it, that fictional scabby lips flower, because a butterfly was perched upon its ivory blossoms and I knew an insect so pretty wouldn't alight on something so ugly. And so, I'd pressed my fingers against the flowers and rubbed their poisoned tips slowly back and forth across my mouth right in front of Mother, staring right at her, and I told her she was wrong. And she lifted my skirt and she raised her hand and she left her telltale red marks across the backs of my thighs. They were still there the next day, tender red weals that made sitting down a chore. That made it impossible to play on the swing in the garden, made it impossible to sit on the wooden go-cart and speed down the grass bank across the road, made me suck in my breath and tense up my shoulders every time I turned over in bed. But the next day, and the day after that and the day after that, my lips stayed as soft as ever. I was twelve when I realised my mother was a liar.

Butterflies, hundreds of them, suddenly fluttered all about me, cutting across the memory and filling the haze at the corners of my eyes with glittering pigments. A kaleidoscope of colours circling my head like a rainbow in flight. Round and round the hypnotic tempest looped as it soared and filled the sky with the gentle trembling of wings, the air quivering as though pulled taut for a moment and then let go like the string of a violin. Like the string of a guitar. Her fingers, Ebony's fingers, plucking the air and making it shudder.

The mirage, the dream, the hallucination, the wishful thinking went on and on. Faster and faster the butterflies flew. Frenzied and beautiful, wings skimming my forehead, gentle breeze touching my cheek. Vivid hues flashed and popped all around me. My wide eyes followed the spectacle as it continued its unbroken path round my head, where I lay like a wounded animal among the grass and the flowers and the contents of my stomach.

I'd shifted my gaze then and looked through the eye of this beautiful storm to the perfect sky beyond, and breathed in its crystal-clear air, enjoying the sensation of its coolness cleansing my lungs and slowing my pounding heart. Something close to peace began to settle around me, calmness cocooning me and holding me gently up to the sky in its palms. The soothing warmth of it spreading like liquid gold across my skin, dripping from my hair and pooling into a molten halo around my head. Angelic. Almost.

But just as all my wild and rampant thoughts distilled themselves, just as they refined themselves and became free of all the impurities you infused there, a shadow was cast. Greyness creeping across the brilliance just like every bad decision I'd ever made, until your gaping mouth seemed to fill the sky and poured out jet-black clouds, suffocating everything in an instant and shrouding all the colour in a darkness so thick I could feel it. Taking everything away with one malicious breath.

And it was then I realised that I'm the butterfly and you're the poisoned flower. Only you're not a lie, you're the truth, you're the ugliest truth, but this butterfly still doesn't seem to understand that there is no sweet nectar to be found in you, only venom. And she tries over and over to find it, holding her breath through the black, trying not to fade away, because she believes that somewhere, somewhere, is the sweetness she craves.

***

I can't quite remember how I got here, lying on the sofa beneath the old dusky-pink eiderdown, staring into the flames flickering in the open fire. Snatches of memories come and go. How I'd woken from a dream on the lawn to find darkness had fallen. How I'd scrabbled for the key in the gutter, moss and dirty water embedding themselves behind my fingernails. How I'd scrubbed vomit from my hair and blood from my hands.

Blood on my hands. Always blood on my hands. Like Ebony's, only different this time.

How I'd stripped off my clothes and stood naked in the kitchen while I'd soaked away the stains of my ordeal in the sink, scouring away the trauma with cheap green soap and years-old bleach until my hands were raw. How I didn't once notice that I was shivering. How I didn't once question why.

How I'd stepped into the shower where the ice-cold water rattled through ancient pipes, shocking me awake, soothing the bruises, easing the swelling. How I'd poured what was left of the bleach into my palm, the smell making my stomach churn and my throat close up; how I'd rubbed it all over me like soap, until my skin tingled and reddened and fought back angrily. How it hurt as it took you away, hurt like hell, but how I was glad. How I carried on. More and more. From the top of my head to the soles of my feet. Frantic, frightened, desperate and determined. Until the bottle was empty and I finally stopped, sinking down to a curled-up mess of a girl in the corner of the shower cubicle, plastic bottle clutched to my chest as visions ripple in front of me like misplaced heatwaves: of the school playground where I saved her that one and only time, a jam-jar clasped tight against her, of Dan as he walked away and didn't ever come back, and the fireplace where Ben had loved me and where he had come undone. And then you. You who took away the little I had left to give.

Now I watch the flames dance in front of me, my eyes staring blankly from the sofa, the fire reflected in them bouncing right back out again. It doesn't warm me. Not today. I'm naked beneath the blanket, naked and cold. My clothes hang on the hot water tank in the airing cupboard, dripping cold water onto the floorboards. They won't be dry before morning. I couldn't wring them out hard enough, hands shaking, losing their grip on the fabric, my muscles refusing to work. As I lie here now, rubbing the corner of the quilt absently backwards and forwards between my thumb and forefinger, its silky softness gently tickling my hand, timeworn thoughts of toasted marshmallows and scorched slices of bread drift out of the fire and scent the air.

I see my little brother, my older sister and me kneeling in front of the glowing coals when the flames had died down a bit and the fire was just right. Toasting forks in hand, fluffy marshmallows or bread skewered on the end, holding them over the embers as long as the heat would allow before our hands were too hot and the air smelled of burnt sugar. Then we'd cram the warm, gooey marshmallows into our mouths, lips and fingers coated pink and white in a sugary mess, and Grandmother's sticky strawberry jam would be spread on the toasted bread and we'd have a sweet feast for supper before curling up in bed, feet searching out the warmth of hot-water bottles, blankets pulled up to our chins, falling asleep as trains rumbled by outside.

Those same trains would wake us in the morning too. The blast of their horns as they approached the road bridge at the end of the pebbled lane bursting into the bedroom through the thin glass of the window, chiming and creaking in their wooden frames and rousing us from sleep, my sister and I sharing the double bed, my brother on a fold-out bed at the foot of ours. In fact, everything rattled; walls, roof, pots and pans and crockery in the kitchen cupboards, the clock on the mantelpiece in the living-room shuffling slowly forwards until it teetered on the edge, tick-tocking and oblivious, the barometer on the wall of the front porch – which we'd take turns to tap each morning, waiting excitedly for the forecast, hoping it'd stay fair – thrumming against the wooden cladding in time to the rock and click of the diesel engine passing by outside.

Sometimes, when we saw a train rounding the headland a little further down the coastline we'd race it and, if we ran fast enough, we'd make it down to the bridge and watch excitedly as it passed beneath, feeling the vibrations travel up through our wellington boots and tickle the hair on the tops of our heads. Sometimes we'd climb on the wire fence at the back of the cottage instead and wave as they roared by, some passengers waving back at us, some looking down at books in their laps, some simply staring out of the window lost in thought.

We spent all our summers there at the cottage with our grandparents. Perched on top of a cliff, set back just far enough from the edge so as not to have to worry about plummeting into the ocean and being washed away in a storm. And the storms here were frequent. Winds whipping up the sea into a frenzy of churning white horses rushing towards the land, crashing onto grey pebbles, pushing them up the beach into a huge seaweed-topped ridge that lined the shore.

We'd always rush down to the beach after a high tide to see what the waves had left behind: plastic bottles by the hundred, thick fishermen's ropes of bright-orange and blue twisted and frayed among the slippery seaweed, smooth sticks of driftwood bleached almost white by the tide, shoes, crates, multitudes of empty sweet wrappers. One day there was a porpoise.

These were our treasures, and we'd scour them collecting sticks for the fire or to use for drawing pictures in the sand further down the beach, picking up feathers to place atop our sandcastles, pocketing shells and turquoise-coloured pieces of sea-smoothed glass to put in a pretty jar, pure-white pebbles and the occasional crab nipping at us angrily all finding their way into our bright plastic buckets.

And we'd walk back up to the cottage, swinging them triumphantly as we marched through the garden gate, tipping the contents onto the crazy-paved patio. Surveying our finds. Chasing the feathers as they blew away on the cliff-top breeze.

I loved the sea in a storm. I loved the power of the waves, the salty spray that blew off their effervescent tops making my skin tight and my hair brittle. The swirling of the gunmetal sky reflected in the eddies. Sometimes it scared me, walking along the beach as a little girl, watching the storm roll in from the horizon and the waves get higher. Sometimes, when the wind was particularly fierce, I'd turn away from the water in fear and walk back to the safety of the cottage with my face turned towards the cliff, or getting a piggy-back ride from Dad, clinging on tightly around his neck, my head buried against his warm back. But mostly the rage of the weather fascinated me, and I'd stand at the tide edge, wind thundering in my ears, the sea a seething mass of grey, and I'd shout at the waves to do their worst. Come and get me. Catch me if you can. They never did. I was too quick for them. I could always get away.

Sometimes though, I loved the calm too. Especially when the evening air was still and the sun was setting, the sky on fire as the perfect circle of orange hanging just above the sea cast a pristine fairy path across the water, connecting one world to another. I would sit on the cliff, legs dangling over the edge, and watch as the sun sank lower and lower in the sky, until only the curving tip of flame remained, balancing precariously on the horizon for a mere minute before diving behind the sea and making way for nightfall. The dusk air would be warm all around me. I'd hear grasshoppers humming in the long grass beneath my legs and the gentle lapping of the waves against the cliff face below. Then I'd hear Grandmother calling from the porch and I'd skip back towards the yellow glow of the windows and the curls of smoke rising from the chimney and the toasted marshmallows and games of cards and the warmth that waited inside.

A piece of coal cracks in the fire and spits out a spark of glowing red into the grate, and I'm back to today again. I can't remember how long I've been lying here, but the clock on the mantelpiece tells me it's almost one in the morning and my bones ache with weariness. The fire is still burning well, its heat pressing against my cheeks and nose, and I can feel them flushing pink in its comforting warmth. The rest of me remains cold though, the fire doing little to stop the shivers twitching through my limbs, although I'm thankful for its valiant attempt and my ability to light it all the same. It is the only heat and the only light in the room. The auburn glow of it like a beacon on the cliff-top. The only sign of life here.

I'm suddenly struck for the first time how remote this place is. There's nothing else around apart from a derelict cottage at the end of the road opposite the bridge, getting closer and closer to the cliff edge as it recedes further and further inland with every attack of the tide. And then nothing, nothing, nothing for miles. As a child, the space excited me, the seclusion gave me room to breathe, to run, to stretch my legs. Now though, I feel isolated and exposed. Vulnerable. Easy prey.

What if he's looking for me? What if he finds me?

I jam my knuckles into my mouth and bite down to stop a scream. My ribs cave in, stabbing me from the inside, stomach tightening, clenching like a fist, again and again, leaving me retching into palms slick with sweat. What if he's looking for me? What if he finds me? What if he finds me? What if he finds me?

I curl up into a ball, instinctively child-like, regressing with such speed into infancy that the lines blur, and there's you with your fists and Mother with her hand and your voices meld into one sharp tongue that lashes me like a whip over and over again, opening all the scars I carry with me with each relentless blow. And I close my eyes and with clenched teeth remember all the reasons why I hate you, and at the very same time all the reasons why I can't.

Ebony

Chapter Thirty-One

I remember the first time she cut herself. I don't mean all the times before that day, when she scraped experimental razor-blade kitten scratches onto her skin. I mean the first time I found her in the bathroom, lying on white tiles smeared with blood that was too red, too much, too real. Deep valleys carved into her arms, chunks of flesh gouged out and hanging lifeless from threads of pale stringy skin. The Stanley knife still there in her limp grasp, a serene smile on her face as I entered the chaos. The screaming echoes of 'fuck!' bouncing off the tiles and being caught by the smudges of a hundred scarlet handprints.

That was the second time I really hated her.

It was a weekend. Saturday, I think. Her parents were away so I called round. She was expecting me. Maybe that's why she chose to do it then, because she knew she'd be found. She knew that what she thought she wanted to happen, the worst thing, wouldn't. Because Belle would save her…again.

I ran to the phone in the hall, fingers shaking uncontrollably as I pressed the white plastic buttons, numbers swimming in front of my face, hoping I'd got them in the right order to call Matty. She was his girlfriend after all, and he also had a car. That was as rational as my mind was able to get right then.

While I waited the endless minutes for him to arrive, I grabbed the cream towel from the rail beside the sink and wrapped it tightly around her arm. Blood-soaked through it in seconds, seeping in perfect circles through the plush cotton like some sinister Hallowe'en tie-dye. I ran to the airing cupboard on the landing, threw open the door and began rummaging for extra towels, wrapping more and more around Ebony's arm, tighter and tighter, until the blood finally stopped seeping and the horror of her missing parts was contained. And then I sat on the side of the bath exhausted, breath coming in short sharp pants, as she lay slumped at my feet in a blissful state of silent agony.

I turned on the hot tap and let it run until steam rose and I could smell its musty heat. As I washed her blood from my hands, as I held them under the scalding water, she lay there and watched me. As I washed the red splatters of her from my cheeks and the water in the sink turned a deep shade of violent magenta, she watched me still. And all the time she smiled. Smiled but never spoke. And all the time I hated her more.

Matty had carried her down the stairs and out to the car to a mantra of 'What the fuck, Ebony? What the fuck?' He'd parked his ancient navy Metro – paintwork rusting to a bright-orange border around its edges as though a decaying sun was glinting off the paintwork – in the lane at the back of the house, in the hope that fewer people would see as he ran awkwardly across the garden with Ebony, her head lolling against his neck, her butchered, crudely bandaged right arm covered over with her jacket, her bare feet dangling over the crook of his elbow, their soles stained red.

I followed behind. Slowly and alone. Silent. Dragging my feet and my rucksack across the wet grass, leaving muddy tracks and bright-green stains on the patchwork. The day was grey and overcast to match my mood, an early-autumn chill in the damp air. I couldn't hurry, couldn't embrace the urgency of the situation with both arms. I could only touch it with the briefest of strokes and then my hand fell back to my side again, bored, uninterested and tired of it all.

She'd been doing this for too long now. This charade, this game. Hide and Seek. Cat and Mouse. Look for me. Find me. Catch me if you can. But she'd always have her fingers crossed so she could never be touched. She wanted someone there to see her, to be near her, close enough to catch a glimpse but to never truly know her. And I'd search for her again and again, as she played her game of Hide and Seek over and over. When she hid from me because I was too perfect, from Matty because he didn't love her enough, from herself because she was too fat, too tall, too plain, too clever, too stupid, too much, and from her parents because she was too scared. Of what I never knew, but I could see it in her eyes. That panic behind their chocolate depths. And each time I found her, each time I brought her back, she was a little more brittle, a little more frail, a little more withdrawn. Fresh silver scars revealed under her sleeves while she picked absent-mindedly at the scabs of the delicate slashes that were still to heal. The butterflies that were once in her jar were now the butterflies in her stomach, because she was too full of fear for anything else to intrude. All those times I thought I'd saved her and all those times she took her broken pieces and threw them skyward, watching them rain down around her in glittering fragments of disorder, reminding me that I hadn't.

Matty had bundled her into the back of the car, roughly and apologetically, with an urgency and a strange kind of gentle impatience in the way he tilted her head so it was resting against the window, and he'd buckled her in. He'd turned to me then, both hands beckoning me so fast they blurred in front of his face. 'Come on Belle!' he'd shouted, his voice cracking as though his throat hurt. 'Come on! Fuck! Fuck! Come on!' He knew this was his fault. His fault and mine.

I'd slumped sullenly into the passenger seat and looked out of my window for the entire journey to the hospital. Passing familiar sights that my mind didn't register because my heart was racing both from fear and from temper. Where there should've been a parade of shops lining the main road, all I could see was the skin and bones of my friend. Where the school should've stood, all the way back in the huge field beside the housing estate, all I could see was the look he'd given me, that look, the one that had started the end of everything. Where there should've been a play park full of toddlers on swings and teenagers swigging cheap cider from the necks of bottles, all I could feel was his kiss. When we passed the cemetery, ironically placed just before the turning to the hospital, all I could see was Ebony's back from the corner of my eye as she'd walked away.

In the waiting room, Matty and I sat in silence. I couldn't look at him and he couldn't look at me. We sat in mutual guilt and the reality of it weighed heavy on our hunched shoulders and shuffling feet, straddling the backs of our necks as we bent our heads and stared at the blue-grey linoleum floor, the colour of a storm, lost in our own thoughts.

I traced a figure eight with the tip of my boot until it left a black scuff mark on the tiles, and I wished I could call Dan. I couldn't though, no matter how much I'd wanted to, because he'd gone. She'd made sure of that. I blamed her entirely for it, even though part of his leaving was a family thing. A new job for his dad, somewhere in the Northeast. I didn't ever find out the details, because one minute he was here and it was all just an idea, and the next moment he had gone, like the worst kind of magic trick. And part of that was my fault. I'm always to blame.

When it was just an idea, when the thought of his leaving was merely a tiny cloud on the horizon with no power to block out the sun, we said it didn't have to mean the end. We could still be together, although it would mean not being together at the same time. But it wouldn't be long until school had finished and maybe I could study or get a job in Newcastle and we could be together properly again. And we'd buy a house and start a new band and we'd maybe get signed and we'd go on crazy tours and see the world, and when we came home again, we could stay curled-up on the sofa for days, watching shitty TV shows and making love.

Those were the conversations we had over and over, and those are the ones I look back on now with a smile, when we were planning out our lives because we didn't know any better. When we didn't know things could ever be anything other than good.

I hadn't meant to kiss him that day and ruin it all. It's just that things had gotten bad. The idea that had been soft and fluffy and far away for so long became more than an idea: it became a cold and hard reality that was a little over a month away. Dan would be leaving with his family, and my heart was broken for the very first time. It was that strange feeling where everything drains from you until you're empty inside, but at the same time, you're full of the worst kind of sadness. So full of it that you feel sick and you can't eat and everything inside is kicking and shoving and pushing and pulling, and in among all the confusion and mix up of emotions, all that's left to do is weep and weep and weep.

He told me on a Sunday night as we sat on the steps of the lighthouse on the harbour, wrapped around each other. Arms melting into arms, legs intertwined, pins and needles niggling at our toes and fingers, sea salt and gulls in the air. I figured that what I felt for Dan was as close to love as I'd ever been and when he told me he had to go I didn't move. I just held him a little bit tighter, pressed my face against his a little bit harder, breathed in his sweet scent a little bit deeper, closed my eyes and told myself to remember his warmth for always.

The day after, on a Monday afternoon when our music lesson had finished, me and Matty walked home. Dan hadn't come to school that day. Too many things to sort out, too many things to pack, he said. Ebony hadn't been in school all week. Not since she'd found out that Matty had come over to my house a few night's previously to help me figure out an English essay. The one about Romeo and Juliet; the one about a nurse and why she was there. I didn't really care why the nurse was there at all, I wanted to stay lost in the drama and the tragedy, so Matty had said he'd come over and we'd figure it out, because I couldn't just talk about love all the time. He was good at things like that. It all clicked with him and made sense, while I just picked through the romance and let that dance around my head for days.

'You were together?' Ebony had asked in school the morning after, irritation flashing in her eyes, their colour darkening from rich chocolate-brown to burnt black. 'Last night? You studied together, just the two of you?'

'Yeah,' Matty had shrugged it off. 'You know what Belle's like, all romance and no focus. I said I'd give her a hand.' He'd gone back to doodling biro shapes on the old wooden desktop in our form classroom, but I could see Ebony was hurt.

'He's good at that stuff Ebs,' I'd said quickly, trying to justify the study session. 'And since he's in my English class, we just figured it made sense to work on the essay together.'

Ebony had looked away then, chewing on a strand of hair as her eyes became glazed with angry, unshed tears.

'Come on Ebony, it's no big deal.' I'd added, when I saw our explanation still wasn't good enough.

Ebony hated my friendship with Matty. She hated that we sat together talking while she wasn't around, hated that we talked at all, hated herself for not being good enough when really, she was better than us at all this stuff. But even though we told her time and time again, our explanations fell on deaf ears and she carried on hating us anyway.

She'd whipped her head around and turned her attention to me. 'You could've asked me for help,' she'd snapped, her voice cracking under the weight of her hurt. 'And you,' her eyes blazed in Matty's direction. 'Why didn't you tell me? If it was all so innocent, why did you keep it a secret?'

Matty had sighed, all too used to this. 'I'm telling you now,' he'd said quietly, resignation sounding in his voice.

'There's no secret, Ebony!' I'd raised my voice in contrast, impatience getting the better of me. 'Matty's in my English class!' I repeated. 'We were just –'

'Save it,' she'd interrupted, and jutted her chin out defiantly. 'I know when I'm not wanted. Enjoy your study time.' She'd pushed her chair back violently and left the classroom. We hadn't seen her since.

Scenes like this played out regularly with Ebony, until we all eventually lost our patience and our willingness to care. When we didn't listen to her anymore, she bought herself biscuits and cakes and the usual piles of chocolate and cola, and hid herself away to make herself sick. I didn't attempt to stop her anymore, because I'd forgotten how to save her and I'd lost the energy to try.

She carried on getting thinner and paler and not really speaking to any of us anymore. Her grey moments would last longer and longer. Hours would spread into days and then into weeks. We tried to call, wrote her letters, Matty stood outside her house one night, shouting softly up at her window for hours, but she didn't respond. Her parents wouldn't tell us anything, so in the end, we gave up and I felt the beginning of the idea of hating her creep into my mind. I tried to catch it and make it explain, but it was too busy festering in a corner just out of reach, repeating too many things over and over, but mostly asking 'why does she always expect to be saved?' So, I stopped trying, and I carried on as if none of this was happening and I told myself she'd snap out of it and that as long as I didn't give in to her attention-seeking she would come back to us of her own accord.

Matty took it badly, the being shut out, the feeling helpless, the explaining to his friends why his girlfriend didn't want to see him anymore, when he had no idea why himself. The band stopped and Dan announced he was leaving. It was all too much. So that Monday afternoon, after Music, when there was just me and Matty left, we shared a cigarette as we walked slowly home, passing it between us, the heat getting closer and closer to our fingertips, narrowing our eyes against the smoke and the sun as we headed down the hill towards the housing estate where we both lived. As we got closer, we slowed our steps, not ready for home quite yet. Instead, we sat on the bench outside the little shop half a mile from where we belonged, and we watched the passing cars for a while, drawing long breaths on the cigarette.

'I still blame you for this.' I smiled, holding what was left of the cigarette up in front of him before throwing it to the pavement. 'You started me on this terrible habit.'

He smiled down at the ground, watching the smouldering end glowing neon in the shade of the bench and the smoke rising for a moment, before crushing it roughly beneath his trainer into the gravel.

'It's going to be okay, isn't it?' he asked into the silence, not looking up. His gentle Irish lilt soft in the air.

I sighed, still staring at the ground too. I knew what he meant; he didn't have to explain. 'I hope so Matty, I really do.'

Out of the corner of my eye, I saw him start to shake. His shoulders juddering up and down, stuttering like someone who didn't know where to start with a conversation, the shudders speaking a thousand words his lips couldn't. And I put my arm around his waist and squeezed him close, resting my head against his shoulder as my own tears came.

'He's going, Matty. Dan's going. Why does he have to leave?'

He shrugged, unable to speak. And then, a moment later, a whisper: 'She's going too, you know. Ebony's going too.'

A sob escaped me then and Matty wound his arm around my shoulders, pulling me towards him until my head was lost in the bitter scent of tobacco that laced his hair, breathing in the undertones of his musky aftershave on each shattered breath. I reached my hand up and held his face to mine, wiping away his tears with the pad of my thumb as we wept silently against one another.

And then it happened. In the blur of a moment. His lips were on mine, fierce and urgent. He gripped my face between his hands, holding me against him, and I kissed him back with equal ferocity. Bound together in this moment. Bound by the uncertainty, the experience, the horror and the loss of everything we'd known as it slowly fell apart around us.

As I leaned my head back, as Matty's lips found my neck, as his hand found my breast, not caring that we were right there on the street. The final building blocks of our kingdom crashed to the ground and turned to dust as I saw Ebony from the corner of my eye. Leaving the shop beside us, drowning beneath her jacket, lost, skeletal, within its folds, head down, clutching a carrier bag to her chest as she walked hunched and slow towards us. The telltale bright packaging of the sweets and crisps inside pressing up against the opaque plastic grinning wickedly at us.

I grabbed at Matty's hand and pushed at his forehead to get him away, desperately trying to separate us. But he resisted for a second too long, and in his hesitation, Ebony lifted her eyes and saw us. She paused, mid-step, left foot behind her up on tiptoes, weight awkwardly balanced on her skinny right leg as though playing a game of Musical Statues. She stared blankly, her unblinking eyes never wavering, the world slowing down around us and crackling like an old movie, seconds expanding and lengthening until time was all wrong and everything was taking too long.

Matty stood, tried to go to her, opened his mouth to speak her name, but her eyes changed in a split second and a fire lit behind them I'd never seen before. Its intensity found its way across the space between us and held Matty in its gaze, frozen and silenced by that look. A look of recognition, of confirmation, of sadness and of pure hatred. Matty's mouth hung open, gaping and fish-like and mute. I closed my eyes and wished it all away.

When I opened them, she was walking away, leaving me and Matty floundering, helpless and disbelieving. As we watched her back receding, Matty turned to face me, a look of resignation dragging his features down. 'Shit,' he whispered. 'Shit Belle, what have we done?'

She told Dan, I know she told Dan, because I never saw him or heard from him again. He didn't come back to school. On the three occasions I called at his house to try and explain, to say sorry, to make it right, he was 'not at home'. And so, he left. No long goodbyes, no 'see you soon', no final kiss. It was the wrong ending, the wrong time for the credits to roll, but I didn't get a say anymore.

I called her the day after Dan left, a week after the kiss. Told her I was going round, told her we needed to sort this out, sort her out, sort out the whole screwed-up mess. But she only made it worse. Brought more chaos as she spiralled out of control. Used herself to teach us a lesson, Matty and me. Let me find her and made sure all I would ever see for eternity when I closed my eyes was her spilling out all over the bathroom floor.

***

I think about this as I wash my hands in the toilet block at the hospital and wonder why I'm here at all anymore. I stare at my reflection in the mirror above the sink and she looks back at me, summer freckles showing through, blue-grey circles beneath my eyes smudging my sleepiness into puffed-up skin, her lips smirking at my stupidity.

Ebony had had surgery on her arm that day I found her. Her parents were called and they travelled the three hours from the Midlands where they were visiting family. Matty and I were sent home. Somebody forgot to thank us along the way but I didn't care anymore. I just wanted to be left out of it now. She had returned to school three weeks' later, frail and diluted, a shadow fading into the furniture. Within a week she caught a cold that turned into pneumonia. A week and a half after that she was hospitalised. That was a month ago.

She got better for a little while, antibiotics fighting the infection her body couldn't. But now, one chest infection too many and she hardly opens her eyes anymore. I can't remember the last time she spoke. Can't remember the last time we had a conversation or what it was about. Can't remember the last time my friend was my friend. And I miss her, oh God how I miss her. And I silently pray that it's not too late to fix this. To fix everything.

Matty is waiting for me outside her room. Neither of us can face seeing her alone anymore. The shock of her image before us never eases, as the contours of her skin dip brutally into the crevices between each bone and then stretch to almost tearing point across their surface, outlining the shape of her skeleton beneath its delicate shroud of pale skin.

The faint scars are there on her knuckles, where her teeth have rubbed again and again against the thin flesh each time she rammed her fingers down her throat, and my eyes are drawn there every time. Away from the horror of her face, towards the telltale signs that something was very wrong and we couldn't, didn't, stop it.

I let out a shaky sigh and Matty steps close behind me, arms circling my waist as we stare silently at our friend. Words escaping us. There was nothing more either of us could say, nothing that would explain things or help them make sense. Nothing we could say that would make anything better. We were beyond that now. Instead, he kisses the top of my head and I stretch my hands up behind me, linking my fingers together through his hair.

Matty and me, we were all that was left. I had to save us now.

Chapter Thirty-Two

Two days after my 18th birthday, I visit Ebony. My birthday had fallen on a Saturday this year, so I'd told her I'd call in to see her after the weekend to let her know all the gossip from the party. She didn't answer, didn't open her eyes, didn't flinch. Nothing. And no matter how many times the nurses assured me she could hear my voice, I'd never believed them. At least not until today.

There was a partial solar eclipse the day I became an adult. The moon obscured the sun. The darkness got in the way of the light and cast a shadow across the stars. But from where I was standing, I didn't see it. The inevitable clouds of an October birthday hung low in the sky, and I forgot about the light show. Instead, I opened present after present, card after card, let my mother fuss over me for the day and let myself believe that it was actually real. That she hadn't, just yesterday, shouted in my face for not coming home for tea, for spending the evening with Matty instead, her spittle landing on my eyelashes, hot bitter coffee on her breath making me want to flinch. But I didn't flinch, not this time. These days I stand my ground, because I'm older and I'm taller and she knows I won't stay quiet anymore. If she knew what I'd actually done yesterday afternoon was let Matty fuck me in the woods, that may have tested her resolve and been a whole other story. But she doesn't.

Matty isn't at the hospital today. He had to stay behind after school to work on an art project he's struggling to finish. Shades of Green, he's called it. A nod to being Irish, he said. A nod to being lazy and just painting pictures with one colour, I disagreed. And we'd laughed together in a way we seemed only able to do when we were alone. Away from the stares and the shaking heads and the whispered judgements of our peers. When there was no pressure on us to look perpetually guilty or eternally sad.

I arrive at the hospital and I bound up the echoing staircase, taking the steps two at a time, to the first floor where Ebony's room is located and in my mind, I tell myself that today is the day Ebony will open her eyes. Today she'll look at me and she'll smile and she might even say something in her quiet, whispery way. Maybe just a hello, a hi, a hey. Or maybe she'll tell me she missed me while she was sleeping and that she's been saving her energy for this, for my special birthday. Just like the years when we turned 16, she'll be awake and she'll have the swirling, animated cocoa depths back in her eyes and her hair will shine and sway and she'll giggle at my stories as she finds her voice again and we'll hold hands as I help her to sit up in bed and she'll never sleep for as long ever again.

I'm smiling my widest as I round the corner on the ward and put my hand on the door handle to her room. But as I'm about to enter, I notice there's nothing there. There's an absence in the room. A big empty space full of nothing. I stop, hand poised ready to push the door open, and look through the square glass window at a neatly made empty bed. There is no stale water jug, no wilting flowers, no tissues or magazines or pens or half-filled-in crosswords on the bedside cabinet. There is no clipboard on the end of the bed with endless charts and unreadable handwritten notes. There's no trace of anything.

I feel a flutter in my chest as my heart leaps its way into my throat and starts closing off my airways, filling the space at the back of my mouth until I feel I might choke. The edges of everything fizzle with blackness and flashes of rainbow colours. I'm hot. Forehead becoming clammy in seconds, palms copycatting soon after, and as dizziness takes hold I push through the door and almost fall into the empty room. It smells wrong: clean and fresh and new. Where's the illness hanging in the air? Where's the sour heat? Where is Ebony? Where is she? Where has she gone? Where have they taken her? My questions trip over themselves and fall in a muddled heap on my lips, writhing around and making no sense.

I stumble around the vacant space, telling myself that maybe I have the wrong room, maybe I'm mistaken. But no, this is it. This is where she was. I recognise the view from the window over the car park, the chip on one corner of the bedside cabinet, the awful fake chair in its precise position beside the bed, angled at 45 degrees and floating somewhere between the left-hand wall and the mattress. And there's the painting on the wall, still askew, of the beach and the waves and the tiny lost person in the corner on the sand. I reach out to it with trembling hands and straighten it. And then, feeling like I've disturbed some vital part of what made me sure this was Ebony's room, I pull the right side down again, making tiny adjustments here and there until it is just right and I've restored the perfect slant of it once more.

It's so quiet without the whirrs and the beeps, the ticking of the clock even louder now the machines are gone. My ears begin to ring in the deathly silence, the weight of it pressing against my eardrums and hissing a stuttered beat in time with my quickening pulse, pressure building inside my head. I spin around and reach for the door, bolting from the room and strutting up the corridor to the nurse's station, anger and violence on the tip of my tongue. They can't have taken her somewhere else without telling me. She's meant to be here, right where I left her. They can't take her away. They just can't. Who said that they could? Who said that? But when I reach the desk there's nobody there. I slam my hands on the pale laminate, making my palms sting, and look all around me for a nurse or a doctor or somebody who knows what the fuck is going on. A nurse I've seen before rounds the corner and begins walking towards me, checking the time, almost walking past me without looking up.

'Hey!' I say, falling into step beside her, not letting her get away. 'Hey, you!'

'Can I h…' she begins, turning towards me. But before she can finish, I grab her hand and half-run half-walk her to the room where Ebony's supposed to be, pointing ahead of me the whole time, indicating the way, trying to make her understand, feeling helpless and pissed off.

'She's gone missing. Ebony's gone missing. My friend. You remember her, don't you? My best friend in the whole world was right here and now she's not. She's not here and she should be here. Right here.' I slap the mattress with my tender palms. 'Right here. Right here. Right. Here.' I punctuate each full stop with a punch of the mattress. 'Where have you taken her? You can't just take her away, you can't!'

I turn to face the nurse and she steps towards me, reaching out her hands, holding me gently by the shoulders at arms' length. Looking at me with an expression which I wish was unreadable, but which I understand straight away. The soft wide eyes, pale-blue like I always wanted, holding mine in a knowing gaze, the sad smile of fake sympathy, head to one side like she gives a shit. I know what's coming but I don't want to hear it.

I press my hands to my ears and squeeze my eyes shut. All I can hear is the rush of my blood throbbing through my veins, the hiss of air trapped in my head, the muffled, distant voice of the nurse as she tries to cut through my astringent screams with gentle words that bounce off me like pathetic cotton-wool excuses. And then I collapse against her, clinging on around her waist, face buried in the clinical smell of her uniform. Sobs mixed with antiseptic, tears like diluted disinfectant.

'When?' I whisper through a new silence when the shock sets in. 'When?'

'Last night,' she replies, stroking my hair, tucking it behind my ear and pressing her hand against the side of my head. 'Amy died last night.'

I crumple to the floor hugging my knees tightly against my chest, leaning heavily against the black tights of the nurse's legs beside me. Shaking uncontrollably in numb silence.

'Belle,' the nurse says gently, prising me away from her. 'She left something for you. She gave it to us a long time ago, when she first came here. For safekeeping, she said. Come on.'

I follow her numbly to the nurses' station. I stand limply as she reaches behind the desk and hands me an envelope. It's white and covered in a printed pattern of overlapping pink butterflies. It looks like lace. Delicate, fragile, beautiful lace. My name is on the front, scratched out by the nib of a fountain pen, the edges feathered and smudged, droplets of black ink, as small as pinpricks sprayed accidentally along the curve of the final 'e'.

My hands shake as I open it. A paper cut rips open the tip of my index finger and turns the torn edge of the paper a vivid red, which seeps into the wings of the largest butterfly. I reach inside and my fingers close around something delicate and cold. A tiny sliver of rope. I loop it over my little finger and pull it out of the envelope. The necklace. The sparkling silver 16th birthday present I'd given her. And there's a letter. Written in her hurried hand, barely legible but so very obviously her. Written before she faded away, when she knew she was going to leave but hadn't yet decided when.

I unfold it, I see the first line, and I hate her.

You should've told her you loved her, my mind taunts. You should've made her stay.

You

Chapter Thirty-Three

It feels like forever since I was last here. The past few weeks have seemed longer than they should have, and at the same time not long enough. I stand across the road from your house and look at it from beneath the woollen hat I wear pulled low on my head, my eyelashes sticking to the soft strands of cream wool. The yellow glow radiating from the living-room window and falling in stripes across the pavement, mimicking the pattern of the drawn blind behind the pane, looks so inviting. My eyes drift to the bedroom window above, all in darkness now, and I wrap my arms around myself as a shiver runs the length of me while I remember how you'd loved me in there. Loved me in a way only you could: beautifully and cruelly. As I step off the pavement and make my way across the street, dread circles me like a vulture and clutches at my stomach, making me feel simultaneously sick and empty. Tonight is where this all ends.

It was yesterday when everything was decided. When I missed you so much it hurt, physically hurt. When my muscles ached so much with the needing of you and when the constant thinking of you scorched a pain in my head so bright I knew I had to see you again. Yesterday when I reached out to you, when I pushed my way through the thick air of our short history, when I ignored the suffocating weight of it and stretched my fingertips through the sticky filth and grime of us to try and touch you again. Yesterday, when I decided to give you another chance, to give us another chance. Yesterday when I found the courage to speak to you. Yesterday when you decided it was over.

Today you told me to collect my things. Today you said you'd have them ready. Today you don't need me anymore. Today I'm worthless and ugly and a waste of space. Today I can remove myself from your life like the cheating little whore that I am. Today I can call round at 8pm, no sooner and no later. Today you will get rid of me once and for all.

Tonight, as I check my watch and count down the minutes, I cross the road under the orange glow of the streetlights and the drizzle misting the air. Tonight, I am covered up, hat pulled down to my eyes, scarf pulled up to my nose, thick coat wrapped tight around me, shielding me from the approaching winter and my closeness to you. Tonight, I am protected. Tonight, I don't try to stop the fear, because the fear is what keeps my wanting at bay. Tonight, as I cross that road, as I raise one hand to knock on your door, I thrust the other into the pocket of my coat and let my fingers close around the cool handle of the kitchen knife I've hidden in there. Tonight, I am prepared.

I knock. I wait. I shudder violently. I shrink into the folds of my winter coat and I wait some more. Nothing. I knock and I wait again, fingers curled around the knife's curved handle in my pocket, fingernails digging into my palm as I tighten my grip. The minutes tick by. You'll be angry with me for being late. So I irrationally reach for the door handle and push it down, heart lurching brutally as it yields to my touch and the door clicks open.

I'm in the living-room now, door wide open behind me. I see two plastic bags packed with my things; clothes, pyjamas, bottles of shampoo, shower gel, toothbrush. I see an empty whisky bottle lying on the carpet beside the coffee table. I see a glass beside it, half full of amber liquid, and I can smell it in the air: first its warming mellow earthiness and then its sharp smokiness like a bitter aftertaste harsh on my breath and quickly coating the back of my throat. I see my name written on an envelope, propped against an empty bottle of beer. 'Belle' scrawled hurriedly in black biro across the thick paper and underlined twice.

I see all this, but you're not here. The space around me is made up of silence and the faint ticking from the watch I bought for your birthday, which lays discarded face down on the coffee table, tiny tick-tocks like faint marching footsteps.

I stand still. I don't call your name. I stay silent in the silence, the weight of it burning holes in the quiet of the room. My silence screaming louder than the quiet can, longer than the quiet can, more angrily than the quiet can. My silence stretching on for endless miles of darkened roadway, reaching out in front of me and disappearing into the depths of the black, screeching and weeping with frustration, while the quiet of the room stares back at me, mouth closed, expressionless and mute. Shrugging its shoulders and saying this is the way it has to be. Everybody leaves, or wants to eventually, and you're just another one. This is how it ends.

I take my knife from my pocket and I throw it hard into the quiet so that it cuts through it and lands with a resonating metallic clatter against the fire on the opposite wall. That knife was meant for softer things. Softer places like the birthday cake it divided up just five months' ago at James's birthday, the flesh of your thigh, or the toughened muscle of your bicep where I'd pictured it slicing cleanly through the sketch of the wide-eyed, raven-haired girl, the soft spaces between your rib cage, where I can almost feel it sinking spongily into your black beating centre. But instead, it lies glinting by the fire, intention gone to waste because you're not here.

Now that the quiet is broken, now that it is standing to attention, taking note, now that it really knows I've been here, I turn carefully around within its walls and take my things. I take what's mine; the carrier bag stuffed with my clothes, pyjamas, bottles of shampoo, shower gel, and toothbrush. I take the envelope with my name on it and stuff it into my pocket where the knife used to be. I take the knife and let it hang loosely between my fingertips. Then I replace your key, leaving it on the coffee table beside the discarded watch and I turn and leave. I don't look back. I don't want to see any more. Instead, I run and run and run.

'You should've told him you loved him,' my mind screeches, scolding me. 'You should've made him stay.'

Part Two: Before You

Chapter Thirty-four

I thought at the end the world would slow down. That it would come to a halt. Freezing in its tracks, stopping mid-stride. With everyone and everything ceasing to exist. But it doesn't. There's a whirlwind. A whirlwind made up of everything you've ever done, the amazing things that life can bring and all the mistakes you've ever made, overlapping into a crescendo of interwoven sounds. White noise and screams.

The pages flip by continuously. Never-ending. Not stopping, not once. And I cling on to the good days, trying to hold the memories in my non-existent grasp. Not wanting to let them go. Not anymore. But the relentless story continues. Plummeting towards an end I no longer want to come. Rushing on towards the darkness.

I clasp my head between my hands, covering my ears with cold, unfeeling palms, squeezing harder and harder to stop the noise. But the noise is inside my head. The whirlwind fills the space between my bones, picking up memories and tearing them apart. I can't stop it

I'm exhausted. All around is black. Fuzzy and endless. I can no longer open my eyes, the energy has long since left me. I don't know if I'm lying down or standing up. I don't know what's coming next but I'm not afraid of the unknown anymore. I'm afraid of these visions. I'm afraid of my life being played out at a million miles an hour. I'm afraid of the jumble of thoughts and having to relive each and every moment before I'm allowed to go.

And it goes on and on and on.

Matthew

Chapter Thirty-Five

Matthew's drunk again. I know because I can hear him curse as he stumbles through the front door. I can hear him bounce off the hallway walls and fall over the coffee table in the living-room below me. I can hear him miss his footing on the stairs, swear and laugh at the same time. I can hear him in the bathroom, vomiting into the toilet. I know that in the morning I will clean it up before the kids see it and I will pretend nothing happened last night. And as I make their breakfast and we curl up together on the sofa to eat it watching Saturday-morning cartoons, I'll tell them Daddy's not feeling very well again. And when Ruby asks, not for the first time, what all the shouting was about last night, I'll tell her, just like I've done all the times before, that it was only the TV and I'll say that I'm sorry I had it on too loud. When

James asks when Daddy will be out of bed so they can kick the football in the park, I'll promise him soon baby, soon. And our weekend routine will play out like this, like it always does, because me and Matthew are getting it all wrong.

Matty became Matthew when he got a job that came with a suit and a desk and required adulthood to become something more tangible rather than just this thing we played at. He'd done well. His love of drawing turned into a love of drawing buildings, which turned into six years of study, which resulted in him becoming an architect.

As for me, I stopped being Belle almost six years ago when Ruby was born. When James came along almost three years' later, the transition from my own person into a mother went unnoticed, mostly because there was no transition to make. The only difference now was that I had made two human beings rather than just one. Well done me. So, Belle became Mummy and Matty became Matthew, who had then, only quite recently, become Matty again with surprising regularity after work most Fridays. He often didn't come home from the office those nights, at least not until the early hours of Saturday morning. Or sometimes he did, and then we'd argue, and he'd leave again. Those were the nights when Mummy had the TV on too loud and the days that followed were when Daddy was poorly.

I don't even know how we got here. I ask myself this same question over and over. On our wedding day, I knew he was the one. Now I know he isn't. I'm the seven-year cliché, only this isn't an itch I'm feeling. It's a burning, prickling heatwave – an allergic reaction. An urge that began nibbling away at me some time ago and has now become more frantic in its insistence. More urgent. Shaking me by the shoulders almost daily and reminding me of the pleasure of feeling again, of being someone again, of experiencing the need in another person once more.

Because Matthew doesn't need me now. He did, for a long time he did, and we held on to each other so tightly because we didn't know what else to do. Ebony was gone, and we'd killed her. We'd made her go, made her so sad that she couldn't stay. What we did, that whole falling-in-love thing, had hurt someone more than we could ever have imagined. So, to make it right we clung to each other. To justify what we'd done we had to make us work. To prove to ourselves that the tragedy of Ebony wasn't in vain, we got married, so that we would become forever.

Summer 2004, not long after he'd got his first real job at a local firm and while Ruby was curled-up tight in my stomach, an undulating lumpy bump beneath the virginal white silk of my wedding gown. The bump, my little Ruby, had started as a little winter surprise, along with the ensuing proposal two months' later as we sat one early-February afternoon drinking hot chocolate from takeaway cups we'd bought at the kiosk in the park. Sitting on a bench beside the mirror-like lake, the beginnings of Ruby already changing me – waist thickening, stomach fluttering, moods swinging – hands wrapped around the warm paper cups, piles of stale bread between us to throw for the ducks, Matty had pulled me close and whispered that he loved me. Then he had pulled me closer and whispered that he'd like to marry me. And I'd said yes without hesitation.

On our wedding night, as we curled-up together in the huge bed of the bridal suite in a remote lakeside hotel in the country, slick with the sweat of a newlywed's first night together, he told me we'd buy our own place soon. Once he was settled into his new job, we'd buy a home for the three of us, where I would have more space to paint, maybe even a whole room of my own to turn into a studio for the pictures I loved to bring to life with oil paints on canvas.

We'd have a place to call our own, he said, instead of the poky little flat we lived in now above the chip shop at a traffic junction, where the bedroom flickered from red to orange to green all day and all night in time with the traffic flow, and where the constant scent of chip fat wafted up through the floorboards and thickened the air. But our own place would be perfect, he said. And smiling at him, nuzzling my head into the comforting and familiar crook of his neck, I believed him.

Just like I would believe Ben years' later.

As the past grew ever more distant and memories of promises made faded, and as Matthew grew older, more engrossed in his work, the history of us mattered less and less to him. His mind matured, became more rational, confident that we were not responsible for Ebony. For the mind she lost. Not really. He didn't need to hold onto me so tightly anymore, and bit by bit his fingers slipped from mine. Slowly, our thoughts, so intertwined over the years, began to unravel. Two separate strands of thread weaving two disparate patterns and moving in increasingly different directions, the space between us widening a little more each day.

He didn't need me to tell him I loved him, and he didn't ever tell me the same. He didn't need to hug me as I stood washing the dinner dishes, his arms wrapped around my waist, lips brushing gently against my ear as he talked in low tones about his day. He didn't need the reassurance that I'd always be there, didn't need to reach out for my hand in the middle of the night, didn't need to pull me close and hold on tight. He didn't need to remember why we did this, why we stayed together, why we got married, why we needed to be forever. I needed to remember, but he chose to forget.

I hear him flush the toilet again and I picture the broken tiles behind the sink, the circles of damp on the ceiling, spreading out like ink blotches on the magnolia walls, the hot bath tap that wobbles and shakes, and the window where the wind whistles through the broken seal and dances across the blind, rattling the slats like prisoners' chains. The faults with our rented house. The house we borrow every month and don't belong to. Because we never did buy our own place. That home of our own never materialised from the promises.

'3am' blinks red on the clock beside the bed. I turn over, reach beneath my pillow to lace the silver strands of

Ebony's necklace between my fingers, and I go back to sleep.

Chapter Thirty-Six

December 2010

I'm drunk again. I struggle to find the front-door lock with the tip of the key, giggling as I miss the target again and again, even though it wouldn't normally be funny being stuck outside in the cold. The taxi pulls away just as I get my aim right, turn the key and fall in through the front door. I giggle again, kicking my heels off against the shoe rack and padding my way softly through the hall and into the living-room, hand trailing across the wall for balance.

I flop onto the sofa, my gaze falling on the clock in the alcove beside the fire. I think it says 3.30am. I close one eye, frown, try to focus and give up. What does it matter about the time anyway? I'm home, aren't I? That's the main thing. I lie still for a moment, legs thrown over the arm of the sofa, skirt riding obscenely high, arm draped across my eyes, trying to stop the house from spinning.

Blurry visions stutter and spin across my eyelids in rapid zoetrope motion; my sister, Melissa, the drinks, the music, the dancing, the guy. I halt the spinning right there and freeze-frame the image. The guy. My eyes fly open and I stare at the swirling Artex ceiling. The guy. I'd let him dance with me, let him put his arms around my waist, let him stand too close, let him buy me a drink, let him make me laugh, let him hug me goodbye. Some stranger in a bar with sparkling blue eyes and a shy smile. And worse still, I'd liked it. All of it.

My stomach lurches and I clamp my hands over my mouth. Acid rises up my throat and my stomach heaves violently as more bitter liquid forces its way up from my belly. I jump up from the sofa and with faltering footsteps run up the stairs, dizziness whizzing around my head like a daredevil on a motorbike. I push through the bathroom door with my shoulder and fall on my knees in front of the toilet. Slamming the lid back, I throw up noisily while the rest of the house sleeps. The pungent scent of recycled alcohol makes me baulk and heave some more until my stomach is empty and I'm leaning breathless and pathetic against the porcelain like some teenage drunk.

My eyes are watering from the effort, nose a dripping, snivelling mess. I reach out a shaky hand to take some toilet tissue from the roll in the holder above my head and that's when I hear him. As I tear roughly at the tissue, the gentle, sleepy sound of a hushed 'Mummy' reaches me through the drunken fog. As I scrunch the tissue into a ball, I hear it again, 'Mummy?' This time it's a question, as though he's not quite sure if it is me at all. I spin round, in the middle of wiping the mucous drips from my nose and the stray droplets of vomit from my chin, and I see James, my beautiful little boy, standing there in the doorway in his new dinosaur pyjamas which almost drown him, favourite toy monkey tucked under one arm, tiny fist of his free hand rubbing his tired eyes, dark-blonde hair sticking up at sleepy angles.

'Are you alright Mummy?' he asks, squinting into the too-bright light of the bathroom through half-open eyes. 'Are you poorly?' And then, when I stare back at him mutely, tissue held across my nose and mouth: 'I'll go get Daddy.'

I scramble across the floor towards him, tugging at the hem of my skirt which is riding up again, aware that the toilet is still full of my vomit and the sour stench is filling the air more and more with each passing minute, and I hold his little shoulders gently in my trembling hands. 'It's okay, baby,' I tell him. 'Mummy's okay. Just a poorly tummy, that's all.' James looks at me in his half-asleep state and nods slowly, eyes closing all the more as the movement lulls him closer to sleep. I press my hand tenderly against the side of his face and hold his tiny waist with the other.

'Come on,' I say, rising slowly to my feet, trying to ignore the faint stirrings of nausea beginning again in the pit of my stomach and the hammering in my head. 'Let's get you back to bed.' I steer him gently towards his little bedroom and tuck his curled-up little body snugly under his dinosaur duvet. He is asleep again before I've left the room.

I tiptoe back to the bathroom, flushing the toilet and heaving once more as I inhale the bitterness hanging in the air. But my stomach is empty and my muscles are aching from their violent contractions. I feel wretched already, and I'm dreading the morning. I stumble into bed, fully clothed and fighting off nausea. And as I roll onto my side, my back to Matthew as is normal these days, and fall into a deep drunken slumber, I don't see the tears that run down his face, the anxious twitch in his jaw or the sadness that keeps him awake.

Chapter Thirty-Seven

The light is too bright so I pull the living-room curtains closed as I pass through to the kitchen. It's almost lunchtime by the time I drag myself out of bed and traipse downstairs in crumpled pyjamas, last night's make-up sliding off my face as though I melted through the night. The house is silent and empty. Inside my head though, the screams and shouts and insults of last night still weigh heavy in the room, sitting atop the sofa, looking across at me and shaking their head in disgust. I roll my eyes at them as I reach into the fridge and grab a can of ice-cold cola, cracking it open and gulping it down, feeling the freezing fizz burn my sandpaper throat. It's not all my fault, I say to them in my head. I'm not the only one to blame here.

I pause for a moment in the stillness of the house and wonder where everyone is. It always feels wrong, the silence. It tells me something's missing, taunts me something's gone, bellows into my ear in a great big yell of nothingness that I'm alone. And I hate being alone.

I shuffle back through into the living-room and slump onto the sofa, scattering the visions of last night and letting them turn to vapour in the air. I pull the TV remote from where it's wedged between the chunky red cushions and flick aimlessly through the channels before settling on a cookery show where some whiny American presenter is making carrot cake. I hate carrot cake.

I take another swig of cola, the fizz tickling rather than burning my throat now, and I let myself sink further into the cushions. There are remnants of pizza on little plates in front of the TV, DVDs of cartoons and children's films strewn across the floor, toys abandoned mid-play, three pairs of shoes missing from the rack in the hall and three coats missing from the hooks above it. There's a note on the coffee table, held down with a half-empty cup of cold tea, words scratched out in a biro that's running low on ink, neat handwriting made into a scrawling mess by the crappy pen. There's Ruby's little pot of glittery lip-gloss laying on its side, lid discarded somewhere unknown, its strawberry perfume wafting faintly under my nose, and there's the musky scent of another man lingering in my hair and on my skin.

The note is from Matthew saying he's taken the kids out for the day and will be back by teatime. He says he's sorry but he had to go. He doesn't say where and I've got no idea when they left. When I try calling his mobile, he doesn't answer. Maybe he's driving or maybe there's no signal wherever they are or maybe they're walking and he left his 'phone in the car. Or maybe he just doesn't want to talk to me. Maybe, maybe, I don't know.

The hangover sadness hits me. That desperate feeling of the morning after the night before, when you remember that your real life is still real, and the alcohol traces in your bloodstream kick-start the sadness you were trying to escape. Only they don't just give it a little nudge, they turn it on full blast, until your entire body is wracked with misery. And it chuckles to itself as it lingers, making your head hurt, your eyes burn, your body shake and your stomach churn. And then it really belly laughs as it makes you replay everything you want to forget.

The shouting was at its worst last night. It was too loud, too violent, too out-of-character, even for us. It was more than just drama this time: it was something very real. It was because he wanted to keep me at home but I wanted to go out. It was because he doesn't need me, and I need him too much. It was because he wants to move on from the past, and I don't. It was because he doesn't care enough about me, and I won't stop clinging on to everything. It was because he doesn't wear his wedding ring anymore, and I insist on sleeping with a dead girl's necklace under my pillow. It was because he's unreliable and I'm pathetic, he's working all the time and I'm lazy. He's a drunk and I'm an embarrassment, he's never around for us anymore and I'm a nagging bitch that won't leave him alone. It was because we wanted to hurt each other. It was because I slapped him across the face and he shoved me hard into the wall.

I had left anyway. Ignoring Matthew, kissing the children goodbye as they slept soundly in their beds, reapplying my lipstick in the hall mirror as I passed, straightening the new dress I'd bought especially for the night – midnight-blue silk, fitted and strapless, hem a few inches above the knee – and heading towards the beeping of the taxi's horn on the other side of the door, heading towards the other man I'm about to meet. The man who puts the butterflies in my stomach and who makes me forget who I am.

Ebony's butterflies. The ones I can't keep. He puts them there, in my stomach so that I won't forget her.

'You look beautiful,' Matthew said as I reached the front door. But I didn't hear him. Or maybe I did, but I didn't want to. Something had snapped and broken in us that night, and I already knew I didn't want to fix it. He doesn't need me, I thought, but someone else does.

I try Matthew's mobile once more. No answer. I throw my phone down in frustration, watching as it bounces off the mound of unnecessary cushions and lands on the carpet at my feet. Why doesn't he need me? I ask myself into the dull light of the curtained room. Birds twitter and fuss indifferently outside as the shadows of leaves and branches on the other side of the window pane shift and sway in hypnotic motion, their outlines cast fluidly, like watercolours, across the fabric of the curtains.

Somewhere in the distance, somebody is hammering at something. Mundane life carrying on as normal. A rhythmical thud punctuated with birdsong. I wish for the nonchalance of those birds and their carefree ability to fly away to somewhere warmer, somewhere better, somewhere fresh and new. I wish for the comfort of the ordinary, the everyday, the thudding of the hammer and the feeling that everything is as it should be. Why is nothing as it should be? I ask silently into the broken hush of the room. Why is it all falling apart? And the monotonous thud of the hammer and the twittering of the birds and all the sounds of the ordinary ignore me and get on with their day.

Resigned to the fact I'm going to be alone today, I reach under the sofa and feel around for the laptop. I find something sticky – a lost toffee of James's, and then something soft – Ruby's wide silk headband, then my fingers find the smooth edge of what I'm seeking and I pull it sluggishly onto my knees.

Lifting the screen up, I turn on the laptop and as it whirrs into life, I wonder what exactly it is that I think I'm doing. But all it takes is a login, a social-media hello, the beautiful face of Ben peering out at me from the screen and a thousand of Ebony's butterflies fluttering in my stomach for me to realise I know exactly what I'm doing.

Ben

Chapter Thirty-Eight

I pull my old battered Fiat up in front of the gate and, leaving the engine running, I get out of the car and go to open it. The gate is huge and heavy, and I struggle with the latch. It takes me all my strength to open it wide enough, but eventually, there's just enough space for me to get the car through. I look ahead of me at the white farm building in the distance and I see his black pickup truck parked in front of one of the barns. Despite the anxiety coursing through my veins, my heart does a somersault. He's here waiting for me, just like he said he would be.

Before I lose my nerve, I climb back into the car. I look briefly at the black hold-all thrown onto the passenger seat next to me, but I refuse to think about what I've done. Inside, the bag is stuffed full of as many clothes as I could fit into it in the ten minutes it took me to leave the house. At the time it seemed like a lot, but now I realise I have hardly anything, except a couple of pairs of jeans, a few tops, some underwear and the birthday cake I thought to buy for him at the last minute. Today is his birthday. Today is the day I left home.

I don't bother to put my seatbelt on before I put the car into gear, release the handbrake and drive slowly down the lane towards the farm. As the farmhouse gets closer and closer my excitement builds. As I pull up next to his pickup, I almost can't contain myself. I open the car door and step out into the late-evening sunshine, my shadow cast long on the ground, and I breathe in the fresh country air. A small rain shower has just passed over and has left behind the unmistakable fresh smell of spring, and the scent of new beginnings.

I walk around the car to the passenger side and retrieve my meagre belongings. When I turn back around, he is there, standing in the doorway of the house, squinting into the sun with a huge smile on his handsome face. Ben. I drop my bag to the ground and run to him, flinging my arms around him in pure delight as he lifts me easily from the ground and spins me around, laughing. I bury my face into his warm neck and breathe him in, and I try not to think about what I've just left behind. Try not to think about my two tiny children fast asleep in their beds, and how distraught they'll be when they wake in the morning and find their mummy gone.

***

It is 5am and the sun burns brightly through the bedroom window. I can see the blue of the sky from beneath the duvet in this unfamiliar bed and it contrasts sharply with the bright-green treetops blowing in the breeze in front of the windowpanes. A vivid yellow band of sunlight is cast across the far wall of the bedroom, its edges illuminating the beautiful old fireplace that dominates the bedroom. There are no curtains: there is no need. The farmhouse is in the middle of nowhere.

I stretch out full length and feel life coming back into my sleepy muscles. I lie still for a moment feeling out of place, unaccustomed to these surroundings. The farmhouse is huge and the layout is higgledy-piggledy, which gives the place its charm, but the rooms are largely bare, save for a few essential pieces of furniture, and it is a stark reminder that this is home to neither of us. Just a friend's place – up for sale for years and empty for just as long – where we can pretend everything is going to be okay. It'll do for now, Ben said. Maybe we could buy it one day, I thought.

Our clothes lie in untidy piles in one of the two spare bedrooms. We'll get new wardrobes eventually, he says, and maybe a new sofa too. The sofas that were left behind in the farmhouse by a long-ago occupant are old and lumpy, and the new throws that were bought to cover the fading floral fabric do little to disguise their ugliness. We'll make it feel like home, he says. Our home. And the thought of it makes my heart turn somersaults.

Rolling onto my side, I reach out and feel Ben's warmth left behind on the bed, the sheets crumpled and furrowed from where he lay beside me just a few moments ago. I hear him in the bathroom splashing water onto his face, getting ready for another day in this brand-new life. The bedding is new, bought especially for us, he said, as he'd laid me down among the sheets the night before. And I vaguely remember they had felt rough and starched beneath my skin, perfect creases still crisscrossed all over their pure-white surface.

A small smile plays across my lips as memories of the night before tiptoe cautiously into my head. I allow myself a brief moment of happiness before the enormity of what we have done surges into my mind like a tsunami, drowning out all other thoughts. There's no turning back now. My mind wanders to home and to my children, and another tidal wave of anxiety rolls over me. I panic. I can't do this to them. None of this is their fault.

I lie for a moment longer, considering my next move and wonder how things ever got this far. I need to get up, get dressed and get back to Ruby and James before they realise I've gone. If I get up now, I can be home before they wake. I can give them breakfast and dress them for school like normal, as though nothing has changed. As though their whole world isn't about to be turned upside down. I can pretend for one more day. For them. I can give them a few more hours in their perfect little world before I shatter it to smithereens.

***

June 2011

I sit in what used to be my armchair at my parents' house. The house I grew up in. Everything about it is intensely familiar: the smell of lavender air freshener lacing the atmosphere, the sliver of Imperial Leather soap in the bathroom that sticks to the sink and has to be picked off using fingernails, the burgundy leather wingback chair my granda sat in every Sunday night as his giggling grandchildren climbed over him, the space on the carpet in front of the fire where Mother decided among a flurry of paper snowflakes that she hated me.

Get out of my sight.

The atmosphere is charged and dangerous and I can almost feel the electricity blistering between us as my parents sit stony-faced opposite me. Some things never change in the house I grew up in.

On the outside, I am composed, almost too composed. On the inside, I am both numb and overwhelmingly petrified. I can't think from one moment to the next. I can't predict what's going to happen. I can only react from minute to minute, bracing myself against the onslaught and spitting out words as they form in my mouth.

It's a few days now since I left home for good. Since I walked away from my marriage and left my children sobbing, clinging onto my legs as I tried to leave, looking up at me with raw, red eyes and little tear-stained faces, begging me in their tiny desperate voices not to go, ripping my heart out until there was nothing left in me, and with every step I took away from them I knew I was ripping their hearts out too. But I had no choice. I was the one who had to go. I was the one who had done all this.

I had arrived at the place I used to call home this morning, making it there early enough so the children were still in bed and they'd never know I'd been gone for the night. My reckless driving had paid off again. I quietly unlocked the front door and stepped carefully inside. Already, I felt like a stranger. Already, I felt like I didn't belong there anymore.

As I'd entered the house, Matthew was making his way down the stairs. As he reached the last step, he'd looked over at me, an expression of pure desolation and despair etched on his face. He'd looked tired and drained. He didn't speak as he walked past me into the kitchen and I didn't know what to say. What could I say? We both knew that this charade of ours was over.

I'd followed him into the kitchen and stood for a moment watching him get the breakfast things ready, carrying on as if everything was normal. Except the tension in the air reminded both of us that everything was far from normal and nothing would ever be the same again.

When Matthew finally spoke, his voice was devoid of emotion. He was almost robot-like in his delivery, impassive and detached, each word like a sharp punch in my stomach. We would tell the children this morning that Mummy and Daddy didn't love each other anymore, he would keep them off school today to make sure they were going to be okay, and after breakfast I would pack the rest of my things and go. He wanted this over quickly. He wanted me out of his sight. I couldn't come here anymore.

I nodded silently, because I couldn't think of anything else to do, but inside I was on fire and screaming. I couldn't leave my children, I just couldn't. How could he expect me to walk away from them? I needed to take care of them. Me. Just me. I wouldn't be made to leave them.

I could feel desperation simmering inside me, growing more intense by the second. In my panic, I screamed at him to leave instead, screamed that he should be the one to go and leave me here with the children. I'd grabbed him by the shoulders and shook him, pounded my fists against his chest and begged him not to take my children away from me. My desperation turned into agonising sobs until I could no longer speak. Until I was retching and my throat was burning.

Yet he just stared at me, a look of pity and disbelief in his eyes. I would be the one to leave, he told me, because all of this was my fault. And inside I fell to pieces, because I knew he was right and I knew this was the end.

***

'I don't know what else I can tell you.' My voice is almost a whisper, struggling to overcome the anxious lump in my throat. 'I've explained it all to you over and over.' I nervously adjust my position in the armchair, grounding both feet on the pale grey carpet, and hug myself protectively as I look across my parent's living-room.

My mother glares at me from the corner of the ancient leather sofa opposite, arms folded tightly across her chest.

'How about *why*?' she spat. 'Why you cheated on your husband. Why you left your kids. Why you think you can come here and expect us to drop everything and help you.'

My throat is dry and the words become a scratchy collection of sounds in my mouth. 'I've told you why, Mother,' I begin again. 'Things hadn't been working out with Matthew for a while, we'd grown apart, we...'

'So you decided to bed the first man who showed you some attention?' she scoffs defiantly, determined to keep the upper hand.

'No! It wasn't like that at all,' I say, my voice finding some power. 'I didn't mean for things to happen this way.'

I glance over at my dad who is sitting silently beside my mother on the sofa. He says nothing. 'I couldn't stop it. We couldn't stop it. It just happened'

'*We?*' Mother raises her voice an octave, incredulous. 'You mean you and that homewrecker of a man you've shacked up with?' She laughs cruelly and begins to clap her hands slowly. 'Ruining the lives of two perfect families. Well done, you deserve each other.'

'We weren't a perfect family, Mother!' Anger begins to bubble beneath my chest. 'Matthew took me for granted, I didn't love him anymore. Why can't you see that?'

'Matthew is a wonderful man,' she insists, 'who treated you like a queen. But you, you're just a selfish, ungrateful piece of work.' She pauses, taking a breath before continuing. 'And what about the children? You didn't once stop to think about them, did you? How could you just abandon them like that? What kind of mother are you?'

She knows what she has done, my mother, and she sits back to watch the fireworks.

'A better one than you!' I yell, standing up, rage seething through me. 'I would never abandon my children, never.' I run my hands through my hair and pace the floor in front of the fireplace. 'Don't you dare accuse me of being an unfit mother. Don't you dare compare me to you.' I hurl the words at her.

'That's enough Isobel,' Dad finally interjects, his tone level and calm, 'Go home,' he speaks again, more firmly this time. 'Go home and make it right Isobel. Make this right with your husband.'

I shrink back down into the armchair, close my eyes and inhale deeply. 'I don't want to 'make it right' Dad,' I sigh, tired and frustrated. 'Why can't you see that being with Ben is what I want now? This is the way things are.'

My mother refuses to listen. 'This is not what the people in this family do.' She has unfolded her arms now and is sitting bolt upright on the sofa. You,' she sneers, boring holes into me with the fierceness of her gaze 'have brought shame to this family. You are not the daughter we raised.' She slings the words at me, each one dripping with venom and bitter resentment.

Nothing I say or do is right. None of the answers I give to their verbal assault on me are the words they want to hear. And now we're going round in circles, the questions and comments fired at me getting angrier and angrier, the lump in my throat getting harder to ignore.

'I need your help,' I plead. 'I need your help now more than ever.' I look from one to the other across the sudden immeasurable void of the living-room 'Please. I'm your daughter.'

But I realise in that instance, as I feel my mother's words slice through me, that they hate me.

'We'd be better off without you.'

And suddenly I'm seven again. And I'm counting coins into Mother's hand and I don't understand and I'm getting it all wrong and I'm in the way and I should just go somewhere far, far away and the back of my legs sting with the sharp slap of Mother's palm as she teaches me a lesson. Yet, I don't cry. I refuse to break down in front of them.

I can see the look of loathing and disgust on my mother's face as she tells me I can go now, and I know I'll never forget it as long as I live. She points at the door, the stab of her finger unchanged since my childhood, the meaning still the same. I'm not welcome here. She turns her back on me, wipes her hands of me and it kills me, but I nod and stand up and walk towards the door. Doing as I'm told. Resisting the urge to scream and run. I catch my dad's eye as I pass and he doesn't look at me with the same revulsion as the others. He looks so very sad, and my heart breaks some more.

Suddenly, I see red. The composure I've been trying so hard to keep is lost. All control is gone and I scream at them.

'You've got no idea what it's like to have a family in ruins!' I scream so loudly that everybody in the neighbouring houses can hear, but I don't care. I finally lose it completely. 'You can't possibly know how excruciating it feels, how fucking unbearable!' My throat is raw, burning with the bitterness of angry words. As I reach the front door, I throw a punch at it in pure, white-hot anger. My fist lands heavily against the glass panel and I feel a sharp pain shoot through the knuckles of my right-hand, but I ignore it. 'I hate you, I fucking hate you!' I drag a ragged breath in over the toxic word and vow that I'm never coming back.

And I'm back in my favourite dark-green velvet dress with the gold belt and patent-leather shoes, rubbing the dirty stains from the gloss with a spittle-laden fingertip, but succeeding only in smearing the shiny surface with more and more dirt as my body hurts from the beating.

The rage surging through my veins is hot and leaves me shaking violently. I flee from the house and into the car, not bothering to fasten my seatbelt before I drive off, tyres screeching on the driveway. I can't focus, can't see the road in front of me. They hate me. I've destroyed everything. It's all my fault and they're right, I deserve everything I get. I don't get far before I have to pull over. I throw open the car door and instantly throw up on the road, stomach lurching brutally as nausea courses through me again and again, until I am empty and there is nothing left.

***

I drive down the lane towards the farm, my car kicking up stones and dust beneath the wheels. The acrid aftertaste of earlier is still on my tongue and the sickness lies heavy in my stomach. As I park the car in between his pickup and the barn, I sit for a moment and look at the building I will now call home. But for how long? Ben and I can't stay here forever. We've both ended up here not out of choice but out of necessity. Neither of us has anywhere else to go. Found out. Forbidden to return home, both thrown together in this place.

I can't think ahead. I can't think past today. I get out of the car and tread slowly over the gravel. All around the sky is bright and the birds are singing, I notice spring's lambs in the fields but my heart is heavy and I take no pleasure from the scene. I am wretched and I am a mess. I reach the door to the farmhouse and walk inside, shoulders slumped, feet dragging across the floor.

I pass the living-room and notice Ben isn't in there, so I carry on down the hall into the kitchen and find him standing beside the dining table. He's facing away from me looking out of the window and as I approach him, I see his shoulders are shaking.

When I'm within his reach, I stretch out my arm and rest a hand gently on his back. When he turns around, I see he is crying, eyes rimmed red, cheeks wet with tears. My heart jumps into my throat, tears of my own instantly spilling from my eyes, and we fall into each other's arms, bodies trembling together racked with grief, each of us holding the other one up, afraid our limbs can no longer take the strain. And we sob against each other's necks, clinging tightly onto one another, tears merging, overwhelmed by the enormity of what we've done. Because this is the reality we've created. This is what we wanted. And to keep one another we have lost everything else. I've lost everything all over again.

***

Ben hasn't come home. It's 11pm and he's still not here. He said he'd be back hours ago. He'd left for work late this morning because I wouldn't let him go, asking for just one more minute of being held close to his warm skin beneath the covers before I lost him for an entire day. I always felt lonely without him here, left in this strange house by myself, unable to see my children for most of the day, trying to be a part of this unfamiliar lifestyle, trying to fit in, trying to make the best of this difficult and surreal situation.

We'd lain together for a blissful and precious few minutes longer, my head resting on his chest, feeling its gentle rise and fall against my cheek, listening to the steady and comforting beat of his heart. Ben's arm draped over my shoulder, stroking the bare skin of my waist tenderly, his fingers tracing lazy circles and giving me goosebumps. I'd closed my eyes and knew that I was right where I belonged. This is why we did what we did, for this moment, for this split second in our lives, for this feeling. And I'd held onto him even tighter.

Ben had gently kissed the top of my head then and stirred slightly. He had to get up and I begrudgingly let him, unwinding ourselves from each other's hold and forcing ourselves apart. I'd watched from the comfort of the bed as he dressed, pulling a mock sad face from beneath the covers and giggling as he'd thrown his T-shirt at me in response. Despite everything, I couldn't help smiling. We were finally together and it made all the hardship and turmoil worthwhile. It made the storm more bearable, easier to weather. Because with him I felt happy. With him, I felt amazing. With him, Ebony didn't matter and Matthew was forgotten. He was my Dan. The one I should've had.

I'd reluctantly climbed out of bed and followed him sleepily downstairs and into the kitchen. Sitting at the dining table and looking out over the fields, I'd marvelled at how bright and strikingly green they were. Today everything was dazzling and intense, like a fog had lifted from my eyes, and for the first time, I'd allowed myself to feel optimistic for the future. Our future. I'd made the right decision and we would make this work. Of course we would.

The room smelled of toast and strong coffee and sunshine. Ben had brought breakfast to the table, and as we ate we chatted about his day. I knew he'd be gone until early evening and the prospect of having to find things to do to fill the lonely hours wasn't a good one. I'd gazed at him sadly, wanting to keep him there with me just for one whole day, and he'd reached out across the table, holding my face in his hand. I'd leaned into his touch as he apologised for working such long hours and promised to be home as soon as he could. He didn't want to stay away from me for too long.

We finished breakfast and I'd followed him gloomily to the front door, still protesting that I didn't want him to go, reaching out and grabbing his hand, pulling him towards me. Couldn't he stay for just a little while longer? He'd squeezed my hand softly and turned to kiss me goodbye, but as I raised my face to his I was swiftly wrestled to the floor and playfully pinned against the ground. I'd squealed in unexpected delight, laughing despite the shock, and made no attempt to wriggle free. And he'd loomed over me for a moment, gazing at me with a look of wonder in his sparkling eyes, as though he too couldn't believe we were here together at last. We'd looked at each other like that in silence for what felt like an eternity, smiles playing mischievously across our mouths. Then he'd leaned down towards me, kissed me long and hard, and whispered 'I love you' against my lips. And then he was gone.

***

Now, I stand at the living-room window and stare down the lane towards the gate at the far end, as if somehow my yearning will bring him back. The light is fading and the fields all around are tinged with the blue light of approaching darkness, and I know that something's not right. I pick up my mobile and try to phone him again, but there's no answer and it goes straight to voicemail. I leave another message. I'm worried. Call me back.

I set down my phone on the window ledge and continue to watch the lane from behind the glass. I touch the silver necklace that rests against my collarbone, running my fingers over the glinting 'E' and letting it jangle gently against the static butterfly. In the emptiness of the room, where the silence is deafening and I can hear my heart pounding in my ears, I am left only with my own maddening thoughts.

Life has been simultaneously amazing and heartbreakingly difficult since I left my old world and came here. Every day I am haunted by that moment three weeks' ago when I looked into my children's smiling faces and told them Mummy and Daddy didn't love each other anymore, and that Mummy wouldn't be living with them any longer. I knew then my heart would never recover from what I'd done to them. Knowing that I'd taken everything that was precious to them and had ripped it away. Knowing that I'd snatched their little world from right underneath them, tearing away their security blanket and changing everything forever.

Darkness falls heavily around the farmhouse and I step away from the window, giving up on my futile searching of the countryside, and I switch on the TV, desperately trying to take my mind off the vast, heavy absence in this rambling house. I stare at the screen but I don't hear the words or see the images. I can't concentrate on anything but the sickening worry in my gut. I look at my watch. It's almost midnight. I try calling again, but again it rings and rings and goes to voicemail. And I don't know what to do. I pace the living-room floor, staring out of the window searching out headlights on the distant road. But it is dark and there is no sign of anybody, anywhere.

I begin to feel scared, really scared, as I realise I am alone here in this strange house in the middle of nowhere and it is pitch black outside. The darkness smothering and close, dense and unyielding. I hurriedly step back from the window, suddenly, irrationally, afraid there may be somebody out there watching me in this isolated place, my imagination playing senseless but terrifying tricks on me. I grab my phone and bolt for the stairs, bounding up two at a time, and run into the bedroom, hiding beneath the covers like a frightened child, mind and heart racing, sweat beading on my forehead. I am lost and I have no idea what is going on. I can think of nothing else to do but grip the duvet tight and close my eyes against the rising fear.

It is 6am when I wake, when the sunlight streaming in through the bedroom window pierces my eyelids and jolts me awake. I immediately remember last night and look beside me. There's a cold empty space. Instantly, I sit up, scrabbling through the bedsheets to find my phone to see if there's any news. And there is. There's a text message from Ben sent only an hour ago. With trembling fingers, I push the screen and scan the words with anguish and disbelief as the message appears in front of me. He's gone home. Back to his old life. He can't do this anymore, he doesn't love me enough and he's not coming back. He tells me I have to leave.

I read the words only once. It's enough, but I still can't process them. Can't fully take in what it all means. I am frozen in this nightmare, the room spinning around me, my surroundings a blur, only his words in harsh focus, so glaring it hurts my eyes. He's gone. Gone. But he loves me. He told me only yesterday morning he loves me. He promised me the world and I believed him. I gave up everything to be with him. How can he just leave me like I don't matter?

I call his mobile again and again and again, frantically, obsessively, until he answers. But when the ringing stops, it isn't Ben's voice that cuts through the dial tone. It's a woman. It's a woman's voice telling me she's his wife. And I don't believe her. Won't believe her. Because Ben doesn't have a wife, he has me. But her words leave bruises against my ear.

The monotonous drone of the dial tone cuts off the heat of the words, like a machine flatlining. Marking the end. Signalling a loss. The sound of the death of so many things. A headache thrums against my eardrums. A low-frequency vibration that rattles inside my skull. Through my daze, I instinctively stumble into the spare room, grab my hold-all and begin searching the piles of clothes on the floor. I know what I have to do.

I am mechanical and robotic, separating my belongings from his, forcing them into my bag, fleeting memories of doing the same a couple of months' ago in a different life daring me to crack. I hurl his things at the wall. I don't want to touch them. Don't want to touch him. But the scent of him finds its way inside me and the memories follow. And I fall apart, collapsing to the floor among the pile of our clothes, shaking and sobbing. And as I lie there, reality kicks me hard in the stomach.

***

Minutes later – hours later, I can't tell – I drag my bag roughly down the stairs, wincing as it knocks against my legs, knowing there'll be bruises later. My steps falter and I lose my footing, falling down the last few steps and adding to the bruising.

I can think of nothing else to do but run away. My chest hurts as though my heart has shattered and all of me has poured out, leaving a hollow space and a trail of useless emotions behind me. I slam the front door and throw the farmhouse key down onto the ground, not seeing or caring where it lands. I heave the bag onto the passenger seat and climb in, hands shaking as I try and fail to put the key into the ignition. I slam my hand hard against the steering wheel, fresh tears of frustration stinging my eyes, and I try again.

And as the key finally turns, as the engine splutters into life and I begin to drive away, as I turn into the gravel lane, I see her standing beside the open gate a little way down the road. Ebony. Only taller, a little less skeletal. Dark hair sliced at the jawline.

Cut my hair. Cut it all off.

What's she doing here? I thought she'd gone. I squint my eyes to peer more closely. Her eyes are too small, mouth too wide, chin not pointed enough, forehead too high. Older. I slowly start to drive closer to her. She shakes her head. She raises a hand. As I pull up alongside her, she punches the window that frames my face as I pass by. The wedding ring glints under the beautiful early summer sky, golden bolts of lightning blinding me momentarily. She screams. I flinch. She punches the side of the car. Again and again. I put my foot to the floor, tyres spinning on the gravel, car lurching erratically away from her.

My knuckles almost puncture my skin as I grip the steering wheel hard. I keep my foot to the floor, engine screaming, drowning out the screaming wife as I drive away.

As I run away. But as I do, I realise I've got nowhere to run to. I've got nowhere to go anymore.

***

Dexter helps me drag everything I have left to the top of the stairs and into the attic room of his townhouse. My forever friend, my rescuer, my knight in shining armour, he's put clean sheets on the spare bed and has made a space for my things in the wardrobe. I smile at him through my daze and hug him, clinging onto him for a little too long but needing so desperately to feel the warmth of another human being. To know that somebody is there and that maybe, in some small way, I still matter to someone. To anyone.

I spent the last couple of nights on Melissa's sofa. Disorientated. Emotionless and devastated at the same time. Feeling empty. Broken. Pieces of me left behind in so many other lives that there's nothing left of me in the present anymore. I am a ghost, a glimpse in the corner of somebody's eye that disappears when they turn to look for me. I couldn't stay long, she said. The house was too small. I'd have to leave soon.

So now I am here, in another town, another house, part of another person's life again, not my own. My own life seems to have been put on hold, like somebody pressed the pause button and walked away, forgetting to push play again to let the movie continue to its happy ending. Because that's what happens in movies isn't it? Happy endings. Eventually, but always, happy endings. This is just the chaos in the middle. The part where everything is all wrong before it is all right again. Please tell me it's just the chaos in the middle. Please tell me everything is going to be alright.

But the world carries on around me as though nothing has happened, and I am stuck in a black hole with only memories and questions to penetrate the darkness. I see his face every time I close my eyes. I see his message in my mind's eye and it won't go away. And each time the agonising memory surfaces brutally behind my eyes it hurts me over and over again, until the pain is a physical ache, not just an emotional torment.

I finish unpacking my life into this tiny rooftop space and go downstairs to join Dexter in the living-room. I've known Dexter for a long time, more than ten years. I sat next to him on the first day of the first job I could secure in the first months after leaving school behind. Brilliant grades wasted on a data-input job, they said. A way to leave the turmoil of education behind, I disagreed. Education and childhood. A job meant an attempt at adulthood. A way to become something Ebony never did. A way to leave all that behind, to be numb and unthinking and to breathe. For a little while at least.

Dexter was blonde and spiky-haired and beautiful and gay. Funny and quiet and serious and loud and brutally honest and gentle and all the opposites you can think of all rolled into one. He smiled as I sat next to him on that first day in my first real job, told me 'welcome to the shithole,' and my nerves scurried away behind the laughter he brought out of me. We barely left each other's sides from that moment. He replaced Ebony and he adored Matty in ways that made Matty uncomfortable, but which left me crying with laughter. My beautiful Dexter.

He still is all those things, but now, more than any of that, he's the one person in all of this that I know will never hurt me. Maybe the only person left I can trust. Now I sit quietly on one of the large sofas by the fireplace in the room where we'd sung karaoke in the past, danced around drunkenly to shitty pop songs, argued over Madonna and

Kylie and nursed hangovers to chick flicks. But now I've retreated inside myself. I'm mute. I can't find the words.

The cat jumps onto my knee, purring and transferring the warmth of her body onto my lap. I stroke her absentmindedly, staring blankly into space, focusing on the middle distance and seeing nothing at all. After a moment, Dexter rises from his seat on the opposite sofa and heads into the kitchen. When he returns, he's holding a can of cider. He sits beside me and tugs at the ring-pull, the liquid popping and fizzing as he passes it gently to me, face so full of concern that I feel instantly guilty for dragging him into all this; but at the same time, I'm so grateful he is here at all.

I drink it down quickly, too quickly. It is sweet and strong and familiar, and I want the alcohol to numb the pain so I drink another can and another. And then I'm crying and clinging onto my friend and sobbing against his shoulder. I can barely breathe, I can no longer speak, I am forcing air into my lungs through jagged inward breaths, my chest heaving erratically, lungs on fire. And I can't stop. Because he's gone. Everything has gone. I gave up everything but in the end, I wasn't good enough for him. And now I have nothing left and I am so, so lost.

Much later, when there's nothing left to say, when no amount of words can untangle the knots of hurt or make sense of the mess I'm in, I slowly climb the stairs to the bedroom. I undress and clamber between the sheets, resting my head on the pillow and taking in yet another new view. And I know I can't stay here forever, yet I don't know what to do. I have no home, no job, no children, nobody to love me anymore. I have no future. I've got what I deserve. I turn onto my side and cry myself to sleep. And I hope I don't wake-up in the morning.

***

August 2011

The days roll by in a blur. Every chance I get I spend it with Ruby and James, but in between these times I mostly drink too much and sit alone while Dexter is at work, staring into space, seeing nothing and feeling nothing. I try to fight my way through the fog but I'm not strong enough and I lose myself in the obscurity, vanishing into a multitude of anguished recollections and shattered dreams. My friends try but they can't reach me. Their kind words bounce off my surface, unable to penetrate an unfamiliar darkness that has become my shield. Because no matter what they say, I am totally alone in all this and I feel every part of that solitude.

In my mind, I go over it all again and again. I gave up everything I had for him and now I am left with nothing. With anger and frustration, I realise what I'd had was never really mine. That while I sit alone in this attic room, my heartbreaking more with every memory of him that haunts me, his heart has found its way back home. Back to where he came from. To a place far away from me. To a life without me. As though he'd never loved me. As though I'd never existed. And it hurts like hell.

And when Dexter comes home from work, we go to the pub, and once again I let the alcohol take the pain away.

*****

My life continues this way for too long. Too many days wasted and nights lost. Then almost as I have given up hope, when I believe my life will forever be the crumpled mess I find myself in now, everything changes, and I begin to step back from the brink. No longer teetering on the edge, but turning away from obscurity to face a future again. An unknown future, but a future all the same.

I find a house to live in. It is tiny, but the rent is cheap and it's available in the next few weeks. Most importantly, it's close to my children, and the thought of being able to be a proper mum again is truly amazing. It's enough to bring the tiniest trace of control back to my out-of-control life. It's enough to save me. And as I move in, I focus on making this my home, my safe place, my sanctuary. A place for me and my little family, and a place for me to heal.

And then one night, when I brave the real world again. When Melissa coaxes me out of my shell, out of the darkness. When I dip my toe into the water of proper living again, I see you. Standing at the bar in a little club in a tiny Northern town. And my life changes again.

Part Three: After You

Belle

Chapter Thirty-Nine

May 2013

Settling myself carefully into one of the unsteady chairs at the old, dark wood dining table in the kitchen of my new house, I open the writing pad I found yesterday, stashed away in the final unpacked box. The one that's been sitting in the corner of my bedroom for weeks because it had nothing particularly important inside.

It's one of those boxes that's full of the little pieces of your life that don't really belong anywhere in particular. The things that can't really be placed in the kitchen or the living-room, the bathroom or the bedroom. It's the keyring with your initial on it that you'll never use but keep anyway, just in case. The spare pens, most of which don't work. The bits of sticky tack and drawing pins with last year's tinsel clinging to them. It's the letters you've been meaning to file away for months, the fridge magnets with well-meaning but useless sentiments and the odd coins. All thrown into the box labelled 'miscellaneous' that you created in the final rush to clear the house you're leaving and take with you to a new place. The place you hope will one day feel like home. It's the box everyone leaves until last. A box of meaningless items with no real place to go. It crosses my mind that maybe I belong in a box like that.

Angry with myself, I shake my head violently in an attempt to stave off the negative thoughts. I stare again at the blank pages in front of me and I feel determined. Tentatively, I lift my right-hand from my lap, surprised at how heavy it feels, and pick up the only pen I can find in that last box. One of my daughter's bright-pink biros, tiny enough to fit perfectly into her nine-year-old hand but lost in my clumsy adult fingers. I don't know why I've decided now is the time. It seems like the right moment to be doing this, so with the pen poised over the paper, I take a deep breath and wait. And there's nothing. I gaze at the page until it blurs in front of my eyes and I have to force myself to focus again. Gripping the pen tighter in my hand until my fingertips turn white, I rest the tip at the beginning of the first line, waiting for something to come to me. Still, my mind is blank.

Frustrated, I throw the pen down, watching as it leaves a crude, inky black graze across the page where my words should be, and I pick up the glass tumbler on the table in front of me instead. With a shaking hand, I bring it to my lips and drain the liquid quickly into my mouth. The vodka slides down my throat with clear, sharp heat. I pour myself another glass, spilling precious tiny puddles of the crystal-clear spirit onto the table as my hand trembles out of control. Fuck. I drain the glass again and wince this time at the sting of the alcohol as I swallow it down. I place the glass and run my finger through the vodka puddle beside it, licking the traces of it hungrily from my hand as it trickles down my wrist.

I look back at the blank paper. This isn't how it's meant to be. I was expecting a never-ending torrent of emotions to come pouring out. Words tripping over themselves trying to be heard, spilling out of my head like a waterfall. But I am frozen. I'm stuck with nothing to say and I don't understand. I want so badly to be able to explain, but I just don't know where to start or how to rearrange the muddle of feelings inside me. I don't know how to see through the symphony of angry colours in my head and make sense of everything in words. I want to start at the beginning, but I don't even know where that is anymore. I am lost before I've even begun.

You see, somebody told me to write everything down. To stop all these hurtful thoughts and feelings chasing their tails, following constantly shifting paths inside my head and colliding with each other painfully time after time, I should put pen to paper and let them escape onto the page. Fill your paper with the breathings of your heart. Isn't that what Wordsworth said? And that's what I'm desperately trying to do. I need to write this letter. I want to tell them everything they already know over and over again, but until they really hear it this time. I want to be given a chance to show them all the things they've already seen, but this time until they really believe them. Because in the end, they wouldn't listen anymore. In the end, they closed their eyes to me. In the end, they loved me a little bit less than before. All of them. Ebony, Ben and You. If I could only tell you the things I never said, maybe one of you would stay.

When this memory takes over everything else, when it punches me in the stomach and takes my breath away, I surrender again. I sit at the dining table in my new kitchen, flooded with bright, beautiful sunlight and with the sound of birdsong drifting in through the open window, and I begin to cry. Silent tears tracing desolate paths down my cheeks, the page shifting as my tears sting my eyes and blur my vision. Everything just seems so unfair.

I put my head in my hands and sob, the tears hot and urgent now, seeping between my fingers and falling in small pools onto the tabletop, seeping slowly into the vodka slick to form a sweet and sour cocktail nobody would ever drink. My whole body shudders, trembling with a curdling mixture of raw emotions that I've been hiding for too long, and my head aches with exhaustion. Yet the tears won't stop. It is they that fall in a torrent, unable to free themselves quickly enough from my eyes, instead of the words I'm searching for but can't find. I can never find them. Everything I want to say is stuck inside. And now, in this new house where I had hoped to make a fresh start, I feel the most alone I have ever felt in the whole of my 34 years.

This is what I've become. Somebody haunted by memories of the best of times, of the worst of times and of things I can't change. Somebody who lies awake at night, thinking over and over the same things, wondering what I could've done differently, how I could've made them love me more, how I could've made them stay. How I could've left them more gently.

In the end, these thoughts manifest themselves into a monster I can no longer keep at bay. The monster I've created then exhausted myself trying to will away to the back of my mind. The monster that's left the shadows behind my eyes and robbed the sparkle from my gaze, letting my thoughts become the tightening in my throat, the constant threat of tears in my eyes, the knot in my stomach and the weight on my shoulders. I have a storm raging in my head and yet I can't let it out.

Suddenly, I'm angry. Suddenly, I hate them for what I've become, but I hate you the most. You left me here in your dark place and this isn't where I belong. I belong far, far away, in a place where the sun shines. A place where I have boundless energy. A place where I smile and mean it. Not this place where everything feels futile and pointless. In this place, the warmth and light of my space has been tainted by the murky depths of yours. I feel empty inside. I feel useless. I feel like a failure.

Heat rages inside me, and in my anger, I swipe furiously at the writing pad, knocking it to the floor, vodka bottle lurching and swaying as my fingertips catch its neck, before it settles itself back on its base with a glassy shudder. The writing pad cartwheels along the brand-new carpet, pristine sheets of paper crumpling, until it rests against the doorframe a few feet away. I take a deep breath to calm myself and exhale slowly as I slump forwards, my head buried in the crooks of my arms, forehead resting on the cool wood of the tabletop, eyes closed trying to wish it all away. My mind is a blur of thoughts that I just can't switch off. My head is thudding with a dull ache that refuses to subside and I suddenly feel so, so tired. An exhaustion I can't describe works its way slowly through my limbs making them feel heavy, and I feel like I wouldn't be able to move even if I wanted to.

I lie like this for a while, feeling the rays of the sun through the kitchen window warming the back of my head and shoulders. Its heat is comforting, like a thick blanket on a cold night or a reassuring hug from a friend. I allow myself to relax ever so slightly into the warmth, moving my head slowly from side to side in an attempt to lose the tension in my neck. It's no good though. Nothing seems to help anymore. I sigh and lift my head slowly, turning it to gaze towards the door where my ruined writing pad lies, and I can't help thinking how I'd love to be back in your arms right now. Back in anyone's arms. To melt into an embrace that would make all this sadness go away.

I had thought you'd be the rock in my storm, but instead, as my waves crashed into you, I smashed into a million pieces against your impenetrable exterior. And now here I am sorting through the pieces of me that remain, trying to put my life back together.

I sit up to stretch out my aching limbs and that's when I see them. The envelopes, almost hidden underneath the table. They must have been wedged between the pages of the writing pad, somewhere unnoticed towards the back to keep them safe. I push back the heavy dining chair and stand slowly, my legs feeling unsure of themselves. Wiping away my tears roughly with the back of my hand, I walk over to where the envelopes lie face down, bound together by a thick elastic band. I crouch and look at them for a moment, too nervous to pick them up, but then I reach out my hand and slowly turn the package over. On the front of the first envelope in large bubble writing is the word 'Photos' surrounded by a huge heart. I'd forgotten all about this one.

When I was packing up my old life, I'd been sure to get rid of any reminders of you. Birthday cards, Valentine's cards, Christmas cards, all the gift tags from all the presents you'd ever given me, all the treasured memories I'd kept from days out, I'd put into large black bin bags and discarded. Photos I'd downloaded of us on my laptop, your telephone number, your Facebook profile, all deleted. All erased from my life to help try and convince myself you'd never existed and that we couldn't hurt each other anymore. But it had never really worked, no matter how much I pretended I was letting go.

I lift the flap of the first envelope with shaking hands, feeling short of breath and with a sudden light-headedness that betrays the anxiety I'm trying to keep under control. I reach inside and pull out the first photo just a little way, holding it carefully between my thumb and forefinger. I see your face then and collapse to the floor, my legs no longer willing to support me. A million memories come flooding back, like a tidal wave washing over me, drenching me in vivid recollections and crushing me under its weight. And it's in this moment that the words come. It is here, when I am crumpled and torn like the pages of the writing pad, that everything bubbles up inside, scrambling to find a way out.

I put one hand to my mouth as if to stop the words escaping and cling to the envelope with the other, holding it tight against my chest, and I let the tears fall from my swollen eyes again, catching the sobs in my hand. Suddenly, I gather up the writing pad and the pen, and on shaking legs I half-run from the kitchen, through the living-room and up the stairs into the sanctuary of my bedroom, throwing myself down onto the fresh white bed linen and burying my face in the pillow.

I don't know how much time passes before the sobs wracking my body subside and I have no more tears left. When I slowly uncurl myself from the tight ball I've made around the envelope of our memories, my muscles ache and my body is stiff with tension. On the pillow are black stains from the remnants of my mascara, salty tears having washed it away, and I remember leaving the same dark stains on your shoulder every time we said goodbye.

Now I feel ready. I sit up slowly on the bed feeling dizzy from emotional exertion and lean back against the solid oak frame, legs crossed on the soft mattress in front of me. Then, placing the writing pad on my lap, I turn the pages over, finding a fresh sheet on which to start, and I once again grip the pen tightly. This time there's no waiting. But there are so many things I want to say to you yet I can't find the right words, so I end up simply writing the most important thing. The thing that says it all. I loved you. I love you. And I hate you with all my heart.

***

I am surrounded by picture-perfect memories laid out on the bed in front of me. Happy faces encircling me like a gang of bullies playing a sick joke. Perfect snapshots of perfect moments in time. The photographs I'd found the other day, well hidden in the back of the writing pad and stashed away in that forgotten box, were going to be my love letter to you in our better times. They were going to be the Christmas gift to show you just how much you were wanted and just how much you meant to me. I'd planned an album showing all our best times, choosing photographs of us at our happiest and hoping to make you see that the world could be a wonderful place. I had wanted to give you something you could turn to in your dark times to remind you you meant the world to somebody. To remind you that somebody loved you.

As I scan slowly over the glossy memories, they come to rest on my favourite photograph. In it, we're looking at each other and laughing, really laughing, and happiness radiates from it like no other photograph taken of us before or since. I hold it close and focus only on you. I take in the laughter lines around your eyes and the huge grin on your face, and I smile a sad smile. This is the man I loved. The man who smiled with me, laughed with me, was silly with me. I loved everything about this person, from his beautiful face to his infectious laugh, the way I'd catch him looking at me like I truly meant something to him and the way I felt protected whenever he put his arms around me and held me tight against his towering frame. I run my fingers gently over the image of you, wishing that you could feel me. Why couldn't we always be like this? Why were so many of our happy times tainted by your fist?

A lump rises in my throat, but I swallow hard and take a breath to steady myself. I drag my eyes away from your smile until other photographs appear in my line of vision. Blinking away the tears, I pick up another image that means so much. Another bittersweet memory of us. It is Boxing Night almost three years' ago, a few weeks after we'd met, when everything was still so fresh and new, and when we still felt a fizzing, nervous excitement whenever we saw each other. That night I was feeling the effects of a little too much cider and had flung my arms around you tightly in tipsy affection. The moment was captured perfectly and our happiness forever frozen in time. In this moment, I hadn't yet learned to hold back the way I would in a few short months. In this photograph we look close, our faces pressed against each other, the happiness obvious in our wide smiles and sparkling eyes. I didn't yet know that this would become an illusion.

I lean my head back against the oak headboard and stare up at the ceiling. This picture stirs up more memories from the depths. An image comes to the surface of the murky waters in my head, of things that happened so long ago now it feels like a dream, the edges of the memory blurred and out of focus from the effects of time. That night in October when we met, when the photo was taken, I was so full of hope for the future. I had never expected to be bowled over by somebody so soon after my life had been turned upside down. I was just finding my feet again. Starting over, or trying to. I'd been hurt and I suppose I was still hurting when we stumbled across each other. But my smile, the mask of confidence I wore when we met on that Hallowe'en night almost three years' ago, did its best to hide that. It covered up the scars I didn't yet realise I had and hid an emptiness that too many heartaches had left behind.

But you knew nothing of this and I knew nothing of you. You saw me only as I was in that moment. No expectations. No preconceptions tainted by my past. You saw the smile you once told me you loved so much, my constant excited chattering, a happiness that radiated from me the moment we met. And in that split second, at the bar in a tiny nightclub in a small Northern town where I first said hello, you got the best of me.

Before I hated you, I loved you. I truly did.

***

I open my eyes and it's dark. Instantly, I scramble into a sitting position, not sure for a moment where I am. My eyes are sore and the skin on my cheeks feels tight and tear-stained. An orange glow from the streetlight is coming through the bedroom window, and I can see its soft light reflected on the glossy surface of the photographs. I look down at myself and notice I am still fully clothed. Then I remember.

I had lain down among our memories, so tired from thinking about you and us. About the ones who came before and the ones who left so cruelly. I was weary from all the what-ifs and of wondering where you are now. Wondering if you're thinking of me the way I think of you. If I cross their minds the way they scorch mine. Such clichés, but I can't seem to stop myself and it's torture. And as I'd lain there drained, all my energy sapped, I must've given in, finally falling into a dreamless sleep.

I realise I still have a photograph in my hand. The one of us laughing. My fingers are cold from gripping it, not wanting to let go despite being asleep, so I place the picture carefully back on the bed among the others and rub the back of my hand roughly, clenching and unclenching my fingers to bring some life back into them. I feel a cool breeze on my face and realise the window is still open. It had been a hot mid-summer's day before, but now that night was here, the heat of the day had been replaced by a cool blackness.

Rising from the bed, I walk to the window intending to close it along with the curtains, to shut out the night and then return to the sanctuary of sleep. But that's when I notice the stars. Usually, the crisp, clear nights of winter are the best time to see the stars but right now, despite the night following the heady heat of a summer's day, there are multitudes on show, taking over the sky like little pinpricks of hope. Lights in the vast dark. The sky looks beautiful and I stand for a long moment, taking it all in.

'Without darkness, we'd never see the stars.' That's what you used to say. And I wish this had been true. I wish that you saw what was in front of you all along. But sometimes you couldn't see through your darkness and, even when you were surrounded by stars, their light didn't seem to reach you. I wanted to tell you the stars are always there. Even on a beautiful sunny day like the one we'd just had, they are up there in the blue sky just waiting for their chance to shine. You might not always be able to see them, but their light never falters.

I was one of those stars, waiting for your darkness to find me and give me a chance to shine. Always hoping that one day you would see my glow through your shadows and realise I was your beacon. But you never did. My light was never strong enough to battle your darkness, no matter how hard I tried. You could never see me for what I really was and eventually, inevitably, I lost my sparkle, my light faded and you would never be able to find me again.

I forever felt like I was standing on the other side of a cavern, staring across at you, shouting your name into the abyss, my voice getting lost on the wind. I'd stretch my arms out to you as far as I could, muscles aching with the effort and me teetering on the edge of something unknown, but still, my fingertips barely reached you, barely brushed your surface. I wanted you to feel my warmth so much. To know that I was there and that you were all I could see. But the more I tried to get close to you, the more you backed away. Until eventually my warmth turned cold, and you turned and ran.

A shooting star streaks across the sky in front of me, and despite my sadness, I allow myself to smile briefly at the rare beauty of it. With a child-like naivety, I squeeze my eyes tight shut and make a wish on that rogue piece of rock. And all I wish is that you'd let me love you. But as I open my eyes again and stare into the sky, at the dark space where the shooting star had been, I realise that maybe I was asking too much. Because right now, standing alone at my bedroom window and looking into the blackness, you feel as far from my grasp as that shooting star, a million miles away in another world. And deep down I know I can't reach you anymore. Any of you.

I finally close the curtains and turn away from the window, childishly hoping there might be some truth in wishing on a shooting star. That my dreams were being heard by someone, somewhere, and not just thrown into the night sky and lost. I climb back into bed and pull the duvet up under my chin, our photographs falling to the floor as I do so. Memories of the seaside cottage I holidayed in with Matthew flutter delicately through my head. How clear the night skies were there, how beautiful the stars, how I thought that that was forever but how Ben had other ideas. And how you took the stars and made them darker. How you stole their magic and forced them to become a beautiful excuse for your fractured mind.

I'm still fully clothed, but I don't have the energy to undress. The weight of the duvet feels comforting for a moment and I curl myself into a tight ball beneath it, wishing for the millionth time you were lying next to me, holding my hand like Matthew used to, or curling yourself around me and nestling into my back like Ben did, or resting your head against my chest, your breath warm on my neck. Tears well in my eyes again and glide silently down my cheeks, dampening the duvet. All I can see are faces. Interlinking. Overlapping. Melting into one another: Matthew, Ben and you. Blurred, muddy and beautiful.

And I think to myself, who is it that I'm wishing for on that shooting star? I don't know. And I think to myself that I can't do this anymore.

Chapter Forty

The sky is menacingly grey with vicious storm clouds bearing down upon us, their fury raging all around. In every direction I look I can see nothing but heavy skies and threatening seas, and a distinct sense of foreboding creeps cold and unwelcome under my skin. The boat is pitching violently as the sea swells with the gathering storm, and I begin to feel scared. I've always hated the sea. Standing on the shore, I love to admire it in all its powerful beauty. I love watching the waves breaking on the beach or crashing into rocks. I love to watch the sun setting all fierce and golden behind the horizon, leaving its violent orange mark on the water and turning the sky into a beautiful glowing backdrop. But here, on this boat in the middle of this storm, I am terrified. I feel panic rising quickly inside me, and I frantically gulp down air to try and quell the nausea that grips me.

I look all around, spinning myself in distraught, dizzying circles desperately trying to find you. I run across the deck of the boat, wind whipping my hair painfully into my eyes, icy raindrops stinging my skin. I reach a handrail at the edge of the deck and cling onto it to stop myself from falling, peering down into the churning grey ocean below, and I scream your name over and over again. I scream it into the sea, into the sky. I scream it so loudly that my throat is raw and I'm left coughing and retching from the effort. But no matter how loudly I cry, my voice is instantly whipped away by the wind, as though it's mocking me for even trying. Angry tears mix with the raindrops, but I won't give in. I turn to face the horizon, raise my head to the sky and using all my strength I scream for you again, feeling like this is the last breath I will ever take. And suddenly, you're there. Suddenly, you're behind me and you're pulling me into your arms telling me everything will be all right. And I cling to you so tightly now. Like I'm never going to let go as long as I live. And you hold me so close and so fiercely that I almost can't breathe, but I don't mind because now I feel safe. Nothing can hurt me now.

We stand like that for an eternity, on the deck of this boat swaying in the storm. My face buried against your chest, the comforting smell of you filling my lungs. Your arms wound tightly, protectively, around me, lips pressed against the top of my head, whispering into my hair that you're here and that I am safe now. And I let relief wash over me. I relax into your arms, I let you take the strain and I don't feel frightened anymore. You hold me until the storm passes and the winds subside, and the swell of the ocean fades and instead becomes a gentle wave lapping against the side of the boat, and the sun gradually appears through the retreating storm clouds.

I turn to face you, but it's not you. It's them. All of them. Morphing into one hideous abstracted portrait: mouths where eyes should be, female mouths on male scowls, eyelashes batting against a chin rough with stubble. Ebony and Matthew and Ben and Mother and you, all dripping from a stranger's skull, skin bubbling and blistering like paint beneath the heat of a blowtorch. I stagger backwards, stretching my mouth open wide until the corners split, and I scream into the nightmare portrait.

I open my eyes and immediately see the familiar curtains of my bedroom, the white lamp on my bedside table, the wardrobes at the foot of my bed and I know, with a strange mixture of relief and sadness, that it was a dream.

Suddenly, I'm too hot. My entire body is burning, my heart is pounding against my ribcage and I can feel a thin sheen of perspiration forming across my forehead. I begin to feel claustrophobic. I kick off the duvet to try and give myself more space. I need air, but I don't have the energy to get up, and anyway I don't think my legs could hold me. I'm gasping now, trying to suck it into my lungs but not being able to. Everywhere feels too bright, too real. The sun is streaming through the thin curtains, pulling everything into sharp focus and it hurts my eyes. I feel dizzy and sick. I rest an arm across my forehead, close my eyes and will myself to take slow, steadying breaths. I concentrate on my breathing for a few moments, focusing hard on the constant rise and fall of my stomach.

I don't know how long I lie like this, but eventually, my heart rate slows to somewhere close to normal and the heat leaves my body. I feel calmer now, although I am still recovering from the shock of the dream, of how vivid it was and how easily I was fooled into believing it was real. How can my mind play such cruel tricks? Not even my own body is on my side anymore. I feel like now I'm fighting a losing battle with myself. I close my eyes and try to sleep again, hoping to be able to escape you this time, but knowing I can't even trust my own self to protect me anymore. Maybe I never could.

***

When I wake, the room is dull and I briefly panic that I've slept through the entire day. I grab my watch from the bedside table and see that it is 12.30pm. I know I need to get up but I still can't face it. I'm so relieved it's Sunday and the children are with Matthew this weekend. It means I don't have to pretend today. I rub my face and shake my head. I need to get a hold on things. I pull back the duvet and head towards the window again. I feel light-headed and have to lean momentarily against the wall to steady myself. Pulling the curtains back a little, I squint into the daylight, but the harsh sunlight of earlier has been replaced by grey skies and the rain is falling in a dismal drizzle. The clouds remind me of my dream and I quickly close the curtains again to shut out the memory.

I remember I am still wearing yesterday's clothes and I feel disgusted with myself. What's happening to me? I catch a glimpse of myself in the full-length mirror on my bedroom wall. I hung the mirror myself just the other day and I felt briefly proud then of my small achievement. Looking at the mirror now I'm only reminded of how you helped me to hang it in the bedroom of my old house. The reflection back then a world away from the image I see before me now. I hardly recognise this person. I'm pale and dishevelled, blue-grey shadows developing beneath my eyes. I look crumpled and hopeless, and I feel even worse inside.

As tempting as it is just to crawl back into bed or to sprawl listlessly on the sofa all day, I decide I should make some attempt to at least try and look like the old me, even if I feel a million miles' away from that girl. I gather together fresh towels from the airing cupboard and head across the landing into my pristine new bathroom, where everything is all gleaming white and modern, and I take a shower. The water feels too hot against my skin, but I don't adjust the temperature. The heat is almost comforting, as if reassuring me that every last trace of last night's dream is being removed. I stand for an age letting the water rush over my face and down my body, letting the steam fill my lungs, until all the remnants of you are sluiced down the drain. And at the same time, I feel like more little pieces of me are breaking off and dissolving, being washed away with you like I'm slowly fading away.

Eventually, I turn off the shower and stand in the steam for a moment longer, squeezing the excess water from my hair, listening to the silence that presses itself insistently against my ears. Always silence. Always alone. Looking up towards the ceiling, I sigh and shake my head, and before tears threaten, I step into the cool air of the bathroom, wrap a towel around myself and head back to the bedroom to get dressed.

From the doorway, I see the photographs and I know I'll have to clear them up, it's no use. I don't really want to touch them anymore or look at their tauntingly blissful images, but I can't leave them scattered all over the floor forever. I pad towards the mess, leaving behind damp footprints on the carpet, the deep cream pile of it oozing softly between my toes. I crouch down, gathering my towel more tightly around my body with one hand, and take a deep breath as I roughly gather them into a pile with the other, trying hard not to look too closely, and throw them quickly into the top drawer of my bedside table. I slam the drawer shut, holding it closed for a minute or two as if scared it will fly open again and I'll be tortured some more by images of you and of us. I should just destroy them, rip them up, throw them out, be rid of them for good. But I know I can't. Not yet.

Satisfied with my cleaning job, I dress and head downstairs, surprising myself at how much better I'm feeling after my shower. I still can't bring myself to put the radio on in case I hear a song that reminds me of you, so I grab a can of cola from the fridge and a bar of chocolate from the cupboard and sit in silence at the dining table. I can't stomach real food these days. I'm losing weight rapidly, my skin is pallid and slick with oil, but I just don't care anymore. The thought of digesting a proper meal makes me nauseous, so I survive on a couple of chocolate bars a day and cans of cola. It works for now.

I look around my large kitchen and wish you were here to see it. You would have really liked this house. It's so much better than the tiny, dark and damp terrace I used to live in. It's light and bright and it has space. The living-room has the fireplace in it that I was always so desperate for, and I wish you were going to be here with me when winter arrives so we could cuddle up on the sofa in front of the flames, watching TV until we fall asleep. The kitchen is full of natural light which pours in through large south-facing windows, and I know that this space would be perfect for setting up my easel, fixing a canvas to it and creating beautiful images from oils and acrylics and as many paintbrushes as I could fit into my hand. Perfect. If I ever felt like painting. Which I don't.

I'd convinced myself that when I moved here, I'd be truly starting again. I'd joke to friends that only good memories would be allowed in this house. And I made a determined start. But that was before I ran out of the energy to pretend anymore. Before I didn't have it in me to keep smiling like everything was okay in my world. Because everything is far from okay and it has been for a long time. Still, I'm trying to make this a proper home, to bring some life into it. But when Ruby and James aren't here filling it with shouting and laughter and tantrums, it's the loneliest place in the world. Silence is where I give up the fight.

Looking around, I realise there is no escaping you. You're here, in every room of my new house. I have subconsciously brought you with me, despite thinking I had discarded every trace of you, leaving our memories behind in crude black bin bags at my old house. But you're here in the camera that sits on the kitchen shelf, the one you got me for my birthday last October. You're here in the mirror that hangs on my living-room wall, another birthday present from you. You're in the beauty products that lie in the cabinet in the bathroom, the ones you bought me last Christmas. You're in the earrings on my bedside table and the perfume I wear. The perfume you chose and that I went through bottles and bottles of because I knew you loved it so much. I still wear it now, but not so much these days. The scent reminds me too much of you, and what's the point anymore anyway?

You're even in the car that I drive, because it's the one you helped me choose. I loved how you looked after me sometimes. How you had the ability to make me feel so special. When you wanted to.

Thoughts of you start to seep into my mind again, an inkblot pattern that I choose to interpret as an image of all the happy times we shared. As I sit here at this table, sipping slowly from my can of cola, I forget all about the bad times and let the good memories come flooding in. For now, I want to remember the best of you and the best of us. I don't need photographs to bring back these memories. They're stored right here in my head, yet I know that I really do need to put you away somewhere. To put all our memories inside a box in my mind and lock it tight, but I don't want to be rid of you just yet. And I still don't know why.

I think of when we first met, full of smiles and laughter and alcohol. I remember you shaking with nerves as you invited me back to your house later that night. I remember our adventures to cities across the country, where we'd fall into bed at a cheap hotel, cuddled up and content for now in our own little world. I remember standing with you on the shore of Loch Lomond, arms wound tightly around each other, my head resting on your chest, looking out at the beautiful scenery and drinking in the remote, unspoiled landscape.

And as the sun shone down brightly on that perfect day, as our breath formed clouds that merged together in the cold February air, I remember thinking how much I loved you. How much I felt it right to my very core. How I wanted to protect you, to heal you, to love you like nobody else ever had, and for you to love me the same way. And I remember how those words still wouldn't leave my lips. They reached their edges and stayed there, never forming from thoughts into words. If only I'd told you. I don't know why I couldn't.

I push this thought to the back of my mind, refusing to let my unhappiness in, and instead, I let all the little things that made us 'us' drift into my mind. How you'd roll your eyes at me and the mess I always made in your kitchen as I cooked, shaking your head and then kissing me gently on the nose as I giggled against your lips. I remember chasing you after your shower, and us falling in fits of laughter on your bed, play fighting. I think of how I always linked your arm whenever we walked anywhere, and of how I'd never let you say hello or goodbye without kissing me.

I think of us lying in your bed, holding each other tight, scratching your back gently until you fell asleep. And I remember watching you while you were sleeping and feeling that overwhelming urge to protect you. To save you. Because I couldn't save Ebony, and I'm not sure I know how to save myself.

I don't let myself think of the harsh words and the fights, of the tears and the fear, or the million reasons why I fled from you so many times.

And I sit here now without you, without anyone and I know that I'll never have any of these things back again. All of those moments I treasured so much, they're all just memories now. Maybe it was all only ever just a fantasy. My foolish fairy-princess dream that I'd hoped would come true for so long. The life I'd desperately sought and that I told myself I'd found, even though the world was fighting against me to show me the truth. Even though I knew everything was wrong in that rose-tinted world, I'd still believed I had my dreams firmly within my grasp. Until reality savagely ripped them from my hands and put them into your angry fists, turning my dreams into nightmares.

Suddenly I'm angry, incensed, ashamed, and I slam my fist down hard on the table, chin trembling, eyes stinging again with angry tears. Because I miss you so, so much. Because I did everything wrong. I always do everything wrong. And it's all my fault. Everything is all my fault.

I drag myself into the living-room and lose myself in TV for an entire day. It's easier than having to face things or think about it all anymore. My mind is numbed by the inane images and I don't have to be reminded that you're gone. That they're gone. I don't have to be reminded that I need to forget. Forget you, forget us, forget them, forget everything. Because I don't want to. Because letting go is the hardest part. And because if I let go, you're gone. All of you will be gone.

Chapter Forty-One

August 2013

The alarm goes off and its incessant beeping penetrates, unwelcome, through the fog of sleep, bringing with it the nauseating reminder that it's Monday morning and I have to face the world again. I reach out and swipe blindly at the clock until I manage to hit the right button to silence it. I lie here, arm outstretched, resting on the bedside table and I try to think positively, though I realise I may have forgotten how.

Another childless weekend waded through in a blur of alcohol and painkillers, the air in my bedroom stale from the stench of perspiration and the fumes leaking from what is now the dregs at the bottom of a large bottle of whisky. My teeth are furred, my tongue sticks to the roof of my parched mouth and my hair lies flat against my head in greasy knots.

I've been doing this for months now. Going into work, going through the motions, getting on with my day, pretending to everybody that I'm fine. But lately, it's all becoming too much. Because I'm not fine and I don't know how long I can carry on with the pretence. Every day it gets harder. Every day it's more of a challenge to smile. And every day I feel myself sinking lower and lower.

So many times over the past few weeks I've found myself sitting behind my desk in the office fighting back tears and fighting the urge to break down. I smile wider than necessary just to convince myself I can. I laugh a little too loudly, a little too much to prove to everyone that I still can. It's exhausting and it hurts.

I'm broken, of that there is no doubt. Everyone can see it. The world is no longer a wonderful place for me and the darkness you carried with you has descended over me too. Maybe it was always there in the background, somewhere far below my surface, but never have such shadows settled around me like this before. Yet, I don't entirely blame you for bringing me here, although sometimes my anger betrays that. I blame myself for not being strong enough to fix you, to make you better, to resist the dark parts of you.

In the end, your pain fuelled my pain, and we turned on each other as fiercely as opposing sides in a battle. Our stained and blemished pasts taking over the flawless future I was determined to pretend we could have. You found all the cracks in my composure and you let the dark pieces of me seep out. You targeted my flaws to turn me into somebody I never was. I'll never understand why.

In the end, neither of us had the strength to let go of our past and embrace the future. And sitting behind my desk in the small and claustrophobic office, staring blankly at my computer screen with the world a distant haze, I'm left trying to process our demise, yet another heartbreaking loss, day after day. Trying to pinpoint the exact moment when everything fell apart. But for us, there were so many moments. For us, we gave in to falling apart almost as soon as we began. And in this place, my workplace where nobody should ever see me cry, the tears of frustration inevitably fall again and I am so tired of them. So very, very tired.

I'm left infuriated and angry, because the image you created of me is unfair and you didn't give me the chance to defend myself. The person you decided that I was isn't real, except in your world where people only ever exist to hurt you. You created a darkness in me that was never there. I fought so hard to stop you thinking badly of me at every turn. To stop you taking what I'd said or done, twisting it into endless knots and tangles in your mind, and spitting it venomously back at me, making me feel small and insignificant. Making me feel stupid and worthless. Branding me with your bruises and making me run from you time and time again.

I had put all of myself into you and me, but you stripped me of everything that I was trying so hard to put back together, until eventually I lost myself in your angry words and repulsed stares. I lost everything because I wouldn't give in or stop chasing an illusion of happiness. I wanted it so much for us. But you punctured my world and let my hopes and dreams bleed out. I was set adrift in the darkness, my life becoming a swirling black mess. And now I'm desperately trying to find my way out.

***

My hand is cold and the pain of a million sharp pinpricks jolts me awake. I'd drifted back off to sleep, arm still outstretched resting on the alarm clock, the circulation cut off by the weight of my head leaning heavily upon it. I sit up quickly and shake my hand violently to get the feeling back. The pain when I try to move my fingers makes me wince, but soon I sense the heat in my fingertips and the feeling returns. I need to get a move on. I need to snap myself out of this sombre mood and focus.

As I begin what feels like the immense effort to get dressed, I open my bedside drawer and immediately see your face staring out. I'd forgotten I'd hurriedly hidden the photographs in there yesterday. My stomach lurches and my throat constricts, and I slam the drawer shut, the lamp resting on top of the unit shuddering with the force. I sit for a moment, eyes closed, breathing heavily as though recovering from some sort of athletic exertion, and I feel the familiar sensation of panic rising; that cold, clammy feeling of dread. I grit my teeth against the onslaught and squeeze my eyes closed even tighter, pushing the palms of my hands against them, pressing harder and harder until tiny stars appear in the blackness behind my eyelids.

Stars.

The thought invokes a sudden rage. Violently, I wrench at the drawer, pulling it open again with the same force with which I'd slammed it shut. And I'm grabbing viciously at the photographs with shaking hands. I'm tearing them apart. Through gritted teeth I'm ripping them to shreds, anger and regret coursing through me hot and unrelenting, driving me onwards in my urgent need to get rid of you. I can't stop. I'm tearing them apart just like I'm torn apart, leaving tiny fragments of us scattered all around me on the bed, unrecognisable portraits of what used to be. Our memories in smithereens, just like the shards of my broken heart. And when the anger finally subsides, I leave us there in pieces, the remains of us strewn on the soft white duvet. And as I walk into the bathroom, I feel a cautious sense of satisfaction.

Chapter Forty-Two

September 2013

The telephone downstairs is ringing before my alarm fires up. I hear its harsh tones puncturing urgently through my drowsiness. Before I even open my eyes, I know something is wrong. I rouse myself quickly and run unsteadily down the stairs, light-headed from the shock of the sudden interruption to my sleep. But just as I reach it, it stops. I wait a moment and it rings again. This time I answer it immediately. Mother.

Within seconds I'm in tears, slumping down onto the sofa, phone held loosely against my ear, vaguely hearing the mumble of the conversation but not really listening. I've heard the first part and that is all that's ringing deafeningly in my ears, the news piercing painfully through my hushed living-room. My grandma has died.

I hang up and stare into space, not able to move from where I've collapsed onto the sofa. I am numb, unsure of how much more grief and sorrow my body can take. I thought the world of her and now she's left me too. Another love lost. Another fracture in my fragile heart. And I feel as though it won't be long before my own heart becomes tired too, unable to cope with any more, and just stops trying to keep me alive.

My tears fall soundlessly and I don't have the energy to wipe them away. They run down my neck and form little pools at my collarbone, the familiar sensation of salt stinging my skin a tragic reminder of the constant sadness I've felt for months now. Maybe years. Maybe even forever. This latest unhappiness merges with the muddy depths of the rest, feeling dense and heavy in my heart.

And I don't know what to do. It is early and the children are still sleeping, I can't wake them yet. On autopilot, I walk slowly up the stairs on trembling legs. I sit on the edge of my bed and pick up my mobile. I suddenly need to be practical, to do something. So I send a text message to Matthew and ask him if he can take the children to school today. I can't do it. I can't pretend to be happy for a moment longer. I just don't have it in me.

The tears are still leaking, an unbroken yet silent stream of sorrow, and I'm hit full force by the pain of this new loss, the reality of it harsh and cold. Yet another person I'll never see again. Another person who I'll never be able to talk to about all the things I think and feel. I lie down on top of the duvet and hug my knees to my chest. I close my eyes and remember her, frail and faded but with a glint of her younger self in her pale, tired eyes. I remember the last time I saw her, when she took my hand between her fragile, delicate fingers and squeezed it with a strength I didn't think she still possessed, telling me I was wonderful. And I smile through my tears.

She understood everything better than anybody else. She didn't judge me when I'd told her the truth all those years ago, as I explained through sobs and faltering words and a million apologies about Matthew and about Ben and about the things I had done. She'd held my hand in that same way and told me not to worry, that everything would be all right. The diluted blue of her eyes sparkling behind her reassuring smile. But now she's gone too, and I don't think anything will ever be all right again.

I'm still gripping my mobile firmly, and through my memories, it occurs to me that I should telephone work and let them know I won't be coming in. I can't go in today. How can I? I've been finding it hard enough working there for the past few months without this to cope with too. I open my eyes and look through the contacts on my phone, scrolling down the list to find the office telephone number. Then unconsciously, completely without thinking, the next person I'm contacting is not work, it's you.

Right now, I need you more than ever. I want you here with me so much. I want you to take me in your arms and make all this pain go away. I want you to hold me and never let me go. Only you can make all this better. If I just reach out to you, maybe you'll come back to me. Maybe you'll see how much you're wanted; how important you are to me. Maybe you'll remember how much you care for me. Maybe I can light a tiny spark in you again, one that used to glow for me, and maybe you'll remember that you love me. Somewhere beneath all the anger and the darkness, somewhere among the shadows, somewhere behind the fists that slam into my face and break my ribs, somewhere beyond the blood you draw and the purple stains you spread across my skin, somewhere far away from the glasses that shatter all around me, maybe you still love me like I loved you.

I'm tapping out the words frantically now. My fingers unable to move fast enough to keep up with everything I want to say. I just need you here. I don't want to do all this on my own. I need you to take the strain for me, to be strong for me. Because I can't do it. Not anymore. And as soon as I send the message, I feel relief pouring over me, coursing through me, washing away the debris of my sadness. Because now you'll come. Because you'll know that I need you. And you'll know not to hurt me anymore.

***

The day passes in a blur. I'm at my parents' house for most of it, feeling as lost as they are, none of us really knowing what to say. I sit in the garden in the afternoon, hoping the heat from the sun will help relax my tense muscles and drive away the melancholy. It's a bright, sunny day, the warmth of the sun draping itself across my shoulders like a comfort blanket, caressing the crown of my head, easing some of the tension as I try to relax in one of the white plastic garden chairs.

I have moved into the shade slightly, positioning my chair beneath the branches of the cherry tree in the far corner of the garden. The delicate pink blossom is long gone, but I watch as a bee busies herself collecting late-summer nectar from a bright-red flower made up of all the shades of the setting sun. I don't know the names of plants and flowers, not unless they're the obvious ones like roses or tulips or daisies. My brother would know, but I don't want to ask him. I don't really want to say anything today.

I tip my head back and rest it against the low back of the chair, so that my eyes are looking straight up into the azure of the sky. The bright-blue peeps between the crisscrossed branches of the cherry tree, an ever-changing mosaic as the branches sway in the gentle breeze. Sparks, like starbursts, occasionally break through as the branches move, making way for the sunlight. The beauty of it feels a little out of place, given the circumstances. But I tell myself that my grandma has made the sun shine today and, as ridiculous as it sounds, it helps.

As early evening approaches, I decide to take a walk on the harbour, a short drive from the house. I need to clear my head. To process everything. I need to be alone with my thoughts for a while, despite having wanted to escape them for so long. As I get into the car, I check my phone again, looking for a message. I've lost count of how many times I've looked at it today. Still nothing. I throw the phone onto the passenger seat and let out a long, dejected breath. I don't know why I thought things would be different. I don't know why I convinced myself I meant enough for you to still care. I feel stupid. So, so stupid. I should have known. You never really cared. Ever, ever.

Just like James's party. Where were you then? Where? Nowhere to be found.

The roads are quiet and the drive takes no time. I pull up in the car park and ease myself out of the car. I can smell the salty sea air, taste it on my lips, and feel the cool summer breeze on my bare arms. As I begin walking towards the harbour I slowly start to relax. The sun is low and casts an orange glow on the lighthouses far away at the end of the harbour walls. I decide to walk out to one of them, to sit on its weathered and worn steps and watch the rise and fall of the sea, by now an undulating grey mass splintered with orange shards in the evening light.

I am alone as I walk slowly along the sandstone pier. In the distance, I can see dogs and their owners running along the sandy beach down below, but up here I am by myself and, unusually, I relish the silence. I stand for a few moments watching boats leaving the harbour to fish, not to return until the morning. I shield my eyes and watch until they become tiny dots in the distance, silhouetted against the setting sun, bobbing freely among the waves. And I wish that I could be as free as they were, not trapped, as though the weight of the world is pinning me down and I am lost beneath it.

I reach the lighthouse and sit facing the sea and the setting sun. I rest my back against its white, curved wall and it feels cool beneath my thin summer T-shirt. The breeze here is stronger and I turn my head into the wind, closing my eyes and letting it blow my hair away from my face. I hear gulls overhead, shrieking into the whispering sky, and I hear the calm sea gently lapping at the harbour wall below me. It feels familiar and for a moment I am almost content. But almost as soon as that feeling arrives it leaves me, and I find myself wishing you were here too. And I wonder for the millionth time where you are and what you're doing, if you're thinking of me the way I think of you, or if I'm just a distant memory.

Dan.

Suddenly, he's right here with me, his bright-red hair, his little-boy-lost eyes, the way he speaks softly, poetically. He intermingles with the sea and the salt and the gulls and the air and I remember the warmth of him, how we wrapped ourselves around each other right here the day he told me he was leaving. A whole other world away, a whole different life. And I wonder all those things I just questioned a second ago, all over again. But for somebody else.

The sun disappears below the horizon and the air becomes instantly colder. Reluctantly, I decide to go back to the car and head home. I'm exhausted and just want the day to be over. I turn my back on the darkening horizon and retrace my steps, walking quicker now, arms folded across my chest to keep out the chill. As I approach the car park I stop sharply in my tracks, feet refusing to move beneath me, heart slamming hard against my chest. Because I'm looking at you. You're right there, across the road. You're walking towards the pub that stands on the main road just opposite my car, not a care in the world. You don't see me. You look stunning and achingly familiar, and I want to run towards you, and yet away from you at the same time. Because you know. You know all about today and yet you don't care. I feel like I don't exist anymore all over again, like I'm nothing. Like my whole life is stuck on repeat. And in an instant, I despise you.

I will my feet to move, to run to the safety of the car, and I clamber inside, breathless and retching. I start the engine, grind the gear roughly into place and drive straight home. Too fast, too reckless, and by the time I pull up outside my house, I realise I remember nothing about the journey at all.

It takes me less than a minute to throw down the car keys on the kitchen worktop, sling the shoes from my feet in the direction of the back door and reach into the back of the cupboard under the sink, scrabbling blindly for what I know is hidden behind my oil paints and the white spirit I used to clean paintbrushes that would probably never see the light of day again.

I push aside the turpentine and the tubes of paints and the first-aid box. I lift containers of fabric softener and washing-up liquid out of the way until my hand closes around the smooth, cool neck of the bottle. It's still three-quarters full and I quickly unscrew the top, close my mouth round the neck and rapidly gulp mouthful after mouthful after mouthful of the clear, burning liquid, relishing the sting in my throat and the heat in my belly. The burn that will take away the pain of everything else.

And I know that the vodka bottle will be empty before the night is done.

***

A week later. I sit in front of my bedroom mirror staring closely at my reflection and applying make-up that I know will be swept away by tears in a couple of hours. Still, I want to make sure I look my best. I want to make her proud. It's the least my grandma deserves on the day we say goodbye. She deserves me, her granddaughter, not the mess I've been lately.

I lean a little closer and press my lips together in a thin line, concentrating hard. I dip the tip of my ring finger into a pot of thick, creamy concealer and press it gently into the dark hollows beneath my eyes, trying to disguise the deep-purple tinge the skin there has taken on lately. It works well, has the desired effect. Good. I'm good at this, I think. Hiding things, covering them up: dark marks, purple bruises, the remnants left by your fists.

I swap the pot for a different one, eyeshadow this time, and begin applying the neutral shades to my lids. This time trying to cover up their swollen redness from hours of crying. This I'm not so good at, and when I step back from the glass to survey my handiwork, I sigh. It'll have to do. I apply one last coat of mascara and take another long look at myself in the mirror. On the outside, at least, I look close enough to being me again. Inside, I'm a million miles away.

My mobile phone lies beside me and my eyes flicker towards the screen as it lights up. All morning I've been receiving messages of support and of condolence. Messages reminding me that I am surrounded by people who are there for me, people who care for me. But there's still nothing from the one person I really want to hear from. There's still nothing from you.

I try to suppress the feeling of sadness and frustration, but I can't. No matter how many friends I have around me, no matter how much I try to keep myself occupied and keep my thoughts away from you, no matter how much I try to smile, I'm always lonely where it matters… in my heart. And today the feeling is even more overwhelming. I just need you so much.

I take a deep breath and stand, pushing my feet into my shoes. Black court shoes. Funeral shoes. Sombre and reserved. Time to go. I grab my bag and a handful of tissues and head out of the door.

***

I am in my parents' car, following the hearse from my grandma's house to the crematorium. I stare vacantly through the windscreen at the coffin and the flowers, the image merging into a blur of indistinct colours as the tears swim in my eyes. My sister and brother are next to me in the back seat. We sit in silence, lost in our own thoughts, none of us knowing what to say or even needing to say anything at all.

We pull up slowly at the entrance to the ugly seventies red-brick building, and I watch the air shimmering around its edges. From the heat of the day or from the heat of the fire? My mind doesn't want to contemplate the question. Grass and trees and blue sky and thousands of dead people beneath the daisy-carpeted lawn, all undulating seamlessly like the swell of the ocean.

The dream. The storm. The melting faces.

I don't like how it feels.

We slowly exit the car and stand for a moment in the beautiful sunshine. The waves of heat roll in to greet me, breaking against my skin, lapping at my limbs, dragging the warmth back with the tide before the scorching day rushes in at me again. Immersion. Drowning under the weight of it.

Sweat beads on my forehead. I lick my lips nervously. And again. The black knee-length dress feels too tight, too hot, and I want to rip off the three-quarter-length sleeves and shove them into my handbag. I want to take off my shoes and walk barefoot. I look around quickly to see if anybody else feels the same. I can't tell.

A butterfly floats awkwardly through the heavy velvet curtain of heat, all misshaped and incoherent in the haze. Its wings stutter clumsily, black-and-red tissue paper beating in the breeze, soaring cautiously on the gentle breath of the warm air. I watch it closely. Follow it with my eyes as it circles me. Once. Then around again. Three times now. Faster and faster. And I spin with it. And I'm dizzy. But I can't stop.

The noise of the whirlwind roars in my ears. White noise. I press my hands against the sides of my head, trying to block it out. But the sound gets louder.

And then it flies at me, ten times the size it was. A hundred times. A thousand. Black wings enormous, about to engulf me. I scream and squeeze my eyes shut against the approaching monster, flailing my hands in front of my face.

'No, no, no! Go away! Go!' The wings lash at my face. 'No! No! Go away! Please, go away. Please!' Still, it comes at me. I hear the rush of air moving all around me with every violent beat of its wings as it bears down on me. Thick, sticky air forces its way into my gaping, screaming mouth. My throat constricts. Bone dry and choking.

And then a giggle. Her giggle. The playground giggle. The little one.

'Fuck off Ebony! Leave me alone! I don't want you anymore. I don't want you!'

Silence.

A hand on my shoulder. A friendly face in an absurd top hat, cheeks rosy red in the heat as black coattails flap in the breeze like giant butterfly wings.

'I'm sorry to interrupt, daydreamer,' he says, 'but it's time to go inside.'

Nobody saw it. Nobody heard. I'm pulled, dazed, out of my day terror by the scruff of my neck and into something even worse. I don't want to be here. I want to run away. I want to hide. I want to close my eyes tight again until it all disappears. Until it's all over.

The coffin is taken from the hearse. And as my grandma's body, tiny and lifeless inside a wooden box, is carried into the imposing building I follow numbly, putting one foot in front of the other, going through the motions to get me to where I need to be, until eventually the sorrow rises in my throat and I break down. I cry tears for her and

I cry tears for you. I weep for all of you, because you never leave my mind. The pain of my losses fusing and becoming a mass of disordered and bleak thoughts. I grieve for you all. And I am crushed.

I cry for Matthew and for all the times we laughed and loved. I cry for Ebony and for all the adventures we'll never get to have. I cry for Ben and for how briefly I felt his love, how I thought he'd be the one to save me. And I cry you. For all the times you made me feel so special, and for all the times you left me feeling scared and worthless with your angry words and repulsed stares. I cry for the sadness in you that I could never understand, and how it could leave you harsh and cold. I cry for all the times I never knew what I'd done wrong, for all the times when I wasn't enough and for the times I was too much. And I cry for all the times I wish I'd just held you tight and shown you I was there.

I cry for the times I let you down and for the times you let me down too. I cry for all the times I wanted you so much but you were never there. For the times I wanted you to hold me close and show me you loved me. I cry for the times you held me away, keeping me at arm's length. And I cry for the man I wanted so much, but who was always too far away for me to reach.

I cry for all the times the words got stuck in my throat, when I loved you so, so much. I cry for all the times my insecurities – my past – got in the way, turning into jealousy. I cry for all the cruel words between us, for the slamming of doors, of fists, and the running away. For all the times I tried to leave but couldn't, because I loved you more than I could understand. For all the times I shed tears on your shoulder and for all the times we clung on to each other, lost and adrift.

I cry for the times when all I wanted was to be your everything, somebody's everything, and for the times I chased you even though I knew you weren't coming back. Because nobody ever comes back. I cry for the friend I lost, not long ago and forever ago, and I cry for my heart that is broken. Regrets pour down my cheeks in never-ending rivers.

But nobody comforts me.

As we leave the service, I place a single white rose on the dark polished wood of the coffin and whisper a last goodbye. And then I can cry no more. I have nothing left to give. There are no emotions left, just exhaustion and weariness. I suddenly want to go home. I want to crawl into bed and let the tiredness take over. I want to sleep until tomorrow arrives and I have made it through another day.

But I can't, because I have to sit and eat afternoon tea in an old hotel, in a function room with a worn carpet and dusty corners and metal chairs with lumpy seat cushions and chipped china mugs on saucers with faded floral patterns. And I have to try to pretend that I can still do this. This whole living, breathing, life thing.

***

The rest of the afternoon passes in a blur of polite conversations with family members and people I don't know, until eventually everybody disperses and returns to their own lives, leaving us in ours. I don't remember a thing about the drive home, except that I was desperate to leave, but I am finally here at last and I am thankful to be putting the key in my front door.

I head straight upstairs to get changed out of the constraints of the black dress. I fumble with the zip at the base of my neck and slide it down to my waist in a less than graceful movement. The dress falls to the floor in fluid folds around my ankles, and I step out of the black circle towards the mirror. I catch my reflection shining out at me from the glass. Blue veins crisscrossing pale skin. Almost see-through.

Standing perfectly still in my underwear, I let the cool air dry my damp skin. The sweet smell of nervous sweat and perfume emanates from me like a bittersweet aura, and I think I should probably shower. Maybe later.

I run my hands across hip bones that stick out way too much and a stomach that's concave and that should be hungry but never is. Somebody I once knew used to look like this. A fading collection of skin and bones. Not me though. It was never meant to be me.

I reach to retrieve my handbag from beneath the discarded dress, and as I throw it down on the bed, I feel the phone inside it vibrate. A message. A heartbeat misses its timing in my chest. It races again to catch up as I fumble clumsily with the zip. As I reach inside, I feel sure that it's you. Something tells me it's got to be you by now, and I feel relieved you've finally got in touch. Finally. A weight lifts from across my neck and shoulders: the burden of missing you that I've been carrying around for weeks finally taking its leave.

But as I look down at the illuminated screen, I see it isn't you at all, it's someone else, another friend asking how

I am. A different person caring for me. Not you. It's never you. And in an instant, I feel small and insignificant, like I don't matter. And from out of nowhere anger surges deep in the pit of my stomach, so hot it burns in my throat. And I venomously send you another message. Because I hate you and I want you to know.

And when I'm done, when I'm satisfied, I've hurt you, I lie down and let my hand drop into the space between the bedside cabinet and the bed frame. And I let my fingers close around the smooth neck of the whisky bottle. And I get drunk. Lying there alone in my underwear.

Chapter Forty-Three

October 2013

I am awake, but I can't open my eyes. I can tell that it is morning by the vague hint of daylight filtering through my eyelids, or maybe it's afternoon by now, I'm not sure. I am aware of a telltale dull ache in my head and my tongue feels swollen, stuck to the roof of my gritty mouth. There is stale alcohol on my breath and I try to swallow to remove the taste, but my mouth is dry and the action is difficult, forced. I am so thirsty and I try to swallow again to ease my parched throat, but it does little to help. I lick my lips and they feel rough beneath my tongue. I chew on them for a moment trying to bring some life back into their scaly surface.

I press my hand to my forehead to try to stop the ache, but the pain only moves to another part of my head, flowing around my skull, vicious and hot. I rest my hand over my face and try to open my eyes. Exhaustion and last night's make-up fuse my eyelashes so that I almost have to physically peel my eyelids apart. They are glued shut as though they don't want to face the day. I raise my eyebrows and my eyelids are forced open a crack. Slowly, between the splayed fingers covering my face, my surroundings come into focus. And this is not my bedroom, not my house.

I close my eyes again to shut out the unfamiliar scene and desperately try to remember. But nothing is coming to me. My mind begins to race and my head begins to throb some more with the effort of thinking. The pounding makes me feel sick and I have to clench my teeth and swallow hard again to control my sudden need to vomit. I feel like my world is spinning at a dizzying speed, and I know that if I move my head the nausea will rise again, so I lay motionless and silently will my memory to kick-start and give me something.

I feel hot now. So hot that the skin on my back is damp. I force my eyes open again and, without moving my head, I look down as far as I can to gauge why I'm burning up. I can see that I'm wearing a grey hooded top and that explains the heat, but I'm aware too that my legs are bare beneath the thick duvet. These clothes aren't mine. A memory flashes through my mind, indistinct and too fleeting to process. A club. The same place I met you. Vodka. Laughter. A house. A house that isn't mine. An urgent kiss. Unfamiliar hands moving over my skin. Hands that aren't yours. A stranger's lips on my body.

I squeeze my eyes shut to stop the onslaught of images. I try to make sense of them, but the pain in my head makes it impossible to think clearly. Everything is lost in the foggy depths of my alcohol-induced agony. I shift slightly in the huge bed and suddenly I'm aware of the sound of soft breathing next to me. Deep and sleepy breaths in and out. My body stiffens involuntarily. My heart quickens and the thudding in my head reciprocates. I hold my own breath for a few seconds, suddenly scared to make a single sound. Who is lying next to me? Where on earth am I? God, what have I done?

I lie still for a minute or two longer trying not to disturb the stranger next to me, but my whole body begins to ache. My muscles feel heavy and sore. Limbs numb and tingling. I can feel warmth from the stranger's body now, adding to my already rising temperature, and I really don't want to move but I know I have to. The heat from wearing this unfamiliar top and lying beneath this heavy duvet is becoming unbearable. I can feel my cheeks are flushed and my forehead is becoming clammy. I need to shift position, to stretch my aching limbs, to remove this top because it's too hot, and in this dizzying mix of heat and alcohol and confusion I feel faint.

Painfully, I shift my left elbow slowly and, using it as a lever, I raise myself up from the mattress a little. As soon as my head leaves the sanctuary of the pillow a hundred tiny explosions go off inside my brain. The attack makes me flinch and a small groan escapes my mouth. I feel the stranger next to me stir and I whip my head round in his direction, realising too late the extent of the pain this will cause. A fire ignites beneath my skull and behind my eyes, and I have to lie back down again before I pass out.

He is facing away from me. I can see his almost jet-black hair resting on the pillow and I watch the duvet rising and falling softly with each breath he takes. I close my eyes and I feel sick. I have to get out of here. I don't want to stay a moment longer in this alien place, next to this unknown man, in this unfamiliar bed surrounded by another person's life.

I slide my legs out from beneath the duvet and sit up painfully slowly until my feet are resting on the soft carpet

409

and I have my back to the stranger. The air is cold. My head feels so heavy and I hold it between my hands for a moment, elbows resting on my knees to take the weight, pain still pulsating through every part of it.

I fumble about on the floor with one hand looking for my clothes, and find last night's dress in a crumpled heap beside the bed. I grasp it between my fingers as though it's some sort of lifeline, a link back to me, and taking an inwards breath I rise gradually on unsteady legs, my peripheral vision an indistinct black haze. I have to lean both hands against the windowsill until I feel I've regained enough sense of balance, of composure, to support myself. My heart is pounding and I can hear the rush of blood roaring in my ears. I feel disorientated, my world chaotic and messy, my head a tangle of thoughts that I can't seem to unravel.

After a moment, I gain control of my limbs and I creep slowly around the end of the bed, black dress hanging loosely in my hand, holding my breath and tiptoeing as best I can with last night's alcohol coursing through my system. I reach the door and open it gently, praying it won't make a noise. Then I step out of the bedroom and close the door behind me. I don't look back. I don't want to see the face of my great big mistake.

Out on the landing, I am surrounded by four doors and I panic. I can't remember which one leads to the bathroom and I have no idea if anybody else lives in this house. Opening a door into somebody else's bedroom doesn't bear thinking about. So, I scan all the doors before heading towards one at the top of the stairs. Opening it carefully I breathe a sigh of relief: it's the right choice and I enter the room, locking the door securely behind me.

I remove the grey hooded top, which is damp with perspiration, and instantly the cold air of the bathroom cools my burning skin. I stand for a moment enjoying the sensation, but I can sense the faint smell of him on my skin and it's unfamiliar and I hate it. I want to strip myself to the bones to get rid of him. But I hurriedly get dressed. I don't want to chance him waking up and coming to look for me.

I turn on the cold tap a little so as not to make too much noise and put my mouth beneath the running water, letting it trickle down my parched throat. I need to wash away the taste of stale alcohol and the taste of him. I wipe the water from my lips with the back of my hand and standing back I look at myself in the mirror, black make-up smudged around my eyes, cheeks flushed, hair wild.

Just over a year since you left.

'Happy birthday Belle,' I whisper to my reflection, and without warning a solitary tear makes its way down my cheek. I grit my teeth. Here is not the place to break down. Don't give in, I tell myself. Don't give in.

I stand, gazing at my pitiful reflection for a moment longer, waiting to gain the courage to step out of the safety of the bathroom and go downstairs. I have no choice but to do it. I need to go now, before he wakes, before it's too late. So, I open the door a crack, listen and wait. The house is still and silent. I leave the bathroom and pad downstairs, treading barefoot on the soft beige carpet, moving slowly and holding the handrail tightly so as not to lose my balance.

The stairs lead straight into the living-room and I briefly notice this is a brand-new house. Newly built, newly decorated in that faceless, impersonal way. The walls the same dull shade of magnolia, the décor uninspiring and bland. No doubt a carbon copy of the house next door and the one next door to that. And a thought fleetingly crosses my mind that faceless and impersonal describes this situation perfectly. Meaningless. Anonymous. Misguided.

I try not to pay too much attention to my surroundings and instead focus on finding my shoes and handbag so I can leave. But my eyes are drawn to a modern white sideboard, and I stare at the evidence of last night's drunken binge. Too many bottles littering its surface, too many cans, too many glasses, too much of everything. I don't remember drinking here, but I must have. My lipstick is on a glass, my handbag is lying among the mess.

I suddenly feel dizzy. Everything is chaos and disorder again, and I feel an abrupt sense of fear. Fear that I'm losing it. Fear that I'm no longer in control. And then, in a blind panic, I'm grabbing my bag and knocking bottles and glasses to the floor. The noise is deafening and cuts through the heavy silence like a piercing scream. One bottle smashes and what's left of the vodka bleeds out, spilling over the edge of the sideboard and soaking the carpet. Certain that he has heard the commotion, I desperately look around the room for my shoes and spot them lying beside the armchair. I gather them hastily into my arms and head towards the front door. And then I stop. There's no key. What if it's locked? My heart surges up into my throat bringing with it a fresh rush of nausea.

I stare at the door handle for what feels like an eternity and almost in slow motion I reach out, grip the cold metal and push down, hoping and praying the door opens, not sure what I'll do if it doesn't. But the door yields and suddenly I'm stumbling through it, out into the cold, grey bleakness of reality.

The heavens have opened and there are huge, dark puddles on the ground. I lurch and sway down the path towards the street, feet bare, gravel sharp and painful against their soles, handbag and shoes clutched tightly against my chest. My dress is short and the rain lashes cold and unforgiving against my bare legs. I look all around and see I'm surrounded by modern red-brick houses, each one identical. Cloned and soulless. Each one fighting for space, packed tightly together as if bracing themselves against the elements. And I have no idea where I am.

I scan my surroundings, frantically looking for a way out and feel certain I am being watched by countless neighbours intent on turning my trauma into their trivial gossip. But I don't care anymore. I feel nothing other than the need to get away from here. I turn left and walk in the direction of what looks like a main road, my steps faltering and unsteady, head down against the autumn storm, rain

414

blowing in wild circles around me. As I reach the road my feet feel raw and painful, but I have to carry on. I have to get away.

I continue on down the main road, thankful that it's quiet. I'm not sure where I'm headed. I'm all but dragging my feet along the pavement now, the effort to keep going immense, rainwater dripping from the hem of my soaking wet dress leaving me cold and shivery.

I need to find my phone. It's in my handbag, but my hands are shaking and wet and I can't grasp the zip. My fingers slip countless times and I curse loudly, angry with myself for being so useless, so tragic. I stop walking and grab the hem of my dress, wrapping it tightly around my fingers and clutching the zip through the fabric, hoping it will give me purchase. I pull the bag open. My phone, my lifeline, is right there and with trembling fingers, I dial Melissa's number. She doesn't pick up. I leave a fragmented, panicked message. I hang up. And I keep walking.

I see a bus shelter ahead and decide to seek refuge from the elements for a moment. I'm so tired and while the icy shower of rain has cleared my nausea and dulled my aching head, the exhaustion of the walk has left me drained and breathless. I stand beneath the shelter, leaning heavily against the scratched and stained plastic, the smell of stale tobacco stirring the feeling of sickness in my stomach once again. My mind is clamouring, trying again to makes sense of the past few hours.

And suddenly there is clarity through the confusion. Suddenly I know. I wanted to drown out your noise. The smell of you, the feel of you, the taste of you. I wanted to replace your stubborn stain with something else, someone else. I wanted to lose myself in someone else's body and maybe then the pain in mine would go away. Maybe then the memory of you would be engulfed by a new image, the memory of someone else, and I could cling on to a new ideal.

I close my eyes, and with an overwhelming sorrow, I realise it's still only you I want to cling on to and not let go. I want to lose myself in you again and again. But instead, I cling wretchedly onto myself for dear life, wrapping my arms around my waist and holding on tight for fear of losing myself to this pain. I'm shivering, every part of me trembling, and I sink slowly to the wet grimy floor of the bus shelter. Skin stone-cold, hair drenched and ragged around my face, the water dripping onto my skin and meandering down my cheeks like icy tears. I wanted it to be

416

you. I wanted it to be you so much. But you've gone. You've left me. And I'm sobbing. And I wait for somebody, anybody, to help me. Rocking softly on this concrete floor.

***

November 2013

I open my eyes and watch the room spin. My vision is blurred, my eyes swollen and raw. I feel nothing. No joy, no pain, no fear, no anger. Nothing. My mind is empty. I am numb. I'm lying on the sofa in my own living-room. I don't know how I got here and I don't care.

The rain is pouring hard from a darkened sky as though it can't fall fast enough. I focus long enough to see it lashing against the living-room window and bouncing off the roofs of the houses opposite. Thunder cracks overhead and there is the briefest flash of lightning.

I close my eyes and blurred thoughts seep through my lids. Faltering memories of last night stuttering and jumping like a scratched record. Some parts misplaced, vanished, incoherent. I remember the smell of the powder; hard, industrial. Threatening and inviting. Hands shaking as I emptied the small bag of white dust onto the toilet cistern in the cubicle of a tiny club along the back lane of a tiny town. I didn't meet you here. I don't go to the place where we met anymore.

The overhead light in the cubicle is flashing, strobing, like the lightning outside. A door that doesn't lock. Clichéd and dirty and needed. A friend said it would help. I said anything to make it all go away. Alcohol just doesn't cut it anymore.

And I'm searching the floor for a straw among the filth, hands scouring through grime and a cocktail of disgusting liquids. Wiping my fingertips on the legs of my jeans, fumbling in my purse for a banknote. Something. Anything. Coins fall to the tiles and spin as I rip out a ten-pound note, laughing manically. It should be a fifty, I think, but this isn't glamorous. This is desperation and I already despise myself. But I don't stop. I can't.

I try to roll the note, but my hands are shaking. I rake my fingers through my hair, pushing it back from my face, holding the back of my head, eyes closed, deep breaths. Try again. Slowly, slowly. A perfect little tube forms from the note and rests for a moment between my thumb and forefinger.

And then I'm kneeling on the toilet seat, leaning forward with the rolled note in my hand and I'm taking a sharp inward breath through my nose and the harsh, bitter taste overwhelms me as it hits the back of my throat and I collapse backwards against the cubical door and wait to feel numb.

And now it is done.

***

It's Sunday today. I think it's Sunday. But as I lose focus, close my eyes again and drift away listening to the thunder, I remember through my semi-conscious thoughts that I don't care anymore.

***

I arrive at work and I want to turn around and go home. My head is aching, my body is cold and shaking, I am tired and I am drained. I slept on the sofa last night, not moving from where I lay all day drifting in and out of consciousness. The shame of the night before suffocating me, sticking to my body like molten humiliation and drowning me in disgrace.

I walk through the door of the office, attempting to smile but the effort proves too difficult. And the question of 'are you all right?' is too much, and I go from being close to the edge to falling from it. I break down, the fractures in my carefully guarded exterior becoming gaping wounds.

And after a long fall, I've finally hit the bottom. After months of plummeting through blackness, I'm as far down as I can go. And it is cold and dark and lonely, and I have never felt so scared.

***

December 2013

I'm sitting in a hard, straight-backed chair opposite a kind face and I don't know where to start. At the beginning, she tells me. But the beginning of what? The beginning of us? The beginning of our end? How I woke up a few days ago on my sofa with no idea how I got there? How I broke down at work and couldn't stop myself? Or three years ago when everything really started to go wrong? Where? Where do I begin? There's too much confusion. Too many places to go and I don't want to revisit any of them. Because it hurts and I'm tired of hurting.

I look around the room, stalling for time. It is all blue and white and decorated with beach scenes: boats and sunsets and driftwood, cloudless skies and endless sandy beaches. I've seen pictures like these before. And suddenly I'm back in Ebony's hospital room, hot and sticky with sickness. And I have to fight to swallow down the lump that's risen in my throat. Clenching my jaw tight to stop me retching, I close my eyes and try to focus on the sound of my breathing, the hasty beat of my heart.

All the time, the kind face stays silent.

It feels like forever until my racing heart begins to slow and the nervous heat in my body subsides. I begin to imagine myself on those endless beaches, walking barefoot, feeling the sand between my toes and the sun on my skin, reaching the cool, shallow water of the tide's edge and wandering lazily between the waves, letting the water lap around my ankles and the gentle breeze blow my hair across my face. But I'm not alone. You're there and you're holding my hand. You're pulling me towards you, brushing the hair from my eyes, smiling down at me and kissing me gently. And then I feel the ache inside me, like a knife twisting back and forth, sharp and intense through the very heart of me, as I remember that I don't have you anymore. Any of you. I have no one.

I jolt abruptly away from the fantasy, focusing on the kind face again, remembering how I had called her from a foetal position on my sofa, curled around the vodka bottle I held in one hand, with the telephone number I'd been given by a friend at work in the other. Taking deep breaths, punching numbers into the keypad, swigging another mouthful from the bottle for courage, waiting for the person on the other end of the phone to pick up and confirm that I was losing it.

Voicemail. I left a distorted message, my voice cracking through the painful thickness in my throat. Please call me back. Please. I need somebody to help me.

Something in the kind face's eyes urges me gently to begin, and unexpectedly, I do. I open my mouth and let my thoughts out. Suddenly, everything wants to be known. All of it. And as I start to release it all, I realise I can't stop. I can't get the words out fast enough. It's like a blissful release of all the things I keep trying to say but can't. But now I'm stammering and spluttering and eventually, the words get mixed up with painful sobs, stumbling over each other in a rush of chaotic explanations, a combination of relief and shame and sadness surging out of me.

I need to explain so much. I need to tell somebody how much I loved you, all of you, despite everything. I need somebody to know how I wanted to be the one to make you see how special and amazing and beautiful you are. How you meant the world to me but I couldn't make you believe it. How I ran away from your sadness so many times just to

422

make you care, always looking for proof that I mattered to you, that you wanted me around, that I was enough.

I need someone to hear how you took hold of my world and shook it again and again. How, as the dust settled from one storm, the whirlwind would begin once more, grabbing my happiness and tearing it violently from my grasp over and over. How I didn't want to give up. Not at first. How I chased your storm relentlessly, refusing to believe I'd never catch up, that the tempest of us would never subside and that what I'd found was already lost.

I want to explain that in the end, I failed you. In the end, through my own desire to be your everything, I let my impatience and frustration drive you away. And how sorry I am that I couldn't reach you. How so, so sorry I am. But that in the end, you didn't want me anymore, you didn't need me enough or love me enough and it was all my fault that I did this to us and there is nothing I can ever say to you to bring you back to me.

I tell her how, when the realisation of this finally dawned on me, I gave up. How I stumbled and fell, my legs buckling beneath me as I watched my dreams disappear, taking my heart with them. How everything came crashing down around me and I was left among the ruins of us, choking on the dust and debris, everything inside of me broken. How all hope was gone. The chase was over. I had lost and I was in pieces on the floor.

And I tell her how this is my story, repeating over and over and over again. The same words, the same chapters, but different characters.

I talk non-stop for countless minutes and she listens quietly and intently, never interrupting or disturbing me until she's sure I'm finished. And when I finally stop, when there's nothing left to say, I meet her gaze and what I see is not pity but empathy and a determination to help me. To get me out of this dark hole I've fallen into and pull me back into the light. But right then I feel useless. I feel like I don't have the strength to drag myself back to the surface and so I put all my trust in her, this stranger, this outsider. The kind face will help. She has to.

My head feels heavy and I feel exhausted, but at the same time, I feel relief that she is here and can help me make sense of all this, and I feel a lightness in my bones, as though the weight of the world is lifting. And through the haze and the sudden weightlessness of my limbs, she is saying something. The words are indistinct at first, incoherent, but she repeats them over and over until she is sure that I have taken them in. And they are the most important words I think I have ever heard, and I cling onto them, holding on tight as though if I let go, they will float away on the wind like lost balloons. She tells me gently that it's not all my fault. Everything is not all my fault. And as the words slowly sink beneath my skin, as they reach the very core of me, I feel myself coming back into focus. And somewhere deep inside, far away in the shadows, a spark ignites.

Chapter Forty-Four

January 2014

I walk down the stairs and out of the little side door onto the slick pavements of the busy street. The air is laced with the crispness of winter, although the sun is bright, and I draw my scarf up a little further towards my chin, pulling my hood over my head and plunging my hands deep into the fur-lined pockets of my parka. I turn left and set off up the icy street towards the harbour, leaving the blue and white room and the kind face behind me for the last time.

I'm not ready for home yet. Instead, I walk down the high street, passing familiar shops and taking in the comforting sights and sounds of my hometown. I breathe in the saltiness of the sea air, let my stomach rumble as the fish and chips scent wafts over from the market place, listen to the gulls shout from the rooftops and watch the pigeons pecking at the ground and cooing in response. I sidestep shoppers rushing through the sales, nod politely at strangers who let me walk past, and try desperately not to open the miniature bottle of Russian spirit hiding in my coat pocket.

As I approach the harbour, I climb the sandstone steps and walk along the top of the outer wall, holding onto the weather-beaten iron railings to stop me losing my footing. It's quiet up here. Far below me the tide is out and the waves break on the shore, their white foam churning the pebbles, and the comforting sound of sea and stone drifts up into my ears. Just like Seamill. A light icy breeze tugs gently at my hair as I pause for a moment to look towards the horizon.

The sky is powder blue and the clouds lay across it like lace, edged in gold from the rays of the low afternoon sun. The sea is dotted with fishing boats, tiny pinpricks in the distance, and I close my eyes to the scene, wanting only to feel the breeze against my skin and hear the rush of the sea below me. To smell the salt in the air and let my senses remind me once again that I'm still alive.

I turn and continue to walk to the lighthouse, making my way carefully down the uneven, weathered steps at the end of the harbour wall and stand in the shade of the ancient building.

Looking out to sea, I lean against the lighthouse and let myself remember all the things you ever said to me. All the amazing times we had. All the times you made me feel so special and so wanted. All the moments when I would silently wish the clock would stop, that time would stand still and that we could stay like that forever. I wanted you so much that it frustrated me when I couldn't reach you, when you were so distant that I couldn't find you. And right now, I want to hold you so tightly and never let you go. But I know I can't. I can't hold any of you.

I pull the bottle from my pocket and twist the lid with frozen hands, breaking the seal. I empty it in two gulps, swallowing hard and coughing against the sting. I can't even hold Ruby and James anymore. Not properly. Not since Matthew thought it better that he takes care of them, for the most part, these days. Because I'm a drunk. A drunk with no job either. Intoxication is frowned upon in some circumstances. Most circumstances. Although I made it through a lonely Christmas that way just fine.

I wince at the heat lingering in my throat and shove the bottle back into my pocket. I feel the familiar ache of loneliness. Of missing you. The dull pain in my chest swelling uninvited into my throat, and I swallow down the choking sensation I've become accustomed to. Memories waiting, biding their time, creeping up on me when they're brought to mind by a song or a scent or a TV show or a million different things that remind me of you. That remind me of all of you.

Of Dan, who broke my heart for the very first time right here. Of Ebony. Of Matthew. Of Ben. And of you. Reminders of what we had and what we lost. And I know I have to let you go, each and every one of you. Because I have clung on to you for too long and because wishing won't bring any of you back. I know I have to lock you away and let the memory of us become faded; an old photograph in the bottom of a forgotten box. Like all the letters loaded with all the things we could never say.

And I know what I have to do.

Chapter Forty-Five

I find you easily enough, even though I've never been here before. It's as though instinct has brought me to you, a connection that will never disappear. My heart is hammering hard against my ribcage, so hard I can feel the fabric of my jumper shuddering with its rhythm. My palms are clammy despite the cold and my limbs feel heavy, liquefied. I'm not sure I can rely on them to hold me up for much longer.

This body doesn't feel like my own anymore. It's like I'm that cliché, that one about out-of-body experiences, sitting up high somewhere on the sturdiest branch of the tallest tree, watching myself far below. Watching the next few seconds and minutes unfold gently like the velvet petals of a flower in the sun, then snapping back again, shutting

430

tight like a Venus Fly Trap who's caught its prey and I'm left flailing and struggling against its vice-like hold.

I wrap a gloved hand around the wrought-iron gate that separates us and push it open, leaning against the soft rounded edges of the timeworn sandstone wall before I go any further. Gathering my thoughts, praying for courage. I want to turn and run away, but I'm stuck. Rooted to the spot. I don't want to be here, not after everything that happened, not after everything I saw. But I know that I have to be. I had to find you. I had to know where you ended up after you left me. And now I see.

You're not too far away from each other, you and Ebony. She's over there somewhere, to the right, where the trees open out into a wide clearing and the sun beats down uninterrupted when the clouds stay away. Where the grass is carpeted in the springtime with purple crocuses, their vibrant petals punctuated with the white nodding heads of snowdrops, and shiny black granite rises from the polka-dot pattern in uniform rows.

Today there are no flowers. Today the grass is blanketed with a dusting of sparkling frost, a million frozen dewdrops suspended from quivering blades of grass like diamonds hanging from a necklace. They glitter silver in the cool winter sun, sharp blades of light piercing through the emerald green of my eyes, and in their lightning flashes, I see the sparkle of the silver butterfly and the glint of the 'E' swaying beside it and the long, slim neck they used to hang from.

I begin to walk forwards slowly, so slowly the muscles in my legs ache with the hesitation of my prolonged movement. It feels as though I'm walking through thick mud, some sort of swamp wrapping itself around my ankles and pulling in the opposite direction, or I'm fighting against the flow of a river that's full to the brim, its current dragging me back. But I continue to move towards you, the brittle grass crunching beneath my feet with each slow step, shattering the jewels and grinding them into the earth under the soles of my boots.

And now I'm here. Close to you after all this time. I stare straight ahead to where you are, tears pricking my eyes, insides folding in on me, churning, shaking, pounding. I feel sick, light-headed with anxiety, but I continue to stare, unblinking, until the vision blurs before me and everything melts together. Until it's all a mess of colours and textures and nothing makes sense, yet at the same time, it suddenly makes perfect sense.

I take off my gloves and ram them into my pocket, the cold air immediately assaulting my bare skin. I close my eyes and raise my right-hand shakily to my mouth. I place a gentle kiss on my fingertips and reach out to you slowly, pressing my fingers against your name, the granite cold and hard beneath my skin.

I trace my fingers over your name, the headstone solid and unyielding as my hands try desperately, foolishly, to get close to you, as if somehow touching these letters will bring you back, will make you real again. Because I didn't want you to go. I didn't want you to have gone. I wanted you to stay. I wanted you to stay with me. I loved you as much as I hated you. And I still love you now.

I crouch down and cling to the stone, saying your name over and over again, the familiar pain of loss burning in my stomach and in my heart, crippling me, taking over me, tearing me apart. And I let it, because I know I have to. Because finally, it is all real. Everything I didn't want to believe has become the truth. All the times I wanted to believe I'd seen you in the distance. All the times I wanted to believe you were still here, that maybe one day you'd come back to me. They were all make-believe. Denial playing cruel tricks on me, refusing to let me acknowledge you were no longer here, that you'd gone and that you were never coming back.

In my mind, an image pierces the foggy greyness of my constant sadness. It's shockingly vivid. Colours and sounds assaulting my senses, forcing me to see. Forcing me to remember. I see the glass, the whisky, the empty bottle of pills. I see me, standing at the doorway, fingers around the knife in my pocket. And I see you, slumped on the sofa, empty bottle lying on the carpet, inches from your outstretched hand, glass beside it, amber liquid sour and sticky inside. I hear the scream, my scream, and I know that I have to face it. The mess that was us.

I remember the phone call to tell them you were dead. The smell of sweat and piss in the phone box I used in place of my mobile phone, which was also dead that day. Punching 999 on the filthy keypad, numbers almost indecipherable under layers of sticky black scum that fills the grooves of my fingertip. The stale, earthy smell of the mouthpiece as I spoke through sobs to a faceless police officer on the other end of the line. How the smell in the phone box made me think of mould, black and fungal, and how I imagined it gathering on you, spores swarming on your skin, growing across your eyes, seeping into you as bits of you fell away.

Like Ebony, spilling out all over the bathroom floor.

And I remember how I vomited in the corner of the phone box until there was nothing left.

I lean into the stone now and rest my cheek against its icy surface, closing my eyes and waiting for the shock to subside. When the images fade and I eventually open them again, I find myself gazing up at the branches of a huge tree, its leaves casting dappled shade across the ground where you lie. And there are birds in the tree and they sing despite the cold. And the winter breeze so full of frost turns soft for a moment and whispers gently through the leaves, making the sunlight dance across the grass all around you. It is beautiful. Peaceful and beautiful. It is how I always wanted life to be for you. And my heart breaks all over again, pouring into the ground, pouring into you as you take the last pieces of me with you. And I know I'll never be able to forgive myself for not being able to save you. And I know that I can never lose anybody again the way I lost you, the way I lost Ebony.

My bag is hanging over my shoulder and I reach into it, bringing out two envelopes. Turning the first one over, I read the word 'Photos' written in large bubble writing on the front and surrounded by a huge heart. I lift the flap and carefully take out the solitary photograph inside. I trace my fingers gently across its glossy surface and, raising the picture to my mouth, I press it against my lips and place a kiss where you are. I turn to face the headstone and kneeling on the grass I place the photograph among the flowers at its base. In the photo, we're looking at each other and laughing, really laughing, and happiness radiates from it like no other photograph taken of us before or after. My favourite photograph. The only one I kept.

The second envelope is smaller and the colour of barely-there blue. It has 'Belle' scrawled across the crumpled and creased front in black biro. It is still unopened. Still unread. I kept it hidden away in the bottom of a box, the one full of things that didn't really belong anywhere. Full of things to be forgotten. But now I need to know. I've come this far and I have to finish this once and for all.

I slide my finger under the seal and rip along the v-shaped line of glue, wondering how you felt when you wrote this. Wishing I could touch you one last time and change all that, while at the same time recoiling from the thought of my skin against your skin and the bruises it always left behind.

The paper inside is thin, tissue-like, folded cleanly in half with a sharp crease across its width, enclosing the thoughts inside for a moment longer. Indentations from the pen on the paper form embossed patterns on the page, words written in reverse, letters scrolling the wrong way. Everything backwards and upside down and wrong.

I do that thing where you take a deep breath and brace yourself against some sort of onslaught, even though you know nothing physical is going to harm you. Still, I clench my jaw, tense up my neck and shoulders and carefully unfold the sheet of paper with frozen hands.

I whimper at the sight of your handwriting. I cower away from it like a frightened animal. I'm expecting the worst. I read your words from the corner of my eye so that I can't see it all at once, just parts of it. Small pieces I can deal with easier.

'*Belle,*

'*There are so many things I want to say but can't. So much I wish I could tell you. But you'll never understand, because I don't understand it myself. I'm sorry. I'm so sorry Belle. I have to go x*'

Hot, angry tears fall onto the page and burn holes in it. The fat saltwater drops too heavy for it to hold, and it falls apart as they drench the paper. I destroy you one last time with my anger, just as you destroyed me by never giving me the chance to try and understand. To try and help you. To save you. To love you.

I crush the soaked letter inside my fist and squeeze until it melds into a tiny soggy ball in the centre of my palm. I hold it there a while, staring down at my closed fingers, unsure what to do next. Watching the light show from the dancing dappled sunspots as they shimmer back and forth across my fingers, faster and faster as the breeze picks up and dries my tears.

The cold creeps up my legs and a shiver makes its way across my body. The breeze turns to stronger gusts, whipping my hair in front of my face and into my mouth. I stand, pulling up the fur-lined hood of my coat and grasping it tightly under my chin with my free hand. I hold the other one up above my head and open my clenched fist into the gusts of wind.

The pale-blue ball rolls around on my palm, twitching, circling, rocking to and fro until the wind whips around me again and carries it away. I hold my hand aloft until pins and needles prick at my fingertips and the cold starts to bite, then I thrust both hands into my pockets and look at you. I look at your name engraved in the stone one last time, the reality of it now imprinted on my mind. And I know I have to go now too.

But I have one last thing to do, and I walk, head down against the strengthening wind, towards Ebony. Towards Amy.

I've been here once before, after Ebony had been turned to dust and poured into the ground. I stood here all those years ago, just as winter was beginning, and said nothing as the last of the red leaves clinging to the almost-naked branches of the trees fluttered to the ground like dying butterflies.

The grave is bare, there are no flowers laid here. Christmas has gone, the leftover decaying blooms cleared up weeks ago, and Ebony's birthday isn't for another couple of months. But I have something to leave now, before I go, and so I crouch down close to the headstone and reach into my bag once more.

'I have something for you,' I whisper, remembering the gentle tone of her voice. 'I hope you like it.'

I pull out a small glass jar, and in it is suspended a tiny silk butterfly. Wings dusted in a pattern of bright reds and oranges with vivid pale-blue and black circles like eyes at each tip, delicately edged in gold and shimmering in the pale-yellow light of the weak winter sun. A peacock butterfly. The ones that fascinated us most as little girls when we nurtured our jam-jar creations. I rest it gently on the grass beside the cold granite bearing her name and smile.

'For you Amy,' I whisper. 'Just for you.'

And as I walk away, as I leave you both behind, I know that I will never come back here again. I realise that nobody will ever truly know our story. The anger, the frustration, the love and the loss, it was ours and ours alone. Yet I would follow you back to the beginning – both of you, all of you – to relive it all again. Because always in those moments when we were lost, you were all I ever wanted.

Part Four: The End

Belle

Chapter Forty-Six

Wednesday 5th March 2014

The TV is too loud in the living-room. I stand over the sink in the kitchen washing the dinner dishes and try not to reach into the back of the cupboard below for the cheap vodka that hides there. I focus instead on the chatter of the cartoon characters in the other room, their high-pitched, rapid-fire babbling grates on my frayed nerves, and I know I'll soon lose my patience. I know I'll storm through and switch off the TV. I know I'll throw the remote control at the sofa, at the table, at the wall. I know that James will cry and Ruby will stay silent and I'll ignore them both.

I think back to the seaside room, the straight-backed chair and the kind face I told weeks ago that I didn't need anymore. Breathe, I tell myself. Just breathe. You've done so well, remember what she told you. Don't fall again. Don't fall into that hole. Stay focussed, stay strong, stay alive. Easier said than done.

I look down at my wrists, skinny chunks of skin-covered bone, hands cut off by the soapy lemon-scented clouds floating on the dishwater. I should eat more, I think to myself as I watch the blue veins snaking across the back of my hand as my skin turns ever more translucent. I never wanted to end up like her, never wanted to be the 'troubled one', the one with the problems, the one who stopped eating and wasted away. My life was never going to be like that. I'm just not hungry, I tell myself. That's all it is.

I try to remember how it felt to be anything other than lost. Anything other than numb. How did it feel to have direction? To have purpose? To feel alive instead of just moving through the days unaware of anything other than wanting the hours to be over and the day to be done? What was that like? I wonder. What was it like to feel hungry? To laugh and smile naturally? To have the energy to run around and act the fool? But I don't remember. Those memories have disappeared along with everything else in my life that was worth keeping.

The job I had, I lost. Just before Christmas, it was. I turned up drunk one too many times, mostly on a Monday morning after a weekend without the kids. I nodded, walked out slowly without protest, didn't try to fight my corner. Because really, I'd have been fighting a losing battle. I knew what I was, what I am, and I knew they knew it too. And I understand, of course I do, but I just wish they'd known how hard I was trying not to be the drunk in the corner. I really was. But when I was alone there was always a room full of people disturbing me from my trying. And even when I turned the TV up to its loudest, or played the noisiest music I could find, they were still there, voices talking over each other in incessant conversation with me. Even when I stuffed cotton-wool in my ears and wrapped a scarf around my head, I could still hear them clear as a bell and see their laughing faces behind the wool that scratched my eyelids and made my earlobes hot.

Ebony would always want me to go outside and look at her latest collection of jam-jar butterflies. 'These ones are the best ever,' she'd tell me. 'The biggest and brightest you'll have ever seen.' So, I would light a cigarette for old time's sake, even though I gave up years ago, and I'd go outside to find her. But she was never there. I'd stand in the yard and shout her name into the night, fingers clasping her necklace, which hung like a permanent fixture around my neck, until the neighbours leaned out of their upstairs windows, told me I was crazy and that they'd call the police. But she never answered. She never waited long enough for me. Each time I tried to find her she was never there. But I kept trying, each time she asked me to. I didn't want her to think I didn't care.

Then there was Ben, who didn't ever say anything to me, but his face would appear each time I closed my eyes, with every blink, with every attempt at sleep, his face would be there, smiling at me. Blue eyes sparkling like some exquisite gemstone, white-hot sparks flying from them and dancing in front of my face. I'd reach out to try and catch them, but I never could. And then there'd be her face too, the one he really loved, kissing him, loving him like I should have been. And after a while, when she saw him looking at me, she'd turn and snarl and she'd throw glass after glass after glass at me until I was a bloody pulp on the floor at her feet, and she'd dance around in what was left of me before swilling me down the drain. And I'd know that I deserved it for everything I had done.

And then there was you. And all I see is your dead body lying on the sofa, skin grey, eyes closed, hand outstretched with nobody to hold it. I'd so wanted to hold it, so wanted to link my fingers through yours, but instead, I ran away. And as I back away from you now, as I turn and run, you run after me. Eyes dead, body limp, feet dragging across the ground asking me to save you, please save you, please. 'I called the ambulance,' I shout at your memory. Sweat standing out on my forehead, insides crumbling to dust and blowing aimlessly around my body like trapped storms. 'I did that for you, but it was too late.' I curl into a ball and shield myself from your angry laughter. 'Please believe me,' I beg. 'I tried, I tried so hard. Really, I did. I tried but I couldn't save you. I'm sorry, I'm sorry, I'm so sorry.' But still your scorn, your ridicule and all the ways you despise me rain down fierce and searing on my body, striking me hard like the hot hands of Mother. And I'd know that I deserved that too.

But then there was the alcohol. That sweet relief. The alcohol would take it all away, would make it all disappear, like a concerned friend who wants to make everything better. When Ruby and James couldn't distract me, when they were distracting Matthew instead – Matthew and her, the new love in his life, the woman who has taken my place – I turned to the new love in mine and I let it burn all the

447

pain away and replace it with a new one. One that I control with painkillers, with sleeping pills, with more alcohol.

I swish my hands around in the lukewarm water and my fingers find the handle of a knife. I lift it through the bubbles and hold it in front of me, wiping the suds away slowly with the cloth, watching bright shards of light bounce off as I twist and turn it before my eyes, casting harsh white lightning bolts on the walls. This was meant for you, I think, before you took away my chance to hurt you. My knuckles turn white, anger and relief with nowhere to go but into my fists, into the strength of my grip. I'd have hurt you that night. Really hurt you. But you beat me to it.

I think of Ebony then, and suddenly, I understand the weight of all her secrets. The pressure inside her of all the things she would never tell me, the constant bubbling lava pool of hidden stories and buried explanations, and the struggle to release it all without erupting into screams and destroying the rest of your world which you're trying, and failing, to protect. I lower the knife back into the water as she comes to me in vivid colour, lying in her bathroom, floor blood-soaked, scarlet rivers of all her fears leaving her body behind and soaking into the white towels that I crush her arm between, blade in her hand, her face blissful and content.

I close my eyes. Grip the handle of the knife even tighter in simple desperation and determination.

And then I'm taking it, this knife that was meant for your soft spaces, and I'm slicing it into my own. Cutting at the flesh of my left arm, gasping at the sharp, bright pain of it, unable to breathe as the agony of the blade takes away all my air. Blood floods the sink, turning the water scarlet, and seeps into the bubbles, a pretty pink bloodshed hue creeping slowly upwards through the pure-white, turning them to candy floss. Spun sugar and gore.

It's a clean pain, a real pain, not a murky shadow of relentless dull torture that drapes itself over you and settles there indefinitely, invading all your spaces and never quite knowing when to leave. This is crystal-clear and understandable. It is finite. I know when it will stop. I know it will heal. And now I know why she did it.

I'm sorry Ebony. I'm sorry Amy. I understand you now. I understand.

'Mummy your arm!' The instant tears of Ruby shock me out of my stupor. She is suddenly there beside me, gazing with pure horror at the mess in the water and the leaking open wound on my arm.

'Mummy! Mummy make it stop!' She's hysterical now and I realise I haven't moved, haven't spoken. And I realise I'm crying too.

Reality rushes towards me full force and almost knocks me off my feet. I drop the knife. It misses the sink and clatters to the floor with the same metallic smash it made against your fireplace the night I found you dead. I stay silent and swallow down the scream that is on the tip of my tongue.

'It's okay, Ruby,' I manage through panting breaths. 'The knife slipped and I cut myself. But it's okay, it's okay.'

I grab the towel from the hook on the cupboard door and wrap it haphazardly around my wet arm. Blood and water and bubbles drip from my elbow onto the floor. I raise it up in the air in an instinctive attempt to slow the blood flow, my fingertips throbbing, but it's working, I think it's working.

And now James is here too, rushing into the kitchen at the sound of the crying, and he stands behind his big sister, clinging onto the hem of her fluffy fuchsia cardigan, crying too. And now my heart, as well as my arm, bleeds.

And I crouch down beside them, hold them close with my good arm, and I breathe them in, their pure, innocent scent. I cling onto them for dear life and I tell them everything's going to be okay.

It has to be okay. It has to. I have to fix this. I have to fix me.

Chapter Forty-Seven

Thursday 6th March 2014

I've trudged the school run in the rain, and now I sit in the car outside the gates, engine running, waiting for the mist to clear from the windows. I'm glad it's raining. I can hide beneath my hood when it does, keep the dark circles beneath my eyes, their red rims, my sallow and sunken features out of view of gossiping mouths and haughty looks.

Ebony laughs in my ear. 'I used to do that,' she says. 'Do you remember? When I was going, going, gone.' Her laughter tinkles, silvery like sleigh bells, inside my head, and I turn the radio up.

'Don't do that, Belle,' I can tell by the blue glint that flashes like a beacon in the corner of my eye that it's Ben. 'We only want to talk to you.'

'You said we had nothing more to say to each other,' my mind screams

Why don't you want to talk, Belle?' You. Mocking? Meaningful? I can't decide. 'Is it because we went away, Belle? Left you on your own?' Definitely mocking. 'You know we wouldn't have gone if we had the choice. But you made us, didn't you Belle? You made us all want to leave you. Nobody wants to stay with you, Belle. Nobody.'

Your face shimmers somewhere just out of sight, and I twist the dial on the radio some more until I can feel the bass vibrating through my chest. Eardrums pulsating. Body alive with sound, trying to drown out the noise. The voices.

They're not there. They're not there. I breathe in and hold it there in my lungs until my ribs hurt and the air gushes out all over the dashboard. They're not real, not anymore. But my good intentions float around the interior of the car, banging against the windows like trapped birds and breaking into a million invisible pieces of nothingness that don't matter.

I force the car into gear, wincing at the ache in my arm, and try to focus on driving. Muted laughter of boys and girls blows through the hot air vents and drifts around the car. It's the schoolyard, I tell myself. It's the sounds of the

453

schoolyard. But the sound is like sleigh bells and mockingbirds, and I know that it isn't.

I squeeze the steering wheel tighter, ignoring the searing pain that shoots up my injured arm, and push the accelerator a little harder. I need to get to the hospital. I need to sort out last night's mess. And the mess of all the months before that. I'm too tired to carry on pretending. I'm just too tired.

The rain falls harder as I pull out of the junction onto the wider main road. I increase the speed of the windscreen wipers and still they can barely keep up with the downpour. I lean forwards, closer to the window to try and see out. I turn on the headlights as the sky turns darker. I see Ebony and Ben and you standing in front of me in the road. I hear you all laughing. I see you all arm in arm. I hear you all shouting at me, words I can't understand, washed away by the pouring rain. I scream. I yank at the steering wheel, swerving to get out of your way.

I feel the wound burst and the blood flow warm and fast down my arm. The car hits a lamppost at the side of the road. My face smashes into the steering wheel. And the world falls blissfully silent.

Chapter Forty-Eight

There's a blackness, but it's shimmering at the edges like the air does on a hot summer's day. There's a warm breeze too, and it's been a while now since my heart turned itself inside out under violent pressure. Minutes, hours, days, I can't be sure. But it gallops for itself now. A thousand hooves thundering across my broken terrain, leaving crescent-shaped marks in my flesh. Lucky horseshoes on a battered body.

A moment ago, I was late. A second ago it was hot and people were crying and I sat in the corner on a hard, wooden seat and opened up a million pages of a nightmare while everything turned to liquid and ran off the edge of the world, dripping into cold, dark space.

But now there's nothing but blackness. Blackness and silence. And I don't know if I'm here or gone. Then through the darkness, I see you. Through my closed eyes, you're there. You're here again, in these dark spaces between sleeping and waking, floating somewhere between unconsciousness and some kind of real life. The difference is that the rage has stopped, the storm has died down, and you look just like you always did. Handsome. Eyes crinkling at the corners as you smile and reach out your hand for me.

There is movement behind you, a faded girl with dark hair and a pale face. With hollowed-out cheeks and sunken eyes and a finger to her lips and a 'shhhhhh' whispered like a mother to her baby. Like waves pulling on pebbles.

I feel my pulse flutter in the hollow of my neck. A butterfly trapped beneath my skin. And like a rush of air to my lungs I know I don't have to go. I turn my back on what's left there in the dark for me and reach for home. I stretch out my hands before me and suddenly the blackness around me becomes liquid and I'm underwater, reaching towards the shimmering surface as faded sounds begin to enter my ears, muffled, thick and clogged, through the ocean.

In the distance, somewhere just out of reach, I hear a tiny voice. A little boy singing a nursery rhyme. Wind the bobbin up, wind the bobbin up. Pull. Pull. Clap, clap, clap. I hear the tinkle of coins, like sleigh bells, metallic and jangling and pretty, calling me louder and louder and louder.

I kick and I fight against the tide and I reach the surface, pushing through the waves above my head. I open my eyes. A shock of bright light, air in my lungs, rushing through me, clean and cold. Filling the dying spaces inside of me, spreading heat through my veins.

I inhale sharply, as though I'm breathing for the first time, and I swallow everything down in a deep, ragged breath, dragging it into the darkest depths of me – all the pages of the horror story and their relentless turning – and I blow it all out into the air, words floating away from their pages, pages floating away from their spine, all of it dancing in the air around my head before disappearing from view.

A machine drones. A machine beeps. Trainers squeak on linoleum tiles.

A fan blows warm air around the hospital room.

James sits beside my bed singing his favourite song, smiling widely as my eyes find his.

'You're back, Mummy!' Ruby exclaims. 'You're okay. Daddy, Mummy's okay again!' She plays with a silver necklace - my necklace, Ebony's necklace - that hangs low around her neck, the shiny 'E' and the butterfly jangling gently together and making a familiar sound.

Like sleigh bells. Like coins.

Acknowledgements

Writing this novel was both a labour of love and, at times, utter torture for me. I began my journey into writing *The Things I Want To Say But Can't* nine years ago, inspired by the book *One Day* by David Nicholls. Sitting in the little back yard of my friend's house in the spring sunshine, tiny notebook and pen in my lap, I began trying out ideas and storylines and allowed myself to wonder if I could really make this happen. Could I actually write a story? A book? A full-blown novel even? Could I fulfil my lifelong dream?

Nine years and almost 90,000 words later, here it is. Completed. And trust me, at times I thought I'd never get to this point.

I wrote in earnest for the first couple of months. Pouring ideas out on to the page, raw and unrefined. Sometimes I doubted myself. 'I'm not an author.' I'd think. 'I don't have any sort of training for this.' Maybe it was all just a silly idea and I should forget about it. But I kept going, despite my doubts, spurred on by friends telling me I could do this, and I *should* do this.

Some days the writing poured out of me so fast that I almost couldn't keep up. Some days the story seemed to write itself, naturally taking me down avenues I hadn't planned out in the pages of notes in my tiny, dogeared notebook, but which linked into the storyline so perfectly I decided to allow it just to happen. And on those days, writing this novel was an absolute pleasure.

On other days, no words would come. I'd stare at the screen of my laptop for hours, cursor flashing, waiting impatiently for me to add something to the page, but my mind remained blank. Some days I could manage only one sentence, if that. And on those days, creating this story was utterly despairing.

After those difficult days, I'd stop writing. For days, for weeks, sometimes for months, so disillusioned was I with the process. Then everyday life would inevitably take over – family, work, friends – and I'd forget about my story, my book, my novel and leave it languishing in a folder somewhere on my hard drive. But it was always there, at the back of my mind, unfinished and crying out to be looked at again.

And then I read another novel, *Beside Myself* by Ann Morgan, and so inspired was I by the writing style that I threw myself back into finishing my own book, my enthusiasm and motivation renewed. First draft, second, third, maybe even a fourth, fifth and sixth, and finally here I am! My work is done. For now. Because despite the sheer hard work that writing very often is, it is also one of the most rewarding things I've ever done, and one of the most difficult to leave behind.

So, I want to take this opportunity to thank everyone who believed in me when I didn't, and who encouraged me when I felt like giving up.

To Lisa, who read some of the very first chapters in the very first draft, and who gave me the advice and reassurance I needed in those early days to carry on. Thank you for being my anchor, my adventure buddy and my confidant over the years.

To Helen, my oldest friend and fellow author (with whom I now share an editor!) We might not see each other as much as we used to, but your enthusiasm for my achievement in writing a novel, your encouragement, and your advice on editing and publishing has been invaluable. Here's to more writing adventures!

To Wayne, Katie, Claire and Tess for keeping me afloat through the hard times and for bringing me back down to Earth when I needed it (or at least trying to!) Thank you for the endless supplies of chocolate, cola, hugs and late-night conversations where we so often tried to make sense of this crazy world we live in.

I couldn't have done this without you, all of you. Your friendship is more precious to me than you will ever know, and for that I thank you from the bottom of my heart.

I'd also like to thank my editor, Amanda Horan of Lets Get Booked, for her fantastic editing skills, her guidance and her belief in this novel.

And finally, I'd like to thank my children for being the wonderful little people they are and for bringing me joy every day. They are proof that, despite the hardships we all sometimes face, there is still beauty and perfection in the world.

About the Author

Carla Christian lives in the Lake District in the North of England. A busy working mum of two teenagers, she has a passion for writing, art and travel, and these interests have been a part of her for as long as she can remember.

Constantly inspired by both the good and the bad in the world around her, she spends much of her time creating in one way or another; be it painting canvases for the blank walls of her new home, sketching pictures to capture memories of the many travel adventures she's been lucky enough to go on, baking fantastical cakes with her daughter, or writing endless beginnings to a million unfinished stories.

The Things I Want To Say But Can't is her first novel.